A RIVER CLOSELY WATCHED

a novel by Jon Boilard

A RIVER CLOSELY WATCHED

a novel by Jon Boilard

MACADAM CAGE

MacAdam/Cage Publishing
155 Sansome Street, Suite 550
San Francisco, CA 94104
www.macadamcage.com

Library of Congress Cataloging-in-Publication Data

Boilard, Jon.
A river closely watched / by Jon Boilard.
p. cm.
ISBN 978-1-59692-381-2 (hardcover)
1. Families—Massachusetts—Fiction. 2. Boys—Fiction. 3. Uncles—Fiction.
4. Masculinity—Fiction. 5. Franklin County (Mass.)—Fiction. 6. Bildungsromans. I. Title.
PS3602.O47R58 2012
813'.6—dc23
                                    2012033895

Book and jacket design by Dorothy Carico Smith.

Printed in the United States of America.

1 2 3 4 5 6 7 8 9 10

This first one is for Angelica.
Thank you for believing.

"He who has listened and has not obeyed is like a man who built a house on the earth with no foundation; the river dashed against it and it collapsed at once, and the ruin of that house was great."
— Luke 7:49

PROLOGUE

THE SKY OVER THE TOWN is purple and stars are like diamonds cut from the moon. Bobby DuBois and Doreen Orlowski smoke as they walk along the railroad tracks, jumping from tarry and woodrotten ties to weathersteeled rails, and running parallel to them just beyond the treeline the river whispers secrets barely heard. They are wildhaired and dirtscruffy and exuding a nearly tangible air of recklessness. Bundles of Japanese knotwood bookend the clapboard covered bridge that spans a narrow and secluded elbow of the river. Blond posts and crisscrossed braces extend from top to bottom chords that parallel the unpaved roadway. The planks of the floor are supported by the bottom chord. Bobby produces a folded hunting knife from the front pocket of his dungarees, Doreen conveys a halfgone bottle of Boone's Farm sweetwine against the jut of her hip. He looks at her and she puts the bottle down and a mosquito lands on the lip of it and then they each take turns with the blade, carving their initials inside the shape of a heart, linking themselves to the history of the place. There is a partial reflection of the primitive structure in the water that's cool and clear and still until a bony rainbow trout catches a softbodied stonefly and the surface breaks and ripples, and shimmers brilliant little bits.

PART I:

"It's wrong of me, but most of what I do is wrong."
—Bobby DuBois

CHAPTER ONE

IT'S RAINING JUST A LITTLE and a riderless white horse gallops down South Main Street and through the common. It has black socks on its front legs. A van from the funeral home stops to let it cross Sugarloaf. The driver of the van has to actually slam on the brakes and the back tires seize up and screech and you can smell burning rubber, the compromised metal drums. The horse gets spooked by the commotion and bucks sideways and snorts.

Bobby and Doreen are sitting on the bench under the maple tree next to the fountain. He has his mouth on her neck and his hand up her yellow t-shirt that advertises Baby Watson Cheesecake and she watches the horse enter the graveyard where the wife of Harry Arms is buried. The panel van pulls away slowly and the driver has his face pressed against the glass of the window, his breath fogging it as he smiles at Doreen. They call him the English Teacher because nobody can understand a fucking word he says. He's a known pervert and she has been the subject of his crude advances in the past. She flips him the bird and he guns his engine, which misfires, and the van disappears.

Did you see that, she says to Bobby.

What now.

That horse.

No, he says. I was otherwise occupied.

Fucking beautiful.

Must be it got loose from Rocasah's.

Should we tell somebody or do something.

Bobby gives her tit a squeeze.

Let's just keep doing this, he says.

She laughs and he does, too. They kiss and after a while he stops pawing her.

Fuck, he says.

I know.

I got to get back.

Me too.

They're on break from their respective shifts in the center of town, at the pharmacy where Doreen jerks soda and, kitty-corner across the street, at the service station where Bobby pumps gas and changes oil and switches out various automobile parts. He's got to throw a new water pump into Henderson's Corvette by five o'clock.

He gets up and adjusts himself.

Fucking blue balls again, he says.

She smiles, snaps her bra and fixes her t-shirt.

The rain has let up now. He pulls her close and she smells like the onion rings he loves to eat with ketchup. They stand there and kiss and she transfers her chewing gum into his mouth so he will think of her all afternoon. Like he wouldn't anyhow after this. But she's a girl who believes in insurance. She puts her hands on his bone-hard chest and gently extends her arms and backs away from him.

Then she turns and walks and he watches her and she knows he's watching her.

Wildberry, he says.

What, she says over her shoulder.

The gum.

That's right, she says. That's our flavor.

BOBBY'S OLD MAN BLACKIE GETS drunk at the Bloody Brook Bar and kidnaps Raymont Redwine. When he tries to escape Blackie chains him to the radiator at his girlfriend's house. She's working a double, slinging beers over to the VFW, and won't get home until late, so he's got run of the place. Bobby calls his old man's girlfriend the human punching bag but she doesn't know any better. Nothing the old man does surprises Bobby anymore so he just sits back and puffs a cigarillo and drinks some Old Crow from a clear plastic cup.

The thing is that Raymont is retarded and everybody calls him Raping Ray—nobody knows for sure if he did it or not and besides it was a long time ago. He's mostly harmless now.

What's this then, Bobby says when he first sees the retard chained to the radiator.

Snatched him off the street.

What you want with him anyhow.

Hell I don't know, Blackie says. It was just a urge.

Jesus Christ, Bobby says. You can't do that to a person.

Blackie gives his son a look as though to say the hell I can't.

You sonofabitch, Bobby thinks.

A heavy silence hangs over the three of them like a blanket.

The old man sits on a pepper crate by the window that's busted and lets in a breeze, warm and stiff like from the hand-driers at the BP Diner. The sky is darker than a state trooper's boot. Professional fighting is showing on the muted black-and-white television in the corner. Sick Sigma is Bobby's personal favorite; he watches him put a choke-hold on GTO. He contemplates his options in terms of loosing poor Raymont Redwine, improbable rapist and societal scapegoat, from this trap that has snared him.

When his old man finishes his whiskey he gets up and hits Ray on the head with the empty bottle and leaves the room and his sick laughter follows him like train smoke. Ray looks at Bobby with his good eye and Bobby blows perfect rings at him. The retard blinks and Bobby wonders about any god's reason for creating a man so obviously ill-equipped for this bad world. God must have a real sick sense of humor, Bobby thinks. He gets up and goes over to Raymont, crouches at his side so they are more or less eye level.

Fuck this shit, Bobby says.

He holds out his cigarillo so Raymont can take a puff, his eye closes as he slowly inhales and then he doubles up in a coughing fit. Bobby rests his arm around Raymont's neck.

Shhhh, he says. Let's not piss him off anymore tonight.

Bobby pats him on the back.

Raymont Redwine settles down after a bit.

Bobby almost smiles. He puts his forehead against Raymont's, and he peers into his one good eye as though it's the skeleton keyhole in a door that leads to a room of vast and unknowable secrets.

LATER THE RIVER IS RUNNING high and good and spitting trout onto the muddy banks and Bobby tells Fat Johnny Klinker about his father and the retard. Fat Johnny laughs his ass off. Bobby also tells him that his uncle Thaddeus got released. He's Blackie's brother, but he's been put away for a very long time, serving his time for a string of misdeeds.

He might try to take me again, Bobby says.

Take you where this time though.

I don't know.

Well, would you go with him.

We always got on pretty good.

Your old man won't let him *see* you, Fat Johnny says, let alone take you.

Bobby knows this to be true.

Bobby and Fat Johnny are not old enough to drive but they acquire Fat Johnny's brother's winter beater that's stored in an old tobacco barn behind the family property. It's a blue 1973 Dodge Charger with a standard 318 V8 and a rusted quarter panel that's patched together with sheet metal. Loud sidestripes, pinned-down hood with a power bulge, anti-sway bars front and rear, fat tires with raised white letters. It used to be cherry but the years have gotten the best of it—and it's been totaled twice by Fat Johnny's brother, who's on probation for operating a vehicle under the influence. Anybody worth a damn ends up on probation or rotting in Cedar Junction, as far as Bobby can tell.

BY TUESDAY A GIANT TREE casts a long shadow on a faded red barn. Bobby's old man emerges from the Hotel Warren. The neon sign out front was vandalized long ago and as a result most of the letters don't work, so when it lights up at night it simply spells "HOT L." Nobody has ever bothered to fix it and now that's what everybody in town calls the place, which over the years has become Stillwater's version of low-income housing as well as a good place to get a cheap drink since there's a bar downstairs.

Across the street Bobby is sitting with Fat Johnny on the steps in front of Leo's TV. They're watching Blackie and smoking cigarillos stolen from the pharmacy. Bobby can smell the pickle shop because it's the end of summer. Dusk surprises like a suckerpunch and Sunsick Mountain muscles up from the banks of the river, all sandstone and moss green, shouldering a blanket of mist. Fat Johnny chugs Boone's Farm thick as syrup.

The old man is alone and he's looking for the keys to his Willys MB. He stops walking and stands there and digs in the front pockets of the pants he used to wear to work, back when there was regular work to be had, mumbling something because Bobby can see his lips moving. Johnny Cash is coming from the bar jukebox, the clack of billiard balls, loud voices shouting. It's Wednesday night and the only place to go in town other than the Bloody Brook Bar. The old man finds his keys and looks up, sees the boys for the first time. He straightens a bit and then changes his mind because who gives a shit what they think after all. He looks up and down South Main Street before crossing.

He clears his throat, spits over his shoulder.

Fuck you doing, he says to the boys.

Nothing, Bobby says.

Don't nothing me boy.

Bobby looks at his father's eyes and they are bloodshot and wild, trying to leave his face, rolling around in his skull sockets like a couple dropped marbles about to disappear down a rusted sewer grate, never to be seen again. It's more than alcohol.

Just sitting here then, sir, he says.

Blackie is a former Marine and he likes to be called sir.

All right, the old man says.

He props himself on the hood of Lou Harvey's vintage El Camino. Even from there Bobby can smell it oozing from his pores, the brown booze that fuels him. His dark hair is mussed and his beard is a few days old. They call his old man Blackie because of his features but the skin of his forearms and hands is fishbelly white in splotches where sparks burned the pigment off him when he was spot-welding train parts for the railroad in Indian Falls—before they laid him off. That was a long time ago, but he's still mad about it. Mad that they let him go, but also mad they hired him in the first place.

He clears his throat and spits piss-yellow and looks at Fat Johnny.

Fuck your pa at, he says.

Fat Johnny's cigarillo rolls to one side of his mouth and he talks out the other.

Not my turn to watch him, he says.

Don't sass me boy.

Fat Johnny laughs like he will but it fades quickly and he looks at Bobby.

The boys speak a secret and silent language at moments like this.

Over to the Rod & Gun, Fat Johnny finally says.

Maybe I'll take a ride and tell him I seen you smoking them things.

Fat Johnny's pa has rules. Everybody knows that. Smoking cigarillos with Bobby DuBois—or doing anything at all with Bobby—will earn him a boot in the ass. Bobby's old man's throat rattles like a busted gear and he spits a chunk of blood and continues.

How'd that be then, he says.

Fat Johnny lets out a long breath that you can see.

Nah sir, he says.

Fuck what I thought.

Fat Johnny doesn't respond.

Is he still got his flock, Blackie says.

Fat Johnny nods his head. His pa is a sometimes preacher.

Blackie laughs aloud because he has found his own private religion.

Fat Johnny takes a final drag and then stamps out the discarded butt with the heel of his boot. It stains the cement in a shape that makes Bobby think of a miniature angel's wings in a dirty snow patch. The old man looks at Bobby and gestures and Bobby gets up and stretches across the sidewalk and gives him the rest of his cigarillo. Blackie steps

back and sticks it in his mouth and inhales slowly with his eyes closed
and his hands on his hips. He stands there like that, like a statue of
himself. Fat Johnny is staring past the train tracks. The local cops roll
by and Westy is driving and LaPinta nods his head at Bobby and smiles,
but not nice. Blackie pops his eyes open and shoots them at his son, and
he ignores the police as they disappear around the bend.

Fuck you get these sticks at boy, he says.

I don't know.

Best not be lifting mine again.

He's a Kool man and these are Salems, but he's too drunk to know
the difference.

Nah sir, Bobby says.

Thought you learnt your lesson last time.

Yes sir.

Blackie has a heavy hand that he knows how to use. He puts his
hand out. The knuckles on it are crudely inked, one green letter per,
spelling out "A-N-N-E."

That was Bobby's mother's name.

There's an unspoken rule against saying it aloud in Blackie's presence.

Give me the rest, the old man says.

Bobby gives him the pack they stole from the pharmacy. It had been
rolled up in his shirt sleeve. He tosses it to the old man underhand and
it hits him in the chest and his reaction time is slow of course and he
barely holds it there. Fat Johnny kicks Bobby and snorts. Bobby looks at
the sidewalk and then he looks at his old man. Blackie gathers himself
and looks at Fat Johnny for a few seconds. Then he looks at Bobby.

Well shit then, he says.

He turns to go.

Guess I'll shove off.

Then he stops and looks at Bobby again and puts his finger to his lips.

Keep quiet about that thing we done, he says.

Bobby stays quiet.

I mean our little houseguest, Blackie says.

Bobby knows he's talking about Raymont Redwine.

Don't drag me into it, Bobby says. That's all you.

Well, Blackie says. Just keep your fucking pie hole shut.

Bobby still doesn't say anything because he doesn't know what to say. His old man appears to be turning a kind of corner in terms of his depravities.

Blackie winks at Bobby.

Until now Bobby had assumed he'd let Raping Ray loose already. That he'd had his fun.

Blackie crosses the street to his pickup in front of Fortier's Barber Shop. There's a paper sign taped to the inside of the big window advertising a potluck at St. Matthew's, where Father Roberts likes to touch the young choir boys and nobody seems to mind. Bobby's no saint but he doesn't believe in a god that would facilitate that type of behavior.

It takes Blackie a full minute to navigate the trick door. Then he pulls himself into the cab and slams the door solid and after a few seconds the slant six sputters then catches. He taps the gas pedal with his foot and the exhaust pipe puffs poison-soaked clouds the color of a dying hog's winter breath. The transmission grinds into reverse and Bobby feels the vibration of it in his bones. Blackie backs into the street without looking or checking mirrors and he drives away slowly.

Fat Johnny spits and looks at Bobby.

Holy shit, he says. Your old man is true fucked up.

Bobby looks at Fat Johnny and shakes his head from side to side.

Never thought I'd say it, Fat Johnny says. But I almost feel bad for Raymont.

Yeah well, Bobby says. Maybe I'm fixing to do something about that.

They stand and walk down the alley to where the car is parked between Leo's TV and Boron's Market. Fat Johnny gets in and Bobby gets in and Fat Johnny starts the engine that runs like a top because he's learning cars at Franklin County Technical, and his brother lets him practice on the Charger in the barn sometimes. He tells Bobby he replaced the points and plugs and distributor cap just this morning. Bobby will still be at the regional school in the fall because there is paperwork involved in transferring and his old man does not have the patience. But Bobby has a natural curiosity about the inner workings of things. He fiddles with the radio until he finds something they both know: Old John Cougar singing sweet about China Girl. Fat Johnny drums the dashboard.

CHAPTER TWO

IT'S EARLY EVENING UNDER STILLWATER Bridge and a sawed-off sun wrinkles pink in an otherwise empty sky. Swirls of dirt and dust kick up in the wake of the 1970 Chevrolet Nova as it carves a path through twisty pine and elm and birch and weeping willow. The two of them laugh like men more frightened than tickled, there is a gloom to it and their hands and forearms are dark and sticky from working on the gearbox of the old American car. Most noticeable are the eyes on the larger man. The way they pierce with a red-rimmed sadness, maybe on the verge of tears, maybe too far gone for that. An open bottle of hooch is on the seat between them. The fumes would get you drunk.

Billy Tucker speaks first, as is his way.

She shifts good and tight now, he says.

That's fine.

Like brand new.

All right.

Good to have you back then.

I can't say yet if it's good to be back.

Billy Tucker shakes his head and laughs. He stops the car and kills the engine.

So what you gone do now, he says. Now that you're out.

Drink and fuck.

Billy Tucker laughs.

I mean for money, he says.

Thaddeus DuBois looks at Billy Tucker and smiles, but you might not have noticed. The slightest upturn at the ends of his mouth, like somebody pulled a string.

Nobody gone pay you for either of those, Billy Tucker says.

Thaddeus laughs.

They both laugh now.

I figure there's other things I can do, Thaddeus says. That won't jam me up.

Billy Tucker agrees.

Can't go back inside, Thaddeus says. Never again.

Right on cue a fat cop on horseback approaches them slowly from the rear. He seemingly materializes out of nowhere to circle the car, but they are not surprised to see him, almost like the encounter is expected. Like they are used to bumping up against the law or challenging figures of authority has become second nature. The fat cop talks into the radio on his shoulder pad and looks the fellows up and down. It's clear that he is not impressed with their general appearance and current disposition. And he knows them, he recognizes them. He says whoa and the horse stops and noses an empty old sap bucket tacked to a tall maple tree.

Thaddeus closes his eyes and thinks on sugar-covered snow.

He thinks more faraway thoughts and keeps his breathing calm.

What you boys up to, the fat cop says.

He is looking right at Thaddeus when he says it but Billy Tucker cuts in.

Just minding our business sir yes sir.

The words he chooses are respectful, but the tone is decidedly not. The horse whinnies, rolls its eyes, coughs a little as though in retort. Tight skin shudders and rolling muscles flex beneath a velvety hide. Broad nostrils blow long tendrils of green snot everywhere.

You can't drive that thing down here, the fat cop says.

He indicates the car with a lazy sweep of his hand, and wonders about Thaddeus DuBois, wasn't aware that he was allowed back in town after the latest infraction. That he had completed his sentence, that he had paid his debt to society—as though that side of the ledger can ever truly be squared up. The all-male DuBois clan is well known to local law enforcement and has been for years and years, generations. He's not sure how to broach the topic.

All right then we'll move her sir yes sir, Billy Tucker says.

Again with the tone. Billy Tucker turns the key in the ignition and the cop unsnaps the holster for his sidearm. It's a standard-issue black Sig Sauer nine millimeter handgun. Thaddeus keeps staring straight ahead and wishes the whole fucking thing away. I can't be here, he thinks.

Hold on there boy, the fat cop says. You can't just do that.

But you said move it sir yes sir.

Well now I said turn it off there boy.

He draws his nine and holds it gingerly like he might drop it. He's only fired it for target practice, shooting empty soda cans and beer bottles at the public landfill. Billy Tucker shuts off the engine and it barks once before going quiet and the horse gets nervous. Thaddeus takes a snort from the bottle and that attracts the cop's attention, too.

A great horned owl sings its five-syllable song in the background and Thaddeus opens his eyes and looks for the telltale silhouette in the black tree shadows, but the nocturnal predator remains hidden. Then the cop's horse shifts his stance and lifts his tail and shits, leaving a steaming pile that stinks. Billy Tucker laughs and punches Thaddeus in the shoulder playfully. Everything is still a game. The fat cop doesn't laugh, though. It's not a game to him—none of this. He takes his position and his duties seriously, and he raises his eyebrows in such a way that the skin of his forehead furrows beneath his sweat-stained hat brim.

He leans in and sniffs.

He makes a face.

You boys been drinking, he says. On top of everything else.

He shakes his head, disappointed perhaps, but not at all surprised.

Thaddeus sits still because he knows better than to put up any kind of resistance at this point but Billy suddenly shoulders his dented door and it opens with a creak and he swings his legs out and runs with just a quick glance over his shoulder and he laughs and the horse bucks and the fat cop fumbles the reigns then drops his gun. Thaddeus looks at it for a long time lying there in the dirt where he could easily get to it first.

SEVERAL HOURS LATER BILLY TUCKER is slumped over a table and Darling Nikki is rubbing up against the thumb-smudged brass pole in the center of the room. Thaddeus is drinking rotgut and chewing ice chips. It's the last of a three-song set and men throw singles at her. She sees Thaddeus and when she finishes her routine she comes over and sits in his lap. It's been years. She tussles Billy Tucker's hair but he's toast. She talks with Thaddeus about the usual things, then goes out back to change into her street clothes.

She helps Thaddeus carry Billy Tucker and they leave him on the bench seat of his old Chevrolet. Thaddeus is hiding out in a broken-down recreational vehicle that stays parked in a barn on his father's property in Leverett. He throws a towel over the stack of dirty dishes in the kitchenette and Nikki laughs and asks why he even bothers. It's different than when other people laugh at him—it's as though he's in on the joke.

Always been like that with her. So she smiles.

Thaddeus tells her about the run-in with the fat cop on horseback.

So he just let you go then, she says.

After I gave him his piece.

Cause he knew you could of used it on him.

I thought of that too.

Well you made the right choice it seems.

There's a first time for everything.

She laughs and pinches his arm playfully and then seems to reconsider.

Hey what about me then, she says. Wasn't I ever the right choice.

At one time maybe you were.

Darling Nikki laughs.

And so then what happened to Billy, she says.

He was already down at the river taking off his shoes and socks.

Fixing to cross it.

I figure.

And go where exactly.

Exactly.

She laughs at the image of Billy Tucker wading across the river.

Well now what, she says.

He looks at her as though he hasn't eaten for days and she is a warm plate of biscuits and gravy. It has been a long time since he has been with her, or any other woman for that matter. He hears it's like riding a bicycle in that you don't forget how to do it.

But he's not yet convinced.

He smiles his teeth at Darling Nikki.

Shit, he says. Now let's do that thing.

All right.

Been a while for me you know, he says. I apologize in advance.

Don't worry baby, she says. I'll help you along.

Darling Nikki fiddles inside her purse and then, using her index finger, she proceeds to rub a small amount of cocaine along Thaddeus' gums, and then she does the same to her own. She puts the transistor radio on soft and dances for him because she knows that's what he likes. That's how he likes to start things off. There isn't much space, but it's old hat for her. She smells pink like cotton candy from the Franklin County Fair when he was a boy and he tells her as much.

After two songs she is naked except for the heels and then she stands Thaddeus up and takes off his clothes. Then she turns around and grabs the edge of the aluminum sink with one hand and puts him deep inside her with the other. She is well lubricated and athletic and she works hard and does what she can for him but there is just no reaching the finish line in his condition. She knows it is his fault and she doesn't take it personally, which is the beauty of it, their relationship, the understanding they have. He pays her what he remembers to be the normal amount and she puts the crumpled, sweat-soaked bills in her purse and lies on his mattress and kicks off her heels and closes her eyes.

She pulls the thin green sheet up to her neck. It smells like mothballs.

That's the old rate by the way, she says.

What's that now.

What you gave me.

Oh shit.

He reaches for his billfold but it's empty.

Gone up since you been inside, she says.

All right but shit.

He opens his wallet up to her so she can see his dilemma.

Not a dime to your name, she says. How you gone to start over like that.

I'll manage.

Shit, honey, I guess you always do.

He looks at her and then away.

Don't worry about the difference, she says. We'll say it's for old times' sake.

She thinks back to when they were an item. The relationship had always been either real good or real bad—four days could feel like four hundred years when they weren't fucking or stoned out of their minds. But he seems to have mellowed during his time in Cedar Junction. Maybe it could work this time around; a girl can dream.

That's her mindset as she drifts off to sleep.

OUTSIDE IN THE CAR BILLY Tucker is snoring and fresh fog is an army of cold ghosts scaling Bull Hill. Thaddeus tries to sleep but his father, Earl Ran DuBois, is over at the main house yelling at his live-in girlfriend again, Thaddeus listens through the window that is propped open with an empty Jack Daniels bottle. He can't discern everything but it has to do with his mother.

Some things never change.

His father is incoherent most of the time and doesn't even know what year it is. He wastes a lot of energy ranting about how she had abandoned him and the boys when she died, when her insides rusted like auto parts from exposure was how Thaddeus pictured it, how some hacksaw doctor had described the cancer that took her away.

That was a lifetime ago, he thinks.

Liz, the girlfriend, simply ignores the old man when he gets like that.

She waits tables over at Wolfie's and Steeplejack's, and occasionally tends bar at the Polish Club. She takes pretty good care of Earl Ran DuBois for the most part, but the old man is certain she's just after his social security. He says often and aloud that she's a whore. He taught Thaddeus and Blackie early on that they're all whores and eventually believing him put his sons at a certain disadvantage.

His father is dying in that room upstairs, hooked up to an oxygen tank. Liz wheels him around the old farmhouse in a rented Cooley Dick hospital bed for his meals and to clean him up because he shits himself constantly. Prior to his latest nickel she used to invite Thaddeus to dinner sometimes, but he declined more often than not. He can't stand to see the old man like that. He told Billy Tucker once that when he's in that bad of shape to just go ahead and pull the plug. Pull the fucking plug on me, he said. Billy Tucker promised because Thaddeus insisted, but that wasn't really going to be an option. Billy always knew Thaddeus was going to end up sliced open like a trout on the riverbank or alone in some deep-dug ditch.

CHAPTER THREE

Two towns over in a poorly lit parking lot outside the VFW a red Willys sits in idle. It's bullshit, as far as Blackie can tell. He looks Kat in the eye, but she is a practiced liar and he knows it. She's a lying goddamn whore. There is a light drizzle building up on the windshield. The truck heater is busted and shooting hot air from the engine full blast at their feet. He doesn't mind because he is used to it, but she's worried that her fancy new boots are going to melt. She got them on layaway at the Brattleboro Army/Navy.

Can't you turn that thing down, she says.

Don't you change subjects on me.

I aint, she says. But my boots.

She shifts her body so she can tuck her legs behind her and maybe save the boots. Blackie grips the steering wheel with his left hand, its knuckles tattooed "H-A-T-E." She smells like a St. Catherine Street prostitute to him. Her makeup is heavy and running from the humid weather and from her long shift over at the Shutesbury AC. She disgusts him sometimes. She looks like a fucking circus clown and he tells her so directly.

A fucking clown from the circus, he says.

Kat doesn't respond because she is on thin ice already.

I seen you walk out with him, he says.

He's referring to Mark, who is waiting in his Buick Regal three spots away.

We was just talking, she says. Honest injun.

She lies like a fucking rug, he thinks.

I swear on my dead dog, she says. And you know how I loved Jelly.

Right, he says. Good thing I showed up when I did.

Shit baby, she says. You know it aint like that.

Problem is, he says. I know exactly how it's fucking like.

She tries to touch the side of his face gently with her fingertips, but he reaches up and gets hold of her wrist and he squeezes until she yelps like a scolded pup and then he slowly increases the pressure.

She cries softly. It feels like she got herself stuck in a table-mounted vice.

Come on Black, she says. You know I wouldn't never.

It's true. She has remained faithful to him all these years—out of fear mostly.

Blackie puts his face in hers and he can smell the spray in her big pile of hair that is now stiff and immovable. It irritates his nose. There are more tears welling up in her dark-circled raccoon eyes. He squeezes more and the bones in her wrist turn to sand. She doesn't understand the stress that he's under, he thinks. Trying to raise a boy in this upside-down world without his mother around to help. They never understand. He can't figure it. Not for the life of him. He's never been convinced it's worth the energy to try.

You fucking cow, he says without unclenching his teeth.

She doesn't say anything back because she knows better. They have been together a long time off and on and she is content to let the storm pass. He releases the steering wheel and hits her with his left hand open and flat, and he's still holding her damaged wrist with his other. She squirms, but not much else because it is no use. The blows sting at first, but she numbs up quick. Mark is watching from his car and eventually gets out and approaches the pickup. It's a full-on one-armed beating by the time he gets to Blackie's window.

Mark raps on it with his knuckles. He's new in town and doesn't know Blackie and hasn't heard anything about him yet. If he had then he would likely just let it go. He would forget the sad, fat and oddly attractive gal who had been giving him free whiskey and bitters all night long. But he assumes this man is like most men.

That this here will be a normal confrontation.

Dude, he says. What the fuck.

Blackie turns and sees Mark and he lets go of Kat and he shoves her to the far side of the cab and tells her to stay put. Then he opens his door and Mark steps back to let him out, which is his second or third mistake depending on how you are counting. The rain is falling hard now. Blackie doesn't say a word, he just slams the heel of his hand up under Mark's chin and there is a muted sound like a bagful of glass breaking. Then with his closed left fist Blackie aims higher and Mark's nose bone gets shoved up and back into his brain pan and the big young man falls backward onto the pavement, his whole head a box of broken parts. He's out cold before he even reaches the ground and the transaction is complete, and Blackie gets back in the jeep. Kat is crying and shivering and shaking her head. Strings of snot like saltwater taffy. Blackie closes the door and looks at her. He doesn't understand women. How they are wired. Just look at her, he thinks. Pathetic. The more he looks at her, the more angry he is getting and she can sense this. She has been with him long enough to know how to read him, not that it has ever been difficult.

But over the years she has learned certain diversionary tactics.

Kat collects herself and lets him stew in his own juices for a minute or two.

Then she indicates the rain pelting the windshield.

The devil's wife is crying again, she says.

It's a line he taught her years ago.

One that never fails to tickle him.

She waits a few beats for his typical follow-up.

Yeah, he finally says. I wonder what she done to deserve it this time.

Kat sighs, relieved, and smiles at him.

Let's just go Black, she says.

Trying to calm him down.

Using that careful tone she often uses.

He looks away from her and out the windshield and at the rain that is hail pellets now. He puts the vehicle in drive and pulls slowly out of his spot without any regard for the critically injured man on the ground next to his vehicle. He drives in silence and Kat calms herself down and slowly works her way toward him until she is against him and she can feel the heat from his body as well as the heat from the busted unit and she doesn't care about her boots anymore. She doesn't care about the young guy with the funny stories who spent a good part of the afternoon and early evening seducing her.

All that matters now is not getting hit anymore tonight.

This isn't so bad, she thinks.

It could be worse, she convinces herself. Much worse.

She's quite familiar with worse.

She puts her hand on his kneecap and he doesn't flinch and she smiles and tastes her lipstick that has been smudged and her own blood and splinters from a newly broken tooth. Dust from the dashboard from when he had banged her face on it.

Ah what the fuck, she thinks.

Kat knows how to get him settled.

It's not rocket science.

She pulls up her red skirt and pulls down her black tights and the cab fills up with her musk. Blackie steers the jeep into the chink-food restaurant just past the rotary.

The place has been shut down for months for health code violations.

He parks out back and kills the headlamps.

Let's go home Black, she says, after he has dumped his mess inside her.

THEY DRIVE BACK TO HER place and the lights are already on throughout but that doesn't unnerve her because Blackie has a key for when he needs a crash pad and if she's staying at her mom's house in Athol. Not that he really ever needed a key, there's not a door built strong enough to keep out a DuBois man. The rain has stopped for the most part. But you can still smell it. He parks in the makeshift carport and opens his door and gets out and she slides out behind him. The driveway is mostly mud and puddles and she worries about her fancy new boots some more now. She walks carefully but sinks a little with each step. She wishes he'd carry her but doesn't dare ask for such a thing. More likely he'd drag her by her hair at the suggestion. A black bat flies low and startles her.

They get inside the house she rents from a one-legged Pollack named Chester. She puts her purse on the table near the door and he tosses his keys there, too, and he smiles teeth like corn nuts. She wonders about that smile and what it truly means. It worries her more than anything. Then she hears an unfamiliar noise upstairs. Different than the usual creaks and groans of an old house. She doesn't own any pets nor have any roommates.

She looks at Blackie.

Don't worry about him, he says. It's nothing.

Him who, she says.

Just stay out of the spare room.

She feels suddenly sick. Lightheaded and also like she's going to puke. She doesn't even know why yet. But she can sense that he has done something awful bad.

She can sense that he has entered new territory.

What you done, she says after a couple heartbeats. Black.

She's trying to get a read on him.

They stand there without speaking.

Mud is dripping audibly from their footwear onto the warped linoleum floor.

What the hell, he says. Come on.

He takes the stairs two at a time and she follows him at a slower pace. He waits for her and then guides her down the narrow hall. As they get closer she can hear the black-and-white television humming in the room that is otherwise empty of furniture.

What the fuck, she says.

She stops.

He stops too and looks at her.

Then he turns her by the elbow and the door to the spare room is closed and he leans against it until it opens and he takes her in there with him and shuts it. There is no light but for the television that only gets two local channels and so her eyes need a few seconds to adjust. Old wallpaper sunfaded and bubbled in places, and peeling back like cancerous skin in others, exposed plaster and lathe and pink gobs of insulation. And then she sees what he has done. Or what he has started to do because it's clear he's not yet finished. She gets sick in her mouth and swallows it back and it tastes bitter like stomach bile. The taste of her own innards makes her even more sick than before. She vomits again and this time lets it out into her cupped hands—pieces of the fried fish sandwich from Wolfie's she had eaten for lunch. Then she collects herself to a certain degree.

She stands there holding the chunks of her own vomit.

It drips between her splayed fingers.

This is what she sees: that boy from down the street is chained to the radiator.

Like a fucking rabid dog, begging for a bullet.

Skin so pale he seems to glow in the dark. He's been missing for a while. It's been in all the local papers. His face is swollen, there's dried blood around his mouth that looks like the remnants of a blueberry pie, his clothes are torn like they've been run through a wood chipper and he is fastened in such a way that he can't sit up straight. Only one of his eyes seems to work now and he looks at her with it—really trains her with it. He does not look at Blackie. It seems he has seen enough of Blackie. His name is Raymont Redwine and his father who he lives with drives a rig up and down Route 91 for the soup company in Indian Falls. She knows the family, but not well. The mother is Amanda. They have pretty much kept to themselves ever since there were some allegations made against Ray when he was a younger man. Kat never believed he had it in him.

Until recently, Raymont would spend his days walking the dead-end street from Kelleher Drive to the treeline, muttering to himself, talking to the birds and whatnot. They say he has the mind of a four-year-old kid. Then she notices the snapped-off broom handle, the channel locks, the thick roll of duct tape, a plugged-in extension chord with a frayed cut end, the jar of petroleum jelly. These things are scattered about on the floor like the crude tools of a handyman in the middle of a weekend project. She looks closer and there among them is a large tooth with a silver filling inside, probably a molar.

She runs her tongue across her own dental work, feeling the newly empty space.

Jesus Christ what you done, she repeats.

Blackie lets out a long and satisfied breath before he speaks.

This aint nothing, he says. We're just messing.

She doesn't understand how his twisted mind works. Never has and she thanks God for it. He steps closer to the retard and Raping Ray flinches away, but keeps his eye fixed on her. Blackie gives him a swift kick with the steel toe of his work boot. Then Blackie squats and picks up the broom handle, pokes Raymont playfully, almost gently.

The retard looks up when Kat drops her regurgitated fish sandwich on the floor and it lands with a sound like splat and then she wipes her hands on the front of her skirt. Then Kat thinks maybe this is a good thing. That if Blackie uses up all of his animosity and violence, or at least a fair amount of it, on poor Raymont Redwine, maybe it will work out in her favor. She'll be somehow spared. She's embarrassed to even think it, it's so selfish. But she starts to reshape in her mind the meaning of this development.

A temporary reprieve is how she thinks of it.

How she tries to think of it.

He deserves everything he gets, Blackie says to her.

She sits on the wood crate by the window and folds her arms across her chest.

Blackie looks at Kat and nods his head up and down.

Oh shit, she thinks. If I call the cops he'll fucking kill me dead.

CHAPTER FOUR

THE NEXT NIGHT THERE IS a keg party over by the river. Fat Johnny parks under Stillwater Bridge. Bobby rolls a joint and they smoke it in the Charger with the engine off and the radio oozing Hank Williams Junior. Fat Johnny changes the lyrics to Blackie and Kat and Bobby laughs at the humorous tribute to his old man and the human punching bag.

The water is running fast because they must have let the dam out again at the Old Squaw Reservoir. There are some drunk flyfisherman in hip boots flicking their leg-thick wrists in synchronicity. The pot is good. Bobby bought it off Tyrone Mayfield, who grows it in his mother's trailer in Ashfield. His mother also runs guns for the local chapter of the Hell's Angels. Tyrone's ambition is to be a biker someday, but watching his mother blow one is as close as he'll ever get. Of that Bobby is certain. Fat Johnny hits it last and puts the roach in the ashtray. He exhales after a while and he looks at Bobby and he laughs.

That is some good shit boy, he says.

Fucking Ryrone came through.

Tyrone has a speech impediment and they think it's funny. They both laugh. They get out of the car and Fat Johnny pops the trunk and Bobby grabs the twelve-pack of Budweiser tall boys that was in a bucketful of ice. Fat Johnny takes off his t-shirt that says King of Beers and puts it in the trunk near the spare tire. Bobby takes off his plain white t-shirt and throws it in there, too. They sit on the chrome bumper and undo their boots. Peel off socks. Bobby closes the trunk and they are just in their cutoff jeans shorts and Double D's caps.

Fat Johnny follows the trail along the bank of the river and Bobby follows him with the beer. Weeds and cattails scratch their bare legs. Then the trail ends and they walk in the water until they have to swim and Bobby floats on his back with the beer on his chest.

Everybody is over by the rope swing. Somebody Tarzan yells and does a cannonball. Bobby and Fat Johnny get across and pull themselves up with tree roots and rocky toe holds. Doreen is there and she comes over and takes a beer from Bobby. She takes the cap off his head and fixes her blond hair beneath it. She smiles at Fat Johnny. Then she smiles at Bobby and takes his hand and stands right up against him. She smells like onion rings, which gets him hungry because he hasn't eaten a meal in a while. It's dusk and there's a fuzziness to everything. They stand there like that and drink beer and look at the river—white foam forming around boulders barely seen, the dangerous bulk of them well hidden. Earlier in the year a college kid smashed his head on one when he tried to shoot the rapids. The farmer who owned the land strung razor wire and put up signs, but nobody pays him any mind unless he appears on the ridge with his pepper gun.

Which, from time to time, he will.

What's up, Doreen says to Bobby.

Nothing.

Where you been at.

Nowheres.

Smoking some.

Maybe some.

Fat Johnny lights a bonfire with an old pallet and pieces of a felled tree. Mike Pekarski brought a bagful of kielbasa from his family's smokehouse off Route 116 and they cook them with crooked sticks over orange flames. Bobby sits on a buttonball stump and Doreen sits on his lap. The sausage is good and spicy and there is grease on his chin that she dabs with the bottom of her shirt. Fat Johnny makes out with Jenny Skibiski. Then it's deeper night and the moon is high and full and illuminating the scene with blue. A couple older kids from Bucktown start acting up, getting loud and smashing empty bottles, real assholes. Fat Johnny gives Bobby a look and Doreen gets up and Bobby gets up and Fat Johnny gets up, too. Doreen holds Bobby's beer and sits back down on the stump, takes a sip. Fat Johnny spits and they stand apart and there's a breeze that hints at the toxin that flows slow from Timmy Boho's single-prop crop duster.

Fucking faggots, Fat Johnny says.

It's about the worst insult you can hurl at a local fellow.

The Bucktown boys look over and start to laugh. The bigger one looks at Bobby and sizes him up and he looks at his friend. Then he looks back at Bobby and he spits. He's made a choice. It's the wrong one, but he doesn't know that yet and the reality is the other option is not too much better. Bobby turns to the side just a bit and spreads his feet apart, making himself difficult to strike, a harder target. But not so you'd even notice.

The fuck you say, the bigger one says to Bobby.

Everybody else gets real quiet.

And Bobby doesn't waste any words on him.

He's got nothing to say.

Bobby's eyes are always most clear and still and empty and black just prior to and during a physical altercation—Doreen calls them his Doll Eyes and they scare her. Then there's a profound hush that settles in on the scene and lasts a few long heartbeats. Bobby and Fat Johnny like to mix it up from time to time; throwing hands is a hobby of theirs and everybody knows this to be a fact. The crowd forms an imperfect circle around them, anticipating the burst of violence. Then Fat Johnny clears his throat.

Time to get gone, he says.

The big one looks at Fat Johnny for the first time. He appears to weigh his options again for a split second and just as he is making his move Fat Johnny reaches up and takes him by the neck with both hands and drags that kid into the dirt and a brown cloud forms around their scrum. Fat Johnny will not let go for nothing. Then the other one steps in to help and Bobby puts his shoulder into it and splits his nose open with a closed fist. The kid isn't used to seeing his own blood and he hollers and cups his hands over his face and so Bobby goes to work on where his organs are, softening them, stealing his wind, until he drops to the ground, whimpers. Bobby crouches over him and hears a rib snap like a dry branch. He breaks his jaw in two or three places. Years ago his uncle had filled a sack with hard dirt and wood chips and hung it from a tree and taught him to fight like a man. At first he used brown leather work gloves but after a time the thin skin on his knuckles had thickened and he didn't need them anymore.

Fat Johnny gets up and they put their heels onto the exposed parts of those boys until they crawl off like bad dogs just beaten. They scramble down the muddy bank. Bobby and Fat Johnny let them go and watch them clean their wounds in the river once they think that they're a safe distance away, sobbing like little bitches. They look up from time to time, neither one says shit now. All the courage and bluster drained out of them.

Lesson learned.

Fat Johnny spits and he looks at Bobby and he speaks.

Pickle smoochers, he says.

That's right.

They laugh and Doreen gets up so Bobby can sit back down but instead he takes her hand and they go for a walk. After a while they stop walking and he leans against a tree and lets her give him head. Then she stands up and puts her face on his chest and listens to whatever is inside him. The dark trees hide things in this perfect part of night. There are fireflies and she gets Bobby to look when she points them out. He almost smiles and nods his head for her, pretending to see what she sees, to feel what she feels.

But what he feels is different and she wouldn't understand.

He's still coming down from the adrenaline rush that accompanies confrontation.

His hands are shaking.

Then she speaks.

I don't like when you fight hey.

That wasn't no fight.

What you call it then.

I don't call it nothing.

Well whatever.

Bobby sips at his bottle of beer and she keeps on about it.

You're gone to get hurt someday, or maybe even worse.

Shit whatever.

You're not like them others, she says. I don't know why you got to act like that.

What others.

Your daddy and your uncle and them.

Bobby spits.

Shit girl, he says. I'm exactly fucking like that.

Bobby says it as though he's proud but he's not always so sure. He figures it doesn't matter how he feels anyhow. You can't choose what you're born into and he just tries to make the most of it. Doreen finally drops it and there is just the sound of crickets and the river and some breeze in the branches a hundred feet above them. Bobby closes his eyes. She is a good and loyal girl, he thinks. She lives in a nice blue house on Captain Lathrop Drive and her parents don't know what she sees in Bobby. He's considered a town boy or a townie. Her parents prefer the college-bound preppy motherfuckers that come sniffing around. They never last long, but Bobby doesn't blame them for trying.

THEY WALK BACK TO THE party and Fat Johnny wants to go ride around. Doreen and Jenny want to come, too. Fat Johnny shakes his head no and so Bobby kisses Doreen goodbye and takes his hat from her head and they swim back across the river. Then they drive around barefoot and shirtless and the air is warm and the entire town smells like a beautiful black mountain of cow shit. Fat Johnny parks in front of Leo's TV and Bobby's old man's pickup is there, too. The Hot L is closing and he is likely taking last call before going upstairs to their apartment. Fat Johnny got them a job throwing hay the next day.

Want me to get you, he says, in the morning.

What time.

He said six to beat the heat.

All right.

Or we can meet over at the field, Fat Johnny says. Whatever the fuck.

Come here is better or else I'll be late.

Bobby gets out and Fat Johnny drives off. Bobby crosses the street and enters the Hot L and Sue is bartending. She smiles at him and his old man is sitting at the bar with a gin and bitter. He is the only one left. Bobby goes upstairs. The old French Canadian couple next door is fighting again. The woman is yelling about this or that, but he can't understand their talk. Something in her voice makes him think of his mother who died long ago in a car wreck. Folks at the drugstore say in whispers that she drove her Ford Pinto off the Cheapside Bridge on purpose because that was the only way she could free herself from Blackie. They don't have any photos, but he thinks she had hair the color of wheat.

Bobby kicks off his boots and tries to get comfortable on the couch. He's starting to fall asleep when the old man bangs on the door because he can't get his key to work again. Bobby lets him in and he looks at Bobby like he's a stranger. The old man pushes past him and sits down hard on the couch and puts his feet on the table, takes off his footwear. There's a hole in his sock and his purple-bruised black-nailed big toe sticks out.

He looks up at Bobby and rubs his face.

Fuck you looking at boy, he says.

Nothing.

Don't nothing me, boy.

Here we go again, Bobby thinks.

He closes the door and pulls the deadbolt that rarely functions properly.

Stop all that racket now boy, Blackie says. I need some sleep.

Blackie tips over onto his side slow like a cut tree and he squeezes a throw pillow between his knees and closes his eyes and a low noise comes out of him like a cow giving milk through a shiny metal machine. There are fresh marks on his face and neck as though maybe Raymont or Kat had put up a bit of a fight and Bobby's glad to know it. Maybe he'll pop up there tomorrow with a set of bolt cutters so he can spring Raping Ray. That poor bastard doesn't deserve what Bobby imagines he's being subjected to, even if what they say is true. He gets a blanket from the closet that smells like mothballs and makes his bed in the chair next to the television that does not always work. The old man is already snoring. He will piss himself and likely worse and be mad in the morning. He'll wake up in his own mess and it will be Bobby's fault and he will pay a steep price.

CHAPTER FIVE

IN THE MORNING FAT JOHNNY hits the horn out in the street. Bobby's head hurts and he goes into the bathroom and pops a couple three aspirin and drinks from the faucet. The water tastes rusty like the galvanized steel pipes that deliver it. The apartment smells like his old man's breath that smells like fifty years of living wrong. Bobby grabs long pants and a green t-shirt and his old man's cigarillos from the coffee table. Blackie is not home, but his stink has stayed behind. Bobby has no idea where his father could've got to this early in the day. He must be off to tend to his prisoner. It's like he's got a new pet. Jesus fucking Christ. Bobby stretches and unbolts the door, opens it and closes it. Fat Johnny is sitting in the Charger with his hazards on in the middle of the street nursing a large cup of black coffee from the pharmacy. He laughs when he sees Bobby.

Bobby opens the car door and gets in and closes it.

You look bad as I feel, Fat Johnny says.

His coffee smells good and strong to Bobby.

Shit, Bobby says.

He closes his eyes and breathes deep and opens his eyes again.

They stay parked there a minute.

Thinking about them Bucktown boys, he says.

Oh yeah.

Maybe we was a bit rough on them.

Right.

They're not so bad.

I suppose not.

Bobby looks at Fat Johnny and he looks at Bobby and he laughs.

Fucking fags, he says.

They hate Bucktown more than Indian Falls but only because it's closer. Fat Johnny puts it in drive and they take 5 and 10 to 116 to Sawmill Plain Road where B. Scoval keeps one of his fields. He is sitting out there on a FarmAll tractor. It's a 1959 140 Hi-Clear. The front wheels have been retrofitted with nineteen-inch tires and rims from a Ford N Series. The little thing is just chugging away. There is an empty grain elevator in the distance, standing tall as a Cedar Junction lookout tower, presiding over Whitebirch Campgrounds, the town's other version of low-income housing. Fat Johnny parks on the dirt shoulder and he shuts the engine down and gets out and Bobby gets out, too.

They walk over to B. Scoval and he sits there pretending to ignore them and they stand in front of him. Eventually he looks up and he's chewing tobacco and he spits out a stream of it. He coughs into his shoulder and it leaves a reddish foamy film in the shape of his mouth on his shirt and then he speaks aloud, to neither of them in particular.

I said work at six not wake up at six, B. Scoval says.

Fat Johnny shrugs his shoulders.

Shit, he says.

Shit nothing, B. Scoval says. I should've hired some Holyoke spics.

No you wouldn't either.

A whole entire family of them. They love an early start.

Come on old timer, cut us a break.

And at this same rate too.

Fat Johnny looks at Bobby and he looks at B. Scoval.

Well shit, Bobby says. We're here now.

B. Scoval spits out a red-brown stream of saliva again.

All right I guess you are, he says. Get on back then you little cock knockers.

There is a trailer with rails of particleboard and plywood hitched to the back, and the boys hop on. He pulls them out to the field where the bales are laid out in perfect rows and Bobby puts the long pants over his shorts. He puts on the flannel over his t-shirt. It's hot and humid already. Muggy as a hundred hells, his old man would say. It's a bumpy ride. B. Scoval slows down and Bobby jumps off and walks alongside and throws bales of hay to Fat Johnny and he stacks them on the trailer. It goes like that for a long while.

BOBBY IS SWEATY AND HIS head is pounding. The sun is burning bold from a cloudless sky. He takes off his hat and wipes his face and forehead with his sleeve. Big summer bugs get in his nose and ears and mouth. B. Scoval stops the tractor and throws Bobby the water jug he keeps behind the seat and the water is cold and good in his throat and on his face. He drinks some more and then he tosses it up to Fat Johnny and he drinks some, too. B. Scoval laughs at their condition. He spits into the dust. Bobby puts his hands on his hips and up on the trailer Fat Johnny stretches his lower back and then he puts his hands on his hips, too. They stand there like that. Then Fat Johnny gives the water jug to B. Scoval and he puts it behind his seat without taking a drink, like a fucking camel. He puts the tractor in gear and Fat Johnny spreads his feet apart and bends his knees a little and Bobby grabs another bale. A spray of pigeons emerges from nowhere and Bobby ducks under the shadow they make and then he watches them disappear. The blood in his head hums and the FarmAll engine hums somewhat and the day seems to hum along, too.

When the trailer is full Bobby stands on the edge with Fat Johnny and holds onto the strings of the bales of hay they just stacked. B. Scoval drives them to the east-leaning barn at the edge of his acreage. There is a small pond with motor oil brown ducks, two sleepy bloodhounds with maple syrup eyes. The hounds look up when the tractor passes, but they are disinterested. Bobby jumps down. There is a piece of two-by-four jammed into a catch to hold the doors shut and he shoves it aside with one hand and swings the doors open wide with the other. A black barn cat scowls orange eyes and disappears into the rafters, one ring from a plastic six-pack holder around its neck, affixed there by some juveniles hoping the cat will get one of the other rings caught on a nail, accidentally hang itself. Bat shit stains the posts and beams like dripped paint. Dust motes obscure and a swallow flaps madly in the high corner where it has nested by a cracked window. B. Scoval positions the trailer and Bobby climbs a support beam to the loft.

Then B. Scoval is cursing a blue streak and tugging at his pantleg that got caught.

Goddamn it to hell, he says.

His pantleg tears and a piece of it is left hanging on the rusted chassis of the old tractor. B. Scoval looks at Fat Johnny still laughing and he looks at Bobby and he speaks.

What's so fucking funny, he says.

You old man.

Twenty years ago I'd show you what's funny.

You were too old even then.

B. Scoval smiles cigar-stained teeth.

You make a point, he says. I am old as dirt.

Then he sits on a chunk of a mulberry stump that's stuck with an axe. He retrieves his pouch of Red Man from the back pocket of his coveralls and he pinches enough for his cheek and he sticks it in there and replaces the pouch where the dungaree fabric has faded around the edges of it and its predecessors over time. He works chaw into its spot and then finally satisfied he spits a bit between his feet. One of the old hounds has risen from the dead and drags himself into the barn and rubs his knotty head against B. Scoval's thigh. He scratches the hound behind its ears and whispers probably about pointing turkey and pheasant and gamecock. Then Fat Johnny bends down and grabs a bale and tosses it up to his friend without warning and Bobby catches it, just. They unload with a familiar rhythm that makes everything else seem all right for now.

THEY'RE FAR FROM THE ROAD and the heat is coming off the blacktop in translucent strip-of-bacon shapes. There is a green four-door Oldsmobile and it's Mrs. B. Scoval. She taps the horn three times. B. Scoval looks up and sees her and he looks at Fat Johnny and he looks at Bobby. He looks at the trailer and appears to be making some calculations in his mind. He's been farming this land a real long time. The trailer is almost full again and B. Scoval shakes his head and spits and then wipes at his mouth with the back of his hand.

Must be lunch time, he says.

Fat Johnny hoots at the sky and Bobby pumps his fist.

B. Scoval laughs at their enthusiastic display.

You boys aint hung is you, he says.

He knows they're a couple of young drunks. But he doesn't know about the other chemicals they imbibe—he wouldn't understand about that. It's a generational divider.

He aims the tractor at the road and lets them take turns with the water jug. By now the water is warm but Bobby drinks it because what the fuck. They follow Mrs. B. Scoval to the house and she has prepared a true spread. Fat Johnny sits on the steps of the porch and Bobby sits on an old tire in the yard and B. Scoval goes inside to get some cold beer that his wife will frown upon. She calls it devil water. Mrs. B. Scoval is a regular churchgoer, which is becoming a rare phenomenon. She serves them cold-cut sandwiches with turkey meat and sliced ham from Rogers & Brooks and provolone cheese from the Italian grocer on Northpoint and lettuce and tomato from her very own backyard garden. There is homemade coleslaw and pickled eggs that she jars every week in summer.

It's shady and there is a slight piney breeze from the hills that seem to roll green and slow to the west. B. Scoval bangs through the screen door smoking a Swisher Sweet and carrying three bottles of Budweiser beer in his good hand, his skinny fingers in the mouths of them. He places a bottle next to Fat Johnny on the steps that need fixing and he gestures for Bobby to come get his and he does. Then he sits back on the tire and B. Scoval sits in a metal chair that bows beneath the weight of him. The lump in his neck goes up and down when he puts his head back for a long slug. Fat Johnny takes a pull, too. Bobby drinks his beer and thinks it tastes different maybe better when you have it after laboring in the sun. Mrs. B. Scoval looks at her husband and shakes her head.

No good doing that, she says.

Doing what now.

Teaching them to drink so early.

He looks at Bobby and he looks at Fat Johnny and he laughs.

Early in the day or early in their life you mean, he says.

She gives him a look.

Either or, she says.

He makes a noise with his mouth that sounds like a stuck metronome.

Shit woman, he says. You can't teach what's already been learnt.

The boys laugh a little.

Besides, B. Scoval says. You know the old saying.

His wife tries to shush him but he waves her off.

Work like a man you drink like a man, he says.

He raises his bottle and Bobby raises his bottle and Fat Johnny raises his, too. Mrs. B. Scoval shakes her head again or still and turns and she goes inside the dark house. B. Scoval finishes his beer and barks her name to bring him another. She eventually brings three more beers under protest and puts them on the card table where the food is. And where a pitcher of stoop-brewed ice tea sits untouched. Ice cubes melting and popping like toy guns when they do. You can hear them popping. But she even knocks the caps off the beers and wipes the mouths of them with a paper napkin. Fat Johnny stands up and gets them and he hands one to B. Scoval and he brings one over to Bobby and they all three raise them up to each other in a salute. Mrs. B. Scoval watches them with her blue-veined hands behind her back. Then she looks at Bobby.

She inspects the bruises on either side of his neck, the size of a man's hands.

Mrs. B. Scoval knows which grown man did that.

You can always stay here, she says. If things get too bad.

She has made similar offers in the past.

The thing is Mrs. B. Scoval thinks she means it, but she has no idea.

Bobby looks at the sky again and then after a few moments he looks at her and she still has him fixed in her gaze that might be motherly, but what would he know about that. The last time his old man got pinched Westy called CPS and they reviewed Bobby's school records as well as what they had on him personally down to the police station and they filed a report. It said next time there was trouble he would have to go into the foster care system since not one of his living local relatives was considered fit to be a parent.

Bobby nods his head slowly and shows her a mouthful of crooked teeth.

Yes ma'am, he says.

But he doesn't really mean it either because, well, he wouldn't know how.

You know that, she says.

Yes ma'am, he says. I believe I do.

But we have rules round here, she says.

Bobby takes a sip of beer and considers the bottle and then he looks at her, smiles.

Oh yes, he says. I can see that ma'am.

B. Scoval spits beer when he laughs and it comes out his nose. Fat Johnny slaps his knees and even Mrs. B. Scoval grins before she turns and disappears again. Then the afternoon goes slow. B. Scoval pays the boys cash and drops them at Fat Johnny's car.

CHAPTER SIX

THADDEUS RUBS HIS EYES WITH his thumbs at dawn's first kiss. He smells coffee and hears bacon fat spitting and there is a small bird outside somewhere singing a song that's like a gift in his ears. He sits up and Darling Nikki is long gone and he doesn't even care. Naked he stands and picks his drawers off the floor and puts them on. An old t-shirt that says Chevys Suck. Barefoot still he steps from the trailer into the dark innards of the old barn. He lets his eyes adjust a moment. There is farm equipment in various states of disrepair lined up alongside the far wall: a thresher, two wood splitters, an engine block, part of a combine harvester and several random handheld items. His father used to work the land before he lost his mind and became obsessed with conspiracy theories. Then a warm triangle of light shows through a dirty window as the sun creeps up over Bull Hill.

Thaddeus blinks and walks like a blind man with his hands out in front of him, making his way carefully to the door that leads to the yard. He opens the door with his lowered shoulder and the day hits him hard in the face. A fine mist has settled on everything and two acres of tall grass and the trees at the foot of the hill. There is a plywood chicken coop next to the barn and three hens pecking at dry corn stop to regard him, but only for a half a beat and then they turn back to their breakfast, watching him nervously, one-eyed and sideways like they do.

The bull cock is shit-black and he puffs up and rushes. Thaddeus laughs inside to himself and throws a foot at the rooster. It is stupid brave and repeats its attack from a few different angles.

Come on now, Thaddeus says. Get back.

But truth be told he has an appreciation for the bird's pluck.

He looks around for Billy Tucker's car but he's gone, too.

His father's girlfriend keeps a garden patch a stone's throw from the house. A square of red tomatoes and green bell peppers and yellow squash and a single tall sunflower that droops under the weight of its own self. He can hear her in the kitchen scrambling eggs with a wood spoon. The radio is playing. It sounds like she's humming a song she knows. She'll be surprised to see him, but she won't let on. He has always liked that about her, her ability to keep chugging along even when life throws her a shocker. He puts his hands deep in his pockets and crosses the dirt driveway and takes the three cement steps, and through the quarter panes he can see her standing over the stove with her back to him. He twists the knob and opens the door and steps inside and she turns and looks at him and then, at first without a word, she goes back about her business.

She remains quiet for a spell.

She didn't even know that he'd been released.

Suppose you hungry, she eventually says.

I could eat.

Thaddeus pulls a chair out from under the kitchen table and sits. Liz cracks three eggs and turns up the burner. The bacon strips are dark and crispy and set on paper towels on a cutting board. There is a large knife that she uses to chop green peppers and tomatoes and onion-grass that she then drops into the pan with the eggs. She is making what his father used to call a lazy man's omelet: all the ingredients but minus the fancy packaging. Liz wipes her hands on her apron and shuts the stove down and gets two plates from the cupboard. There is bread in the toaster. She makes a plate for him and one for herself and she joins him at the small card table. She is wearing jeans rolled up at the bottom and a big flannel shirt with a tattered collar and red and black checkers.

So how is he, he says.

Oh you know.

Yeah I guess I do.

His father is a miserable prick and even worse now that he's insane and paranoid with old age. Thaddeus scoops eggs and vegetables onto a heel of toasted bread. Liz watches him and uses her fork and chews slowly and takes a sip from her coffee. The man on the radio is talking about the weather. He talks about a storm out to sea. They named the storm after a woman, which Thaddeus thinks is appropriate. He has never seen the ocean but he likes to swim in a fast river or a shallow pond or over to Old Squaw Reservoir, which had swallowed up some of the old towns when he was just a lad.

You like that bread, she says.

It's damn good.

It's from Hebert, she says. That's the new French baker in town.

Good.

It's a short loaf with a crunchy brown crust that flakes when he pulls it apart with his hands. He smears it with the sweet, thick cream butter that she has set before him. Neither one of them is much good at small talk, but they are trying to catch up.

Your pa don't like the French, she says, laughing a little bit.

Thaddeus nods his head up and down as he chews.

If I remember correct, he says. He don't like nobody much.

Now she nods her head up and down.

No, she says. Not much.

Then she offers him coffee.

All right.

She stands up and wipes her hands on her apron and gets a cup from a hook over the sink and goes to the pot on the stove. She pours and Thaddeus eats and watches her and the steam of the coffee rises into her face, which is pretty and round and chestnut.

Her skin is smooth as polished wood from a cabinetmaker's shop.

You like it black, she says.

It's an old joke between them.

Not as much as my pa.

She looks at him and smiles and laughs. He laughs a little, too. She puts the coffee next to his plate. He is nearly done with his food, and Liz gets the pan with the eggs and with the wood spoon she shoves the last of it onto his plate. There is some stuck to the pan that will need to soak for a while. He nods his head at her and makes a small sound of approval from his throat. She gives him four more strips of fat-backed bacon that has been drizzled with brown sugar and another piece of toast that is cool to the touch now.

You can stay out there as long as you like, she says. He'll never even know.

All right.

Not that it's my place to say.

Yours as much as anybody's.

He finishes eating and pushes back from the table and drinks his coffee and looks at what some folks in town call his father's nigger girlfriend—but never to her face. He sometimes uses that word to describe her but he never thinks of her in a negative way. It's a descriptive word to him, as commonly used as some others that are less offensive, like referring to somebody as tall or short. He has been up against the true niggers inside.

She stares into her coffee cup and blows on it and takes a sip. He is a smart boy and a dangerous one, too. In and out of detention facilities his whole life. Even a stint in the mental hospital up in Brattleboro. They called it a retreat and a court had ordered it. But the doctors had released him and determined that Thaddeus was simply a product of his environment, and it was hard to argue. She knows the type well and has always had a soft spot. It's impossible to imagine Earl Ran DuBois raising sons any different than the way Blackie and Thaddeus turned out. She hates to think it, but it's true. And yet Thaddeus is the pope compared to that other one. She is of the opinion that people are born with their bags halfway packed anyhow. And that these boys were going to be rough-cut regardless of parenting. And now young Bobby chasing fast in their footsteps.

She shakes her head when she thinks of the boy.

Liz has always felt that he is slated for something better.

So they let you out, she says.

Well, he says. There's a place I'm supposed to stay at.

Like a halfway house.

Right, he says. But I got about halfway there and turned back around.

Liz laughs.

You don't suppose they'll look for you here, she says after a while.

She had suspected he was on the run because, well, he's always been on the run.

They will turn over some stones, he says.

But not right away likely.

No, he says. Down to Billy Tucker's first and maybe a couple other spots.

Oh I know them other spots too I guess.

He finishes his coffee and puts the empty cup in his lap and crosses his legs. He yawns and stretches his arms and rubs his eyes with his thumbs again. It feels fine to have his stomach full. It feels fine to have a conversation with a relatively sane female person.

So what else, Liz says.

I'll just have to keep moving like I do, he says. You know.

Uh huh.

I suppose that's the thing.

Liz finishes her coffee too and stands and takes their plates and forks to the sink. She runs the tap and tests the water with the soft tips of her fingers. She squeezes green liquid soap from a plastic container. Thaddeus can smell it. Small bubbles emerge from the nipple of the bottle when she sets it down. She uses a yellow sponge.

Blackie been by much, he says.

She does not answer right away, caught off guard and perhaps a bit troubled.

Oh no, she says. Not seen him.

Thaddeus notices that she doesn't sound disappointed.

How about his boy, he says. Bobby there.

She pauses and water runs over the plate in her hands and then she starts again. Bobby is more like Thaddeus, she thinks. He has some saving graces. Could maybe be all right with a little bit of luck. The key would be to remove him from his current situation.

Get him away from his father.

From this goddamn place.

No not here, she says. But I seen him in town when I go looking.

How's that.

Sometimes I'll bring him something, she says. To make sure he's eating all right.

Thaddeus nods his head at her, but she is facing away from him. She would do that, he thinks. That is exactly the kind of thing he would expect from her. She is a fine fucking woman and deserves a better life than the one she's living in Earl Ran's house.

I'ma take him, he says. The boy.

She takes a moment to let this bit of news sink in.

That's a good thing, she eventually says. I suppose.

Us against the world, he says. You know.

Not the whole world.

He shrugs his big shoulders at her and looks out the window. The rubber branches of a weeping willow are brushing against the glass with a hard gust from the northeast. She shuts the water down and removes her apron and hangs it over the back of the chair where she had been sitting. She moves around the kitchen smoothly and without effort like she is on invisible wheels. She dries her hands on a towel on the refrigerator door. Puts her hands on her hips and looks at Thaddeus for a while until he looks back at her.

Then she gets nervous and turns away from him.

There is a thump upstairs and then another. She looks at a brown spot on the ceiling from where the top-floor toilet has leaked from time to time over the years, some kind of broken seal or gasket. Liz remembers that she needs to get in there and check that out. Then she looks at Thaddeus. He stands up and puts his chair back under the table.

Well thanks for the grub, he says. That feels just fine.

She nods her head and he leaves without a word through the same door that had let him in. The sun is now high and hot and backed by bright baby blue. Liz watches from inside the kitchen as her fat chickens panic and Thaddeus slips back into the big red barn.

THERE'S A DRY WELL A couple hundred feet from the barn, not visible from the house or the road. The grass is tall and wide and yellow and Thaddeus flattens some of it with each step. The hole is protected by a circular pile of mismatched stones measuring maybe a foot and a half from the ground. A crude contraption of wood and rope serves as a pulley system. There is a tin pail tied to the unseen end of the rope. The accessible end is frayed and coiled around itself in the dirt like an angry snake lying in wait. Thaddeus lifts the rope and drapes it over the cross-log and pulls it taut, gives it a jiggle. He can feel the weight of the thing he seeks. He jiggles again until he feels it get loose from the weeds and roots that have taken hold through the years. Then, hand over hand, he raises the pail.

It rises full of pebbly creek mud and twigs, blind and see-through centipedes. He flips it over and shakes it so the muck spills at his feet. The smell is rank. He drops the pail and pushes at the pile with the toe of his boot. There is a small cloth satchel, once green and now barely recognizable, held closed with thin ties. He wipes it on his pantleg and fumbles with the ties, unfolds it. There is the cash that he years ago stole from the tin box at Douglas Auctioneers and hid away. Billy Tucker had been contracted to lug antique furniture around and Thaddeus came by to give him a ride and it was simply a crime of opportunity.

It isn't much, but it will hold him over for a stretch.

CHAPTER SEVEN

RAYMONT REDWINE IS SWEATY AND naked and Blackie stands him up. His legs are weak and bruised; he wobbles a bit. He puts his small hands on Blackie's shoulders. The skinny fingers of a piano player minus the necessary dexterity. The heavy metal chain around his ankle is too tight and his circulation is cut off so his foot is swollen, misshapen, blue to the point of being purple. The other end of the chain is still hitched to the radiator that juts uncomfortably from the plaster of the wall. Raymont is done crying. His tear ducts are empty. He's waiting patiently for this man to start in on him again. And then for him to someday be done. The television is playing professional fighting but the sound is muted. The picture is full of static, flickers colors.

Don't worry none, Blackie says.

Raymont doesn't feel any less worried.

There's a plastic jug of industrial-strength bleach at his feet. The kind you'd use with a mop to clean a kitchen floor. Blackie produces an X-Acto knife from his shirt pocket and holds it to Raymont's face. Raymont looks at the blade for a moment. Then he remembers what it is to bleed and he shits himself and his waste is soft and black and runs down his leg like pure liquid. It drips on the floor, it puddles. For the life of him he can't think of what he did wrong to this grownup man on the same street.

He had seen the man from time to time, that's all.

But it must've been something awful bad.

Blackie takes a step back when he sees the mess and laughs out loud.

Shit, he says. Look what you done did now motherfucker.

There is a bucket of cold toilet water and he picks it up and pours it over Raymont, who convulses against it, a shiver that comes from someplace deep and starts from the floor and runs through his pale body like an electrical current. Then Blackie punches him in the stomach, folds him over, drops him to his knees. He puts his hand in what's left of Raymont's thinning hair and stands over him, shirtless.

Blackie's bare chest and stomach and shoulders are splotched angry with red. He holds Raymont in a headlock and puts out his cigar in his good eye. Then he lets him loose. Blackie regards the television screen for a few minutes, distracted from his task. He enjoys a good contest. While it's a welcome rest for Raymont, even he understands the basic concept of temporary.

JUST A FEW MILES AWAY as the crow flies Earl Ran DuBois is watching his neighbor weld a snowplow to his Ford F250. He must think I'm stupid, Earl Ran thinks. There is some hint of an angry god pissing beer-yellow dawn on the fog over Bull Hill. It was his wife's favorite part of the day before she died. The neighbor is out there already with his machine and a flash of light and then another. There are sparks like little stars that hit the cement floor and bounce upward and disappear. A flatbed from McCoy's stops and turns onto Route 63 toward Lake Wyola where Earl swam and cavorted as a child. Then it's quiet again and he closes his eyes just for a minute to find a sliver of peace in that time, and when he opens them the neighbor is looking at him with his mask and Earl Ran will bet his life that the sonofabitch is smiling wide behind it. With only the dark scar of Leverett Road between their old homes they are alone again in the valley. Then the neighbor starts in again. That bastard. With that thing he is stealing Earl Ran's memory.

It's a fucking memory-stealing machine, of that he is certain.

How else could it be happening.

He pulls himself out of the rented hospital bed.

His oxygen tank trails behind him like an old dog.

There's a black phone in the kitchen that doesn't always work. But Earl uses it anyhow and hopes the voice on the other end is a real one. He's out of breath and it takes a few minutes to spit it all out so they can understand. So they can register his complaint.

This is Earl Ran.

I'm not supposed to get excited.

Hold on.

All right.

He's out there again with that goddamn memory-stealing machine.

Well it's got to be him.

Because it's only us between Bull Hill and Leverett Mountain.

Nothing can penetrate that.

I don't care what you say.

That's right.

You remember me.

Sure you do.

Out at the old schoolhouse.

They think it's funny. LaPinta and that other one. Earl doesn't know what they say because he won't let them in the house and he certainly won't go outside. The last time he opened the door for them they took him to Cooley Dick and stuck tubes in him. Their car is parked in his driveway as though he's a criminal. LaPinta finally crosses the road and talks to the neighbor. They chew tobacco and spit at a skinny barn cat that arches and runs. The other one sits in the car and writes things down on a piece of paper.

They're in on it too, he figures.

Of course they are.

The house is probably worth something to somebody. It was built in 1817. There is a problem with the plumbing sometimes, but other than that. There is a low water table. His wife did some research when she was alive and the town was supposed to come out and look into it but Earl could never figure out her system. She was a smart old girl and he was always more of a hands-on type. After he put her in the ground his life went straight to hell. Not only that, but his bastard neighbor is stealing his well water on top of everything else. All those people taking showers over there. They won't leave a drop sometimes. It's all part of the plan. Earl Ran didn't just fall off the cabbage truck.

He doesn't think I'm onto him, Earl thinks. But he will soon enough.

CHAPTER EIGHT

JUST OUTSIDE THE FRONT DOOR of Sammy Blue's Diner is a telephone pole. There's a paper sign on the telephone pole and a fairly recent Polaroid picture of Raymont Redwine looking slightly bewildered, standing in his yard. It claims he's been missing for a week. There's a phone number if you've seen him. It says he's a gentle soul and couldn't hurt a fly. His parents have checked Franklin County Medical Center and Cooley Dickenson Hospital in Northampton. Friends and family have fanned out to search the nearby fields and swamps and wooded areas. State cops dragged the reservoir and the river and the tri-town manmade pond. It's unlike him to just wander off. He's very routine-oriented and predictable. Never spent even a single night away from his parents. Authorities suspect foul play. Possibly a vigilante act of retribution for past accusations, however unfounded.

Blackie laughs when he sees the flier.

People are so fucking stupid.

They're exactly like sheep.

But he enjoys the term: foul play.

It's not really much of a diner. It looks like somebody years ago parked his aluminum camper on the sidewalk, put it up on cement blocks, pulled the tires off and abandoned it. Exposed brake drums are rusted and cobwebby; orange extension chords run out of two open windows, underneath the thing and finally attach to a generator on a plywood platform that makes an awful racket when it kicks in. The inside isn't much better; gutted from the original and converted to form a kitchen and a seating area. Mostly kitchen, it seats maybe six people. This morning there is only one customer.

Sammy Blue is running the grill. His wife is taking orders. There is a blue pen behind her ear, a notepad in her waistband, a thin gold cross on a chain around her neck. This last was a gift from Sammy. They've been together thirty-five years, married thirty-four.

The place smells like eggshells and coffee grinds. Blackie asks for a menu, but the fucking cow tells him there isn't one. He never heard of an eatery without a menu. She pours him a cup of coffee, stands there with her thick-veined hands on her hips, treats him like he's a nobody. He can see in her eyes that she thinks she's better than he is.

Fucking cow, he thinks.

Well, she says.

Well what.

What can I git ya.

I said a fucking menu'd be nice.

She rolls her eyes at him. The cook is watching him now, too. He's smoking a cigarillo and the ashes are piling up at the end of it and about to fall off. Short sleeves of his white t-shirt rolled up further. A grease-splattered apron. Blackie stares right back.

Are you fucking kidding me.

I don't have time for this bullshit, he thinks.

Get me some eggs, he says.

Scrambled okay.

Yeah hey.

Toast.

Wheat.

Bacon.

Sausage and some hashies if you got them.

Of course we got them, she says.

I'd know that if you had a fucking menu wouldn't I.

He says it loud enough to get a rise out of her and to see if the slob in the kitchen would come to her rescue. But the cook simply finishes his cigarillo and starts to dismantle the filter military style. Not a Marine, no fucking way, but maybe Army, Blackie thinks. The waitress ignores his comment and goes away and the cook starts cooking and Blackie scoops sugar into his coffee and sips it. A radio is playing softly somewhere in the back. He can't make out the song exactly. He doesn't want to let it go but he will for now—the menu issue. He mostly wants to eat so it must be their lucky day. And no need to draw attention to himself now and ruin the good thing he's got going.

The way he looks at it, Raymont deserves everything he gets for what he did.

And he has now put that soft-skulled boy on the road to salvation.

He laughs at the thought.

It started out innocent enough, but he can't stop now.

Then he thinks about the fucking menu again.

These fucking people, he thinks.

He can't stand to be around people sometimes.

CHAPTER NINE

AROUND TOWN THEY CALL HIM a war hero but don't really know shit about it. All they know is he went over there for a time and then came back in one piece. And of course the obvious question everybody has for him after a couple drinks is did he blow up any sand niggers in the desert, but he doesn't speak about what he saw, what he did or did not do. Westy fell from a helicopter on his third tour in Afghanistan and he still gets headaches.

He shoots at the big buck, but misses a cunt hair to the right. It's a ten-pointer. The burp of the Winchester echoing in his ears, Westy watches the deer dance across the meadow and into the gloaming grove. He lowers the shotgun, the hot muzzle of the thing aimed at the ground. He kicks dirt with the toe of his boot and spits a long stream of tobacco juice, some of which dribbles into his beard, already stained with it.

Fuck me, he says.

Westy doesn't really have the temperament for such an endeavor; he knows his way around firearms and can outlast most folks in the New England backcountry, but the problem is that he is at the core a restless and social beast and he can't sit still. Manning a deer stand in complete seclusion and silence for hours at a time goes against his every instinct. But more than anything else he's also a finisher and he has come to kill a fucking deer so, using the makeshift ladder comprised of pieces of scrapwood nailed into the thick bark of a hundred-year-old elm, he re-climbs the tree and repositions himself in the four-foot-by-six-foot aluminum box that has been situated high among the muscular-bending branches for as long as he can remember.

After all the commotion he has caused it will be a while before the sounds and smells of nature resume their typical patterns and help to camouflage his presence. That is always the risk of taking a shot. He leans the Winchester in the corner, removes the pouch of Red Man from his jacket pocket and sits on a crate. There are dozens of old beer bottles littered about the sawdusty floor, stuffed with the remnants of past chaws. He picks one that still has room and raises it to his mouth and, using just his tongue, shoves the lump of tobacco into the opening and partway down the neck of the bottle.

He learned guns from an older cousin. As kids they took target practice on a dune in the public landfill, trying to break the big black birds that were constantly scavenging and savaging plastic bags of rubbish. But the birds were impossible to hit and eventually the boys would tire of missing so Westy's cousin would suggest cans.

What kind of cans, Westy would say as if on cue.

Afri-cans, Puerto Ri-cans, maybe a couple three Mexi-cans.

And they would share a laugh together.

He has always felt the local brand of racism to be different than what you hear about down south, for example. Still born of ignorance, it's more of a passive enterprise, lacking the venom and animosity, no white sheets or burning crosses around these parts.

EARL RAN. EARL RAN.

Where did you go off to.

It's Liz. Earl doesn't want to talk to her right now. He closes his eyes and thinks the slow thoughts of a scarecrow. Then she wants to know how long he's been standing out here. His legs are numb. She starts to cry. She gets behind and pushes him toward the house. She wants to put him in Kozy Korners Nursing so he can die quiet with the rest of them. There's a brochure she carries around and he tears it up and she always gets another one.

She cleans blood off his face and fixes his hair, which needs a good clip. I should go see Fortier, he thinks. I hope the wait isn't too long because I can't sit.

There is an old man in Earl's house. He doesn't know who he is or what he wants. He is following Earl from room to room and there he is in the bathroom. He looks afraid and tired. He looks drained. Earl yells at the man to stop following him and he yells right back. Then Earl is covered in gasoline. This is in the toolshed that he built with his own hands. He's underneath the lawnmower somehow. The grass does need to be cut and there used to be a kid in the neighborhood who would do it for five dollars. He wonders what ever happened to him. There is a crowd of people now and Earl can hardly breathe. There are hands everywhere. He closes his eyes and tries not to panic. He tells them about the man in his house. Following around and mocking him, sonofabitch.

Sonofabitch sonofabitch sonofabitch.

He's not supposed to cuss.

Sonofabitch, he yells at the top of his lungs.

He's not supposed to yell.

The strangers disappear and the curtains move but the neighbor doesn't come out. There is a coyote crying off in the distance, probably dying of mange. He'll see him on a fence post tomorrow with flies buzzing around his asshole and birds scratching at his eyeballs. His is a sad song but at least he knows what's coming. It's a harvest moon, too.

Earl is leaning on a broom handle that he puts up to his shoulder like to unload a round of birdshot into his neighbor's upstairs bedroom. His hands are never steady anymore. That used to be a thing of pride for him. Then the slow-wafting fumes from across town at the pickle shop, large vats of green cabbage heads rotting brown.

Liz says that he shouldn't stand in the yard in his underthings.

The sun has made his shoulders red. She puts on a pot of coffee and grills him a cheese Danish from Hebert's, that French fuck. She reads to him from the *Hampshire Gazette*. She tells him about how Todd Bartos was killed when a tree he was cutting snapped vertical. Earl saw that happen one time. Jesus Christ and Todd was not one to do a sloppy job.

It was a fluke. Truth be told, Earl could think of somebody who he'd rather would get killed in such a fashion. He glances again at the house across the way.

CHAPTER TEN

AFTER ANOTHER DAY SPENT LABORING for B. Scoval, Fat Johnny counts his money and puts the heads facing the same direction, which is one of his superstitions, and then he folds it and puts it in the front pocket of his jeans. Bobby doesn't count his and he closes his hand around it and puts it in his pocket like that. Fat Johnny gets his keys from the top of the rear tire and opens his door and gets in and Bobby opens his door and gets in. Fat Johnny starts the engine. He removes his cap and runs his hand through his hair. Bobby sticks his arm out the window. Fat Johnny puts it into drive and punches the gas and fishtails off the shoulder and kicks dirt and stones into their wake. He really opens it up on the straight away and he smiles. The car rights itself and they follow the pink setting sun.

Where to, Fat Johnny says.

Bobby wants to avoid his old man if at all possible.

He can smell himself and he can smell Fat Johnny, too.

Could use a bath, he says.

Fat Johnny turns right onto 116 and then right again onto 5 and 10. He turns left at the Sheli Deli where the smell of fried chicken emanates from angular tin smokestacks and then he takes a hard right down toward the manmade pond. It's supposed to be for residents of the tri-town area only, but niggers and spics from the Holyoke and Springfield have started using it, too, dirtying the water so many of the locals won't even get in anymore. It's late in the day so there is a chain keeping the metal gate shut to vehicles. Fat Johnny parks and they get out and put their shirts and long pants and boots and socks into the trunk. They walk barefoot across Hank Zukowski's pumpkin patch and cut through his yard littered with auto parts and landscaping equipment and bags of trash that collectively resemble a miniature mountain range. There is a treeline and the train tracks past the rabbit run and a dirt path and then the pond. Out in the middle is a sun-flaked white dry dock. On the side farthest from them sits the beach area and an upended lifeguard chair and a fenced-in shithouse that you can smell from a mile away.

Bobby removes his cap and Fat Johnny removes his cap. The water is shallow so they wade until it is deep enough to swim. Then they race to the dry dock. Bobby beats Fat Johnny by a couple strokes and Fat Johnny grabs at Bobby's feet as he pulls himself up onto the worn green turf covered platform. Then it is dusk and they sit there listening to the deep exhortations of bullfrogs. The smoke of a Boston & Maine yet miles away but running fast is visible over the sharp tops of conifer. Then Bobby can hear its rumbling and he can see it skirting the edge of the pond. A whistle blows and its song endures. This line is mostly used for hauling coal and piggybacking service. Fat Johnny is oblivious as he fingers a splinter in the bottom of his foot. Bobby watches him work it.

What you got there Sally, he says.

Fat Johnny's mother's name is Sally.

Fucking cunt, he says. I got a sliver see.

He looks up at Bobby with a pained expression. Displays his foot that is red where he was pinching the skin between his thumb and pointer finger. It looks infected.

That looks bad, Bobby says.

Looks like I got snakebit.

Then the sun is completely gone and the smuggler's moon is reflecting in the water that smells like a pocketful of pennies. They swim back to shore and get their caps and they walk back through the treeline and over the tracks and across Hank Zukowski's yard. Zuke is inside now because they can hear the television and he will come out

with buckshot because he is a paranoid old fruit so they tread carefully.
At the car they dry themselves with their t-shirts and sit on the crooked
chrome bumper that is like a funhouse mirror and they drink a couple
warm beers that were nestled in the spare tire in the trunk. They don't
say anything for a long time. Then Fat Johnny clears his throat.

Doreen closing the pharmacy, he says.

Yeah.

Then you gone see her.

For a spell.

Want to ride around till then.

Shit all right, he says. Why not.

Big Ben is working over at the package store in the center of town
and he sells them beer and a pint of blackberry brandy through the
back door that has cowbells on it.

Where you boys drinking, he says.

Just driving around.

All right but you didn't get this from me.

Shit, Bobby says. I guess we know the fucking drill all right.

I'm just saying.

What are we fucking rookies.

Big Ben closes the door on Bobby and the bells ring and he makes
a funny face through the window. That fucking guy. Fat Johnny laughs.
They park next to the town common and get out and sit on the park
bench near the polished stone commemorating a battle fought long
ago. In the dead of winter a band of 350 Frenchman and Indians
advanced on an English settlement, silently scaling the palisades and
overpowering the sentinel. Blood flowed that day. Bobby opens a beer
and flips the cap into the wishing well. Fat Johnny follows suit. It's the
same as dropping a coin as far as they're concerned but they don't speak
their wishes aloud so as not to ruin them. Bobby closes his eyes and sits
back. He can hear the milking machines from Melnik's, the soft low
moan of cows getting emptied. Fat Johnny goes to Rogers & Brooks for
a couple meatball subs and a bag of chips. His cousin's husband works
there and he will not charge family. Ratso's a pretty good shit like that.
They finish the beer and the sandwiches and the chips.

Fat Johnny remembers about a party over to Hoosac's Road so they leave their empties and wrappers in a pile under the bench. They get into his brother's car and he starts the engine. Then Westy and LaPinta park across the street and they see the boys. Westy makes eye contact with Bobby and he gestures with his hands for them to wait a minute. Bobby looks at Fat Johnny and he makes a face and leans back in his seat. Bobby looks back at the cop car; Westy and LaPinta are talking. Westy is half out of the driver's seat with his foot in the street and his hand on the top of the door. Then they finish talking and he gets all the way out and stretches his back and puts his hat on top of his head. He fiddles with the radio on his belt and it emits a static sound and he makes his way toward Bobby and Fat Johnny. He comes to Bobby's window and Bobby pulls his arm inside and Westy leans down and puts his face in Bobby's. He smells like aftershave. There is razor burn on his neck and blood on his chin. His breath is a pot of black coffee.

The Latin words Semper Fidelis are inked onto his forearm.

Ah yes, Bobby thinks. The fucking war hero.

You boys doing, Westy says.

Nothing.

Westy looks at Fat Johnny and then back at Bobby.

I seen you after doing nothing all night, he says. It aint a pretty sight.

He laughs because he thinks he is funny. Fat Johnny is looking out his window, away from Westy. Bobby is looking straight ahead at the clock that hangs over Pioneer Bank. Westy's radio statics and he curses softly and reaches down without looking and decreases the volume. Westy is filling up the window now so Bobby can't see past him, but he hears LaPinta close his door, too. Then LaPinta is standing in front of the car smiling with a load of chaw in his cheek and shaking his head like a true redneck asshole. He puts his heavy foot on the chrome bumper hard and the car bounces up and down.

Fat Johnny looks up.

Shit man, he says in protest.

Hey potty mouth, LaPinta says. You even old enough to drive yet.

He spits some of the juice from the tobacco resting against his gums.

The brown gob of spit lands on the hood of the car and will eat at the paint job.

Then Fat Johnny shakes his head again and he taps the gas pedal and the engine roars to life and it startles LaPinta because it idles so quiet and he suddenly pulls his boot back off the bumper and stumbles backward a bit and Bobby laughs into his open hand. Then Fat Johnny lets up on the accelerator and he looks over at Westy and he smiles.

Well, he says. My foot can reach the pedal.

Westy just looks at him without speaking.

Must be I'm old enough then.

My foot can reach your ass boy, LaPinta says. And don't think it won't.

Then Fat Johnny looks away from Westy and stays looking out the window. LaPinta comes back around to where Westy is standing and they talk back and forth so Bobby and Fat Johnny cannot really hear them. LaPinta calls them little fuckers and some other things along those lines. Westy tells him to calm the fuck down and go inside. LaPinta looks at Bobby and he looks at Fat Johnny and he makes his hand like a gun and he points it at each of them in turn and makes a popping sound with his mouth.

Everybody in town calls him Super Cop because he takes himself so seriously.

Now you fucks is on my radar, he says.

Oh no, the boys chorus.

I got a memory like an elephant, he says.

Fat Johnny speaks to Bobby but loud enough for everybody.

Ass like a elephant maybe, he says.

Bobby laughs into his hand again and LaPinta's face turns red.

You little fucks best watch yourself, he says.

Fat Johnny adjusts his rearview mirror.

Maybe some town hours would do you good, LaPinta says.

On weekends and after school he shuttles local delinquents around town to pick up trash, at the drive-in movie theatre, the Dwire Lot, alongside Route 91—it's basically slave labor. Bobby and Fat Johnny have extensive experience working on one of his crews as a result of some of the more minor offenses they have committed over the years.

Westy takes his partner by the shoulders and turns him around and gives him a little shove toward the town hall building. The police station is in the basement. There is a short set of stairs. Bobby has been inside there for the wrong reasons before and his old man practically has a lease on the drunk tank. One time Bobby and Fat Johnny and a gang of other townies filled party balloons with the acetylene stored in metal tanks and used for torches, and they blew them up down there and you can still see the black marks on the wall just outside the front door. LaPinta takes the stairs down two at a time and Westy puts his big square face pretty much all the way inside the car with them again.

You best mind that shit, he says.

He reaches in and turns off the radio so he can have their undivided attention.

He's a touch hole but he is the law round here, he says.

Agree with that first part anyhow, Bobby says. About the touch hole.

Westy tries not to laugh.

All right but if I wasn't on shift this right here would be ending different, he says.

It's true and the boys know it. Westy isn't so bad.

Yeah we know hey, Bobby says.

What's that.

Fat Johnny and Bobby look at him and speak at the same time.

Yes sir, they say.

All right. Now get this heap off the road.

Fat Johnny starts to protest but Bobby hits him on the shoulder and he shuts up.

Don't want to see you driving round again till you got your license, Westy says.

Then Westy makes a point of sniffing the air in the car.

And drunk driving at that, he says. At your age.

We aint drunk yet, Bobby says.

Westy looks at Bobby and shakes his head. He came up in this town and he knows that everybody drinks young and hard and everybody drives drunk. It is a way of life here. Simple as that. He straightens up and stretches his back. All Bobby can see of him now is his shiny black belt and his Sig Sauer and his radio. His thick-fingered hands are on his hips. He asks about Blackie's whereabouts but Bobby throws him some lies.

Then Westy asks about Uncle Thaddeus and Bobby denies any knowledge.

Westy knows bullshit when he hears it, but he dismisses the boys nonetheless.

Go on now, he says. Before I change my fucking mind.

Fat Johnny puts it into drive and he pulls away from the curb very carefully. Bobby can see Westy in the side mirror. His face takes on a warm red hue from the taillights. He is watching them drive away. Bobby turns on the radio. Fat Johnny accelerates when they get by the Tilton Library and Bobby's head snaps back against the seat.

Then Bobby looks at Fat Johnny and he laughs.

That fucking guy, he says. What a beaut.

Bobby deepens his voice to sound like LaPinta.

My boot will find your ass boy, he says.

Fat Johnny keeps laughing.

His dick will find your ass most likely, Bobby says. That fruity motherfucker.

Queer as a three dollar bill.

Bobby laughs and Fat Johnny laughs, too.

PART II:

"He's my blood, and if I can't have him then nobody can."
—Blackie

CHAPTER ELEVEN

EARL RAN DUBOIS WONDERS ABOUT his sons and where he went wrong with them. Neither one amounting to much or willing to do an honest day's work. He tried to teach them about personal responsibility and moral accountability. Nobody could argue that. But there was something deep in them that they couldn't escape, was how he saw it. From their mother's side, he felt certain. She'd had a mean streak wide as the turnpike.

He remembers a time at the river when they were just boys. He brought his canoe and intended to catch a fish or two, let the little roughnecks cavort. It was a dark afternoon. He paddled out a bit and told them to sit still so as not to capsize the narrow handbuilt woodrig. So they did as he said for once and they sat still and he closed his eyes and he only opened them again because it was so goddamn quiet. And sure as shit there was Blackie calmly leaning over and holding Thaddeus underwater. The younger brother was thrashing about under the surface, but it was hardly even perceptible.

Boy what the fuck you doing there.

Seeing how long it takes.

For what then.

For him to die like that down there.

So matter of fact. Earl hoisted Blackie by the shoulders and deposited him farther back and Thaddeus came up gasping, sobbing, hair matted to his face. He pulled him onto the boat. He didn't know what to say to either of them so he didn't say anything. He sat there looking at them. The little fuckers ruining his chance at trout.

Liz fetches him a beer.

Thaddeus stopped by, she says.

Oh.

He gone to see Bobby, she says. To take him.

Earl Ran looks out the window. There are stormclouds.

Who in fuck is Bobby, he says.

His memory comes and goes, but she tries to keep him informed anyhow.

He puts the beer away in three swallows. He's not interested in these people she is telling him about. All these strangers she insists on telling him about. He shakes his head.

You hear me, she says.

Then he has a sudden and infrequent moment of clarity.

He hears her all right. He doesn't say anything though. Not much to say on the matter. He washed his hands of it a long time ago. Them boys is on their own. He doesn't feel that he should be accountable for the sins of his sons. There is some thunder in the distance. A jagged yellow line appears over Bull Hill. The snapping sound of a tall dry tree that's been split in two. He can almost smell it burning. He counts it getting closer.

The storm.

He lets out a long sigh that whistles at the end.

It's gone to get messy, he says.

She's not sure if he means the storm or something else altogether.

IT'S TEATIME AT THE SMOKEHOUSE. The married ones started calling it that because it sounds respectable, but the beverages served are much stronger. Blackie produces a fifth of rum. Scotty Lorenson brings a bottle of Jim Beam. Baker shares a case of beer. Mike Pekarski Junior closes the store out front and then joins his friends in back. He retrieves a tattered and stained cardboard box from one of the walk-in freezers and places Andouille kielbasa links and a chunk of cheddar cheese with a sharp knife on the cutting board nearest Scotty. Help yourself boys, he says. Scotty cuts sausage and cheese for everybody. They sit on metal stools near the sliding wooden door. Mike Junior's dad used to lead cows in through that very entrance and hit them on the head with a sledgehammer, peel off their skin, chop them up for eating purposes. The process now is much more humane, but the floor is sloped to capture and drain cattle blood. There are several meat hooks hanging from chains bolted to the ceiling.

Blackie ruminates on the benefits of a well-organized slaughter.

He's not a regular at these Friday afternoon affairs, but he came up with the fellows here and so the door is always open to him as long as he provides some drink to share. Those are Mike's only parameters—local boys with booze always welcome.

But Blackie's presence makes the others noticeably uncomfortable.

The men eat and drink in silence for several minutes.

Then Blackie starts to cough and it goes on for a while.

When he's done he takes a long pull from the warm fifth of rum.

You all right, Scotty says.

Shit yeah, he says. I'm all right.

Mike Junior laughs.

That's not what I hear, he says.

What's that then.

Westy's asking after you for one thing.

Ah the fucking war hero, Blackie chuckles. Guess I should be fearful.

He saw some shit over there, Mike Junior says. Four tours.

I'm a fucking Marine too, Blackie says. Don't forget that.

Well did you ever see any action in the corps.

Nah, Blackie says. Too young for Vietnam and too old for Bosnia.

Well he saw some shit over there I guess, Mike Junior says.

Well, Blackie says. I wonder what he wants to see me about.

What you been up to that goes against the law, Scotty says, is the real question.

That's a long list.

Blackie looks at Mike Junior.

Like putting some guy in a fucking coma over to the VFW.

It seems everybody has an opinion all of a sudden.

And now your brother been coming around too.

Blackie sniffs and hands the fifth of rum to Mike Junior.

My brother hey, Blackie says. I guess I know what he wants.

I hear he wants to take Bobby again.

Blackie sets his jaw.

What about Bobby then, Mike Junior says. If you have to go away or whatever.

Well, Blackie says. He's mine goddammit and if I can't have him nobody can.

CHAPTER TWELVE

THE SIDING OF THE OLD Victorian is painted purple. The trim around the windows a shade or two darker. It looks odd to him, that festive color. It has been a while, but he enters like he owns the place. Sue looks up and then at Thaddeus and her body shivers; it starts from her toes and works its way up. She tries to compose herself, pulls a bronze lever and pours herself a shot of beer, holds it at the ready. He puts an elbow on the bar and tries a smile that doesn't fit his face. It's a face that has seen a lot. It's not a nice face to her.

But she's well aware that a certain type of woman finds him irresistible.

The proper frame and square jaw and all.

Looking for the boy, he finally says.

She throws back the shot and some of her hair gets caught in her mouth.

She pulls the strands back into place behind her ear.

Not even a hello, she says.

Hello then, he says.

Hello.

How you, he says.

Been better.

Well, he says. Now I'm looking for the boy.

I aint seen him.

She's surprised at how calm she sounds. Her voice doesn't crack like it usually does when she tells a lie. Thaddeus looks over his shoulder and then right back at Sue.

He lowers his voice.

All right then, he says.

Sue swallows hard.

Well, Thaddeus says. I'ma go up and collect his personals then.

You taking him on a trip, she says. Disney World maybe.

Yeah something like that.

He remembers now that Sue has always been a smartass.

That's nice, she says. But I guess I can't let you just go up there.

He looks at her and she looks at him and then down at the floor.

I guess you can't stop me, he says.

Sue looks at the telephone and he sees her do it. He waits until she looks at him.

If Black goes away, he says. You don't know where some judge will stick him.

You don't neither.

Come on now, he says. I got a pretty good idea.

Uncle Thaddeus does not fondly remember his years in juvenile detentions. Although he did learn how to fend for himself and how to bide his time. But the kid deserves better than that. He has half a brain and can maybe use it somehow. Sue shrugs her shoulders and reaches beneath the bar and places a single key in front of him.

He's wearing a wrinkled t-shirt that says It Aint Gonna Lick Itself.

Sue shakes her head, noticing it for the first time.

Now where's somebody go and get a fine shirt like that, she says.

He looks down at the t-shirt, but ignores her question.

Real classy, she says.

I could of got in without this you know, he says holding up the key.

He likes the idea of busting up a place that Eugene owns.

And he likes the idea of breaking down a door. It's been a while.

Who'd pay for that then, Sue says.

He smiles at her and she does not believe it for a minute, that smile, and he takes the key and pinching it between his thumb and forefinger he heads upstairs. The room looks like he imagined it would: small and dirty and unkempt. Empty beer cans on the floor, coffee containers filled with ashes. He gets a pillowcase and stuffs it at random with articles that seem to be his nephew's—clothing, a toothbrush, a half roll of toilet paper.

CHAPTER THIRTEEN

LESS THAN AN HOUR LATER he's in Indian Falls and he approaches Bobby's girlfriend. She is clearly nervous and he doesn't blame her for that. She is a pretty young thing. She is clean and blemish free and reminds him of a housecat the way she eats her ice cream.

Stabs at it with her pink tongue.

You know who I am, he says.

Course I do, she says.

Oh all right.

Don't everybody, she says.

Shit I guess.

She doesn't really look at him yet. Her ice cream is melting down the cone.

So you're his girl, he says.

Well.

My nephew Bobby that is, he says.

Doreen smiles. Nods her head. Finally looks at him.

Yeah, she says. I like the way that sounds.

Well, he says.

Doreen looks away and then back in his eyes.

Well, he says. You got to let him go for a spell.

Let him go.

She doesn't like the way that sounds.

That's what I wanted to say, he says. Why I stopped.

She looks at him and he looks at her. She reaches across the table to the napkin dispenser, sees the elongated reflection of her face in the chrome side of it, and gets one and then two napkins. She cleans the ice cream that is melting down the cone and onto her hand and wrist. Peppermint stick ice cream. Smiles at herself in the thing.

Checks her teeth.

What you mean, she says.

I'm gone to take him with me.

What for.

There's things he's gone to get stuck in the middle of.

Like what.

Related to his old man, he says.

And stuff Bobby done.

Nah it aint what he done.

But where you gone take him then.

See now that's the other thing.

He watches her clean up the mess. She's very tidy. He's impressed with her, but at the same time she seems a bit too self-assured. He has never much liked confident females, but maybe that's because he hasn't been exposed to many in his lifetime.

You know how his old man is, he says.

Yeah.

And the trouble he can cause.

Uh huh.

So I can't let on the whereabouts, he says.

Well then I'll come too.

He laughs and then he catches himself when he realizes she's not joking.

No, he says.

No.

No you can't either, he says.

Why.

Number one because you're not cut out for it.

She knows that he is right but she can't imagine being without Bobby for even a single day. Not an hour or a minute or even a second. Not a moment. She misses him now but sitting here with this man she feels like she is with him in a way. His uncle makes her nervous but there is something familiar in his demeanor. It scares her but she also finds it comforting. To think that Bobby could be like this man someday or already.

And number two because you're just a girl, he says.

He sighs and sits back and raises his arms in the air, yawns.

So anyhow I was driving by and seen you a sitting here, he says.

He absently gestures at the chopper he stole from a filling station that morning.

Oh, she says. That was you.

She had seen the bike. Actually had heard it first and looked up and seen it slow down. She looks at her feet and puts her ice cream on the white plate on the table. Done with it. A speck of it on her bottom lip. He wants to touch her pink lip with his finger. He wants to in the worst way but he won't.

This is Bobby's girl after all. Just a fucking child.

And so I figured I'd ask you to tell him, he says.

Tell him what.

That I'm coming soon to get him, he says.

Uh huh.

Soons I take care of a couple three things, he says.

Oh well, she says. I think he knows by now.

Word has been getting around town. Thaddeus knows this. Been here his whole fucking life when not in the system. He knows how this place works. That's the problem with a one-horse town, he thinks. Everybody always in everybody else's business. He shrugs his big shoulders and leans back in his chair. He holds his coffee in his lap. There are people sitting at other tables and they are looking at him sitting there with her and they are whispering behind their hands. When he looks up they look away. They know who he is. He is used to this kind of attention and it hardly ruffles him at all anymore.

I suppose you right about that, he says. That he knows I'm around.

Yeah well.

That's why he's steering clear, he says. I get it.

Doreen offers him an innocent look.

I know, he says. You don't have to say it.

A tow-headed little boy, maybe six years old, comes out from the side entrance of the Creamy. He's carrying a cardboard box in one hand and a knife with a wooden handle and a dull-rusty blade longer than his skinny arm in the other. He parades back and forth like that in front of the patrons, showing off. Then when he's sure all eyes are on him he proceeds to cut the thin clear tape and flatten the cardboard, making a big production out of it, getting the enthusiastic audience behind him, a true showman. Fighting back a smile he puts the cardboard on the top of an existing stack near the door.

Thaddeus laughs and claps louder than anybody else.

The boy looks at him startled and disappears inside.

His moment stolen.

Thaddeus sits up and finishes his coffee in one swallow and puts the empty cup on the table. He leaves his hand on the cup for a moment or two. Then he takes it away and he stands up. Doreen looks up at him and he sadly realizes again that she is merely a child although it is clear from her emotional attachment to his nephew that she is already behaving like a woman in certain ways. He tries to fight back the thoughts that are entering his mind. But she's on the verge of true womanhood. He can practically smell it on her. He closes his eyes and breathes her in. The things he could do to grow her up.

He commits her scent to memory for lonelier times.

He opens his eyes.

All right then, he says.

All right, she says.

She does not know what else to say and neither does he. He pushes his chair closer to the table and then he turns and walks away and she watches him. Everybody else watches him too and then they look at her and frown. She looks at her feet and closes her eyes. She slumps into her seat and into herself as much as possible. If Bobby were here he would tell them all to fuck off, she thinks. She knows. The motorcycle barks to life and the back tire spits little stones and then it fishtails onto the blacktop. Uncle Thaddeus isn't wearing his helmet and he shifts his weight and pulls back hard on the handlebars and the front wheel lifts up high and he rounds the bend like that riding only on the back tire, and Doreen's cheeks blush red at the sight.

CHAPTER FOURTEEN

BOBBY TRIES TO IMAGINE WHAT it's like to be chained to a radiator and to get shit on by a perfect stranger. He is convinced that despite any of Raymont Redwine's past indiscretions, his intended fate, while certainly unexceptional, was not supposed to be this horrific. That Blackie's imposing himself upon the helpless man is nothing less than the cruel and savage act of a bully. A person born so delicate is supposed to be cared for, not like in the wild where the weak and slow are chased down and slaughtered. It's what separates us from the animals, he thinks. But he also has the notion that there is no wilder place than the mind of his father. The old man has messed with the natural order and now Bobby feels compelled to right things somehow. He closes his eyes and sets his jaw.

FAT JOHNNY DRIVES UP NORTH Main past Cannonball's house and the high school and Hardigg Industries and Al Gula's yard that is filled with trash because he is protesting the town. They cut across 116 past the drive-in movie theatre that shows porn most Saturday nights. Last weekend Richard Freeline smuggled them in the trunk of his car so they could watch Oriental girls shooting ping-pong balls out of their bald pussies.

They hang a left on Lee Road and cross the Route 91 overpass and make another left onto the drag strip. The corn is eight feet tall by now and the alfalfa fields all around them look empty and dry and brown.

Fat Johnny stops the car and guns the V-8 four-barrel and he looks at
Bobby, who reaches under the seat and feels around for the bottle of
Southern Comfort. It is a half-full pint and it is warm and it sloshes
around and Bobby twists off the cap and takes a pull and hands it to
Fat Johnny and he takes a pull and looks at Bobby and then he takes
another. Then Bobby kills the bottle and twists the cap back on and
tosses it out the window and he can hear it smash on the road behind
them. They sit and idle for a little while longer and there's a breeze that
smells like a wet dog.

I hear your uncle been around, Fat Johnny says.

Me too but I aint seen him yet.

Gone to snatch you up and run you away.

I heard that too.

My pa seen him.

Not at the church.

Fat Johnny laughs.

No not likely, he says. Just around town.

Doreen seen him the other day too.

So what the fuck.

I guess we'll just see what my old man has to say about it.

If he's around to say anything.

Blackie hasn't been by much and Bobby knows exactly fucking why
and he has been sleeping where he can, trying to avoid the old man and
Uncle Thaddeus for the time being, but he knows it's inevitable. Then
Fat Johnny floors it and the rear tires scream and burning rubber stings
Bobby's nose and the car jerk-backs and Johnny rights it with a couple
half-spins of the steering wheel and they fly down the gray stretch with
the chain-link fence now on the one side and the flattened field on the
other. He slams the breaks where it ends at a line of trees and Bobby tries
to hold himself steady on the dashboard. The car stalls and Bobby looks
at Fat Johnny and he is laughing so hard that there is not any sound
coming out. He likes to go fast. Bobby fixes himself in the vinyl seat.

Shit boy that was sweet, Bobby says.

Fat Johnny can't say anything because he's still laughing and Bobby
laughs, too.

There is a spotted skunk coming across the cabbage field and Bobby watches it sniffing around. It doesn't see them right away. Fat Johnny has to piss so he opens his door and the skunk looks up and stamps its front feet and raises its tail but they are out of range. Bobby saw one spray while doing a handstand once. Fat Johnny leaves his door open and he undoes his trousers and he pisses on a clump of thistleberry bushes and that makes Bobby want to go, too. He gets out and the skunk is heading in the other direction now toward a brush pile near a stone wall and Bobby opens his fly and pisses right there on the dirt shoulder of the road. There is a clump of shit nearby that is from a black bear. Bobby studies the dirt and mud for prints but does not see anything. His old man used to hunt but he never took Bobby. Bear and deer and turkey and pheasant. He favored a bow and arrow because that's as close as you can get to the feeling of killing something with your bare hands, watching it die, he said to his son once. The key is to drop the animal close range, he always told Bobby, so that you can feel the life slip out of it.

Fat Johnny gets back in the car and Bobby gets back in and they close their doors at the same time.

Bear shit out there, Bobby says.

Thought they just shit in the woods.

Bobby fakes a laugh.

Fat Johnny jiggles the key that is already in the ignition.

Getting me a sweet ride when I'm sixteen, he says.

This one does the trick.

Big bro won't part with it.

Even with a suspended license.

He figures that won't last forever.

Well nothing does.

It's got nuts but I want a girl-getter too.

Bobby nods his head and Fat Johnny is right that his brother's car is not the most impressive looking after all it has been through. The engine starts after a few tries. Fat Johnny is concerned that he set the gap wrong on the plugs. A narrow gap may give too small and weak a spark to effectively ignite the fuel-air mixture, he tells Bobby as though reading it from a manual. Bobby laughs. They turn right and through a tunnel of droopy willows and into the dusk and down the access road that slices Gary Milewski's forty acres of property in half. It is a bumpy ride over stones and holes and tractor ruts.

Bobby breathes in the combination of alfalfa and cabbage and Williams's sweet corn. A skinny Puerto Rican is wrestling with a long black hose that's attached to a tank on one end and a mammoth sprinkler on the other, shooting water in random patterns, a rainbow forming in the resulting mist. After the fields it is residential and they get onto Plain Road until it puts them back on Lee and they follow that up the hill to where Max Bush parks his rigs. Young Max emerges shirtless from beneath the belly of one like some beasty newborn with oil on his face and a rag in his hand. He sees Bobby and Fat Johnny and smiles, waves them over. Fat Johnny eases up next to where he is standing and puts it in park and Bobby turns the radio down and Young Max leans on the roof.

What's up, he says.

Just tooling around.

Gone to Hoosac's tonight hey.

I expect we're gone to see what's about.

Them boys from Bucktown been looking for you.

Looking for who.

For those that sent them packing the last time.

Bobby laughs and Young Max laughs and Fat Johnny spits out the window.

I hear they're plotting their revenge, Young Max says.

Shit, Bobby says.

That was but a taste of what we got for them, Fat Johnny says.

Fat Johnny reaches under his seat and produces about nine inches of a rip-sawed old baseball bat. He holds it up so Young Max can see. Fat Johnny holds it with his right hand and strokes it with his left hand and he gives it a funny kiss.

This one, he says. She never lets me down.

Young Max's eyes get big and he laughs into his hand.

Oh shit, he says.

Fat Johnny puts the stick away and he gives Young Max his serious look.

What you got anyhow, he says.

Nothing much.

What's that.

Well we could huff if you want hey.

Fat Johnny shuts off the car and he and Bobby get out and follow Young Max to the structure about a hundred feet from the road. There are tools on the pegboards on the walls and red toolboxes and fifty-gallon barrels of old oil and white buckets of sand. An old truck seat rests on cement blocks and Bobby and Fat Johnny sit on it. Young Max goes to the workbench and fiddles around with some pink goop to get his hands sort of clean. He comes over to where they are and he drags an empty bucket and he flips it upside down and sits in front of them. There is a bottle of clear liquid model airplane glue and they pass it around and sniff at the thing until it is gone.

If Young Max's father caught them there'd be a shitstorm—he's old school and won't abide by any such nonsense. Bobby slouches down so he can rest the back of his head on the seat. He's tired and wants to close his eyes, wants to sleep for a while now.

Oh fuck, Bobby says.

His mind is not working right anymore from the glue.

His heart bounces inside his ribcage like a bee caught in a plastic cup.

Nobody else says anything because they have lost the facility for language.

Young Max hunches over the bucket with his elbows on his knees and his eyes closed and his nose starting to bleed. He is a straight-up huffer. Fat Johnny points at him and Bobby nods his head up and down. Blood is falling in drops that are pooling red on the woodshaving-covered floorspace between his steel-toed boots. There is a bullfrog and he warbles and croaks his fuck-me song. Bobby closes his eyes and listens to him beg for pussy. Fat Johnny falls asleep because Bobby hears his breathing get heavy. Every now and then a vehicle passes by but they can't see the lost boys tucked away in the makeshift shed behind broken eighteen-wheelers. It is the perfect setting. Then the darkness is complete and Bobby dreams about jumping naked and alone from the Stillwater Bridge by the light of the moon into the cool moving water of the Swift River.

CHAPTER FIFTEEN

BILLY TUCKER HANDS THADDEUS A cold bottle of beer that he's just opened with his teeth. They are smoking Swisher Sweets and sitting on a sideways tree trunk near the gravel pit in Bucktown. In the distance some kids are taking the sand dunes on Jap motor bikes and you can hear the high-pitched whine of two stroke engines being pushed too hard. Power lines overhead hum and crackle electricity from time to time, startling the small black birds that perch there, sending them into fits. The men watch this and smoke the cigarillos and drink the beers and they do not look at each other or speak for several minutes. Then Billy Tucker leans forward and puts his elbows on his knees.

Fucking hotter than a thousand hells, he says.

Thaddeus finishes his beer and throws the bottle and it breaks against a rock.

Yeah, he says

There is a fine black dust settling on the world around them.

Billy Tucker wipes sweat and soot from his forehead with the back of his hand. He reaches down to the plastic cooler at his feet and puts his hand inside and comes up with a bottle. He uses his teeth again to pop the cap off and he spits it into the dirt and then pushes it deeper with the toe of his work boot. He hands the beer to his friend. Thaddeus takes it and puts it right to his lips. They are getting good and drunk now.

Well so you gone make a run with that boy.

When I find the little fucker I will.

Where will you go.

The million-dollar question.

Neither man has been out of the county much before. It is a very small world to them. A mosquito flies into Billy Tucker's nostril and he shakes his head and puts his beer down and tries to get it out with his finger. He curses and Thaddeus laughs. What's doing over to the Hollywood, Thaddeus says.

It's Billy Tucker's favorite bar, where he just came from.

Oh just a bunch of no good drunks, he says.

One less now.

Billy Tucker laughs.

Oh all right then I see how it is, he says.

Any talent over there at least.

I was talking to this one broad from Hatfield.

Was she pretty.

In two ways.

Thaddeus knows the punchline all too well but he waits for it anyhow.

Pretty ugly and pretty likely to stay that way, Billy Tucker says.

You mean pretty from far and far from pretty.

Right.

The men share a laugh.

Pudge still run that joint hey, Thaddeus says.

Yeah him and Whitey Reznik now.

From Bucktown.

That's right.

Shit that boy could play some football.

Yeah he could at that.

Thaddeus and Billy Tucker made the team in high school until they got expelled for smoking pot in the bathroom and doing a couple other wrong things. The idea of hitting the snot out of people their age had appealed to them back then but the discipline and structure of organized youth sports did not.

Should see him now, Billy Tucker says. Whitey.

Yeah what.

Fat as fuck.

No shit hey.

Father time catches up with all of us.

Amen brother.

Thaddeus laughs and finishes his beer and throws the bottle at the same rock as before. It smashes into pieces. He's sweating now, too. He finishes his cigarillo and drops it onto the ground and a last thin wisp of smoke escapes it. Billy Tucker puffs on his. His face is red and his neck is red. He gets some ice from the cooler and rubs it on his head.

Blackie will be pissed if you get Bobby, he says.

He's already pissed and I aint even got him yet.

He was born like that wasn't he.

Thaddeus scratches his chin that is covered in stubble sharp as barbed wire.

That's a fucking fact, he says.

I mean he'll want to settle it with you.

It will come to that someday and it was always bound to.

Billy Tucker nods his head up and down. He befriended them both as boys and he never recalled any brotherly love between them. Not even the slightest hint of it.

CHAPTER SIXTEEN

SMITTY SEES HER FIRST AND taps Dennis on the shoulder. They're sitting in his mother's Pontiac Sunbird, parked under a willow tree, taking turns with a bottle of Jim Beam. Doreen is crossing High Street on foot. She's wearing a snug pair of cut-off jeans and a dark blue tube top. Smitty's arm is still in a cast and sling. Dennis had to have his jaw reset and there are wires and pins in there now. He has to take his drink through a straw. And the doctor had joked that anytime he passes through an airport metal detector he'll set off alarms now—as if he has anywhere to fly to.

Dennis doesn't see the humor in it just yet. He feels like some kind of freak show. But he has been learning all he can about Bobby DuBois and the rest of his dysfunctional townie clan. Revenge is on his mind. What he has learned is not very reassuring—them boys are a rough bunch. He is not convinced that he is ready to take them on in any kind of feud just yet. Maybe when he heals up some. But then he and Smitty spot Doreen. It's as though she has been presented to them as a gift, an offering. He puts a lot of stock in fate and shit.

Holy fuck, Smitty says.

Is that really fucking her, Dennis says. That bitch from the river.

It's difficult for him to speak, he spits when he talks now, and even harder for other people to understand what he's saying, but Smitty is already accustomed to it.

Fuck yeah, he says.

They can't believe their good fortune.

Oh shit that redneck bitch is gone to pay, Smitty says.

Bust that ass cherry wide open.

So he knows we been there.

So that motherfucker knows hey.

Let him know.

They feel brave and indignant and feed off of each other's anger. They are not considering consequences. That level of critical thinking is at least a couple years away for them. They get out of the car and follow her on foot past Ruddock's Fine Jewelry and Green's Grocery Cooperative. She's doing a bit of window shopping so they hang back.

Bobby had told Doreen to avoid downtown Bucktown for a while but she likes the little shops and needs a new pair of sneakers for work. He knows how these things can play out and she should've listened. That's her thought process when she first sees them, those boys—she recognizes them from the party that night down at the river. What she doesn't recognize yet, however, is the look in their eyes. Very soon it will be something that stays with her forever. Doreen is naïve to the true menace of unchecked male aggression. So she dismisses them and figures they will maybe shadow her for a bit and talk some amount of shit.

There's an abandoned storefront next to the five and dime. A nest is wedged between the old sign and the wall, and a young bird has fallen after testing its fragile wings. Doreen kneels beside it and purrs as the mother bird, still perched at the edge of the bowl-shaped collection of straw and twigs, tries to warn her away.

CHAPTER SEVENTEEN

BOBBY OPENS HIS EYES AND his lap is warm where he pissed himself. He feels anxious and unsettled and uncomfortable and he attributes these sensations to all the drugs wearing off. A warm breeze carries with it the scent of knotwood blossoms, which makes him think of Doreen. He tries to put her out of his mind because fond thoughts can be such a burden. Young Max is back to work because Bobby can hear the rhythmic revolutions of his standard ratchet a hundred feet away. Bobby shakes Fat Johnny and he starts.

What the fuck, Fat Johnny says.

Fat Johnny rubs sleep seeds from his eyes and sits forward and shakes his head. Bobby stands up—it takes him a minute to get his legs under him—and he shows Fat Johnny what happened to him and Fat Johnny laughs and checks himself. He did not have such an accident. He looks at Bobby again. The dark stain extends almost to his knees.

Boy you pissed yourself, he says.

Right.

Shit boy you are sure huffed out.

Fuck that.

Bobby rubs his pants where they are wet.

You got some extra drawers back there, Bobby says.

Yeah I likely do hey.

They walk out of the structure and there is Young Max under the bonnet of a rig with a yellow drop light in one hand and a crescent wrench in the other and a wad of tissue jammed up his nose. The knuckles on his wrench hand are freshly stripped of the top layer of skin. He looks up when he hears their steps and he hops down and puts the light on the fender and it slides off and lands on the ground. He picks it up and stands holding it and his face is illuminated in that spooky way that kids do around campfires.

Hey, he says.

Back at ya.

You boys up and out.

Look what you did to your boy, Fat Johnny says.

Young Max looks at Bobby's lap and laughs a little but it is a sad kind of laugh.

Shit man I been there, he says and means it.

Young Max reaches out and Bobby claps his open hand and Fat Johnny does the same. Then Young Max hops back up on that rig and gets to work, tap-tapping the generator with a rubber mallet, tugging on the loosened belt. His father will be checking on his progress soon and he won't stand for any lollygagging. Without turning his head Young Max calls out their names and they stop and look at the backside of him.

See you boys at Hoosac's, he says.

All right then.

Fat Johnny pops his trunk and next to his spare tire he does have an extra pair of cutoffs that are streaked with engine coolant and tie-rod grease but it's better than human piss so Bobby takes his pants off and stands there in his underwear until Fat Johnny hands them over. A car goes by and honks its horn and they hear somebody hoot but they don't know who it is. Bobby puts on the shorts. They are too big but he cinches them with a length of blue nylon rope that he cuts with his foldout buck knife. He puts his wet pants in the trunk and Fat Johnny closes it and looks at Bobby. He shakes his head and removes his cap and runs his hand back across his shiny scalp.

He regards Bobby's slight frame.

Nothing but a goddamn scaredy-crow, he says.

Shit.

It's no wonder boys take you lightly till they feel you sting.

A little piece of leather but I'm well put together.

It's something he heard his uncle say once and he liked the way it sounded.

Bobby sucks in his stomach even more than normal and shows Fat Johnny how much extra space there is in the waistband. Fat Johnny steps forward and punches Bobby in the gut and it takes his wind for a second or two. Bobby chases him around and flings some mud at him and Young Max laughs and yells for them to leave. If his father sees any evidence of them, even on the road, it will raise his suspicions. The car starts hard again and Fat Johnny curses and wishes he had his motherfucking toolkit.

CHAPTER EIGHTEEN

MAYBE I'M BRAZEN, THADDEUS THINKS. It's just daylight but difficult to tell because a thick curtain of clouds shields the sun. He's walking around the center of Stillwater. Past the police station even. Eventually he'll have to take to the backcountry and he knows this. It is a simple fact. But for now he is enjoying his freedom. And the ability to smell outdoor smells. Trees and car fumes and dog shit. The pickle shop. He doesn't care much what. It's better then smelling nothing but men all day and night. Man sweat and man shit and bad man breath. Thaddeus sits on the bench in the town common, looks at the fountain.

He reads the inscription on the plaque bolted to a boulder.

Dedicated to a white man who killed a bunch of red men many years ago.

My old eyes deceive me, a voice says.

Thaddeus looks up and Roger Syska is standing there in his white gloves. Roger raises and lowers the American flag in the common every day and has been since god knows when. He must be a hundred years old now. It is an honor that he takes very seriously. He folds the flag meticulously and stores it in his house across the street.

Roger, Thaddeus says.

Roger smiles drugstore-bought teeth that don't fit quite right in his mouth. He holds a white-gloved hand out to Thaddeus and the younger man takes it and they shake.

It's a good day my friend, Roger says in Polish.

Thaddeus agrees with him in the little bit of Polish he remembers.

Then they don't say anything to each other for several minutes. Thaddeus looks at Roger and the old man stares off into nothingness. His eyes are glassy.

Roger turns to the flagpole and uncoils the rope. Hand over hand he slowly lowers the flag. Thaddeus watches him. When it is low enough to reach Roger unclasps the corners of the cloth from the rope and he folds it. He tucks it under his arm. He wraps the slackened rope around the pole, turns to Thaddeus, smiles.

Goodnight my friend, he says.

Goodnight.

Roger takes short steps that seem to last forever. Thaddeus watches him wait for a pickup to pass and then look both ways again and again and then cross North Main Street. His house is two-story with gray shingles and white trim and a black shingle roof that sags in the middle. There are brown leaves all around his yard that is mostly dirt and long tufts of dead cuntgrass. There is a wife inside those walls that rarely shows her face.

Thaddeus is sure that Roger is in a time warp. That he doesn't see Thaddeus as the dangerous man he has become. In the old man's fog-marble eyes he is still simply a mischief-making town boy, when the most severe punishment his various misdeeds would earn him was a belt-whipping. It is refreshing almost to be seen like that. He sits on the bench and closes his eyes and the punch-drunk sun warms his face.

CHAPTER NINETEEN

BOBBY'S OLD MAN IS OFF doing god knows what but at least ducking the police. The human punching bag is nowhere to be found either. He has a pair of red bolt cutters acquired with the six-finger discount from Elder Lumber. Bobby goes upstairs and the door to the spare room has a new lock on it so he kicks the shit out of it. After three tries the hollow core door splinters around the deadbolt and it swings open and he can hear the retard wheezing in the corner. After his eyes adjust Bobby finds him. Jesus fucking Christ.

Raymont is on his haunches, naked as the day he was born.

A bowl of dog food set where he can reach it.

Jesus, Bobby says. Relax.

Raymont doesn't relax.

I aint gone hurt you none, Bobby says.

Forgive the retard for not believing him.

I'm here to cut you loose, Bobby says.

Raymont's eyes are wild and he clearly doesn't believe Bobby or understand that he means well, and who can blame him after what he's experienced these past weeks. They look at each other and Bobby waits for the retard to get used to his presence. He looks like hell. The old man has been putting him through the paces for sure. Then Bobby takes a couple steps closer and Raymont doesn't flip out or anything. His breathing slows.

I'ma let you go home now, Bobby says.

He grabs the chain where it's wrapped around the retard's ankle but it's so tight the skin has practically grown over the links like you sometimes see with a tree that's been long-burdened with a hammock or a backyard swing. So instead he snips where the chain is attached to the radiator. But the retard doesn't make a move, as though he doesn't realize he's free to go. He stares at Bobby without blinking.

Go on now, Bobby says.

He still doesn't get up so Bobby reaches out to him and he takes his hand. He helps him stand and Raymont can't fully straighten out yet and it's a good thing there are some old clothes in a pile in the closet. Bobby gets him into a pair of pants and a shirt that are both too big. With his arm over Bobby's shoulder they go down the stairs and out the front door. It's slow going but Bobby doesn't want to dally in case his old man returns from wherever he is. If Blackie catches him in this trespass he will blow a gasket for sure. He will not tolerate what he will interpret as an act of treason. But Bobby figures that he will likely be departing with Uncle Thaddeus soon.

As they step out the front door Raymont all of a sudden throws his hands up against the glare of the day and he starts to whine. Bobby shields the sun for him, too.

Raymont calms down after a little while.

Come on, Bobby says.

Raymont follows him, dragging his bad leg.

Bobby knows he can't just walk up to the retard's house without getting himself involved and possibly arrested and he would certainly be incriminating his old man by proxy and so his plan is to simply get the retard down to the street and point him in the right direction. His hope is that Raymont will take himself home.

They eventually make it to the street and there aren't any cars and Bobby untangles himself from Raymont but he seems stuck. Bobby nudges him but he resists. He's like an abused dog that has become so used to his mistreatment that it is almost a comfort to him. Bobby has heard about this phenomenon. It's a pretty fucked up thing. He hears a car coming so he drags Raymont down to where there are some blackberry bushes and the retard sits down behind a clump of them and starts to cry without tears.

Go on home, Bobby says.

Raymont doesn't move a muscle.

Go home you dumb fucking retard, he says.

He kicks at Raymont and spits at him too in an attempt to scare him off.

He throws a rock at him and hollers.

Go fucking home.

But Raymont Redwine is all done being scared.

Bobby leaves him there like that because he doesn't know what else to do.

CHAPTER TWENTY

THE NEIGHBOR HAS GOT ABOUT ten acres that puts his property line at the foot of Bull Hill. He's growing pumpkins and squash over there now, watering them with my goddamn water, Earl thinks. Then Earl drives his car into the middle of them and leaves it there to teach the sonofabitch a lesson. He originally intends to back it out but the thing won't start up again. Earl is no good with a clutch anymore. Liz usually drives him. He bought the car brand new in 1965. Then the neighbor pops the hood and fiddles with the carburetor.

Earl tries to stop him.

I don't need your goddamn charity, he says.

The neighbor shakes his head and then he shakes his fist.

DuBois men don't take handouts, Earl Ran says.

The neighbor curses at Earl and wipes the sweat off his face and shoos him away like a mosquito and if Earl Ran was a younger man it would be different. Blue smoke puffs out of the exhaust pipe. The neighbor gets in and reverses out of his patch and onto the road and into Earl's driveway. He parks the car carefully. I know it's a trick, Earl thinks. Then his head hurts. The neighbor's wife gives him a glass of lemonade that probably has rat poison in it so Earl throws it back at her. When he opens his eyes again the Red Sox are on television and he's in his chair smoking a Swisher Sweet.

He is not supposed to get excited.

She says that she is his girlfriend but she is old and fat and the skin on her face is like a leather saddle fresh from the tannery. Liz was a beautiful black girl from Holyoke. Earl doesn't listen to the imposter. She vacuums around him and he won't even move his feet. He doesn't know where they all come from and what gives them the right. The smell of bacon. Earl had a dog named Rexall when he was a boy. That damn thing could hunt, he remembers. They went after turkey mostly. But when it was his time he took him to a spot they liked and put one in his brain so he could go quick and painless. It's a hard thing but you got to do it. Earl Ran is not one to shirk a responsibility like that. There is blood on his hands now and she wipes them with a dishrag and asks him where he's cut.

Where you cut Earl Ran, she says.

He grunts.

Show me where you cut yourself, she says.

She inspects him and he ignores her. She gets the first aid kit and the rubbing alcohol. When she is satisfied she gives him a smug look and he closes his eyes.

Don't you close your eyes at me Earl Ran.

THERE IS A COW IN his yard, got loose from Melnik's. Some boys from over there try to rustle her up but she doesn't want to go. They apologize to Earl and he spits at them. She eats the weeds in his yard while they strategize over tall cans of Budweiser that they better not leave behind. They finally get a rope on her and she lifts her tail and shits. Then it's cold. It looks like Mount Toby but he's not sure. He sits on a flat red rock. There are power lines and blue sky and an eagle. His feet are tired. He can smell himself. There is shade under the tower but he doesn't think he can make it that far. This is getting so hard every day. He'd jump off Cheapside Bridge if somebody'd only drive him.

CHAPTER TWENTY-ONE

THEY GO NORTH ON RIVER Road and then west on Hoosac's Road even though there is no sign telling them that. Shacks and sheds and Ozzy Sansome's half-breed father's lopsided trailer. Then nothing but deep dark woods and Fat Johnny kills the headlights and he takes it slow. He knows this road like the back of his hand. They can feel in their skeletons where it turns from pavement to uneven earth. Fireflies so big you can count them congregating in clusters. Bobby turns the radio volume low. It is several long minutes until they see the bonfire and the shadow people that they are so often a part of.

Bobby updates Fat Johnny on the retard.

Fuck me, Fat Johnny says.

Right.

So you just left him there.

I didn't know what else to do.

Well shit you done enough I guess.

I fucking hope so.

There's a cherry 1967 Chevy Nova and a 1974 Pontiac Trans Am. There is a Ford F250 and Lance VanKampen's beat-up old Silverado. All parked at strange angles with their bold noses jammed into the foliage. Fat Johnny finds a good spot where they won't get dinged by a fellow reveler. He turns the key off and he gets out and Bobby gets out and they walk toward the fire. They cannot make out the faces yet but they hear some folks calling their names. Then Carol Ward comes running up and she puts her arms around Bobby. She is just some town girl he messes with sometimes. No big deal to him.

Hey you, she says.

Hey.

Hey Johnny.

Back at ya, he says.

Fat Johnny walks off and leaves them alone to talk or whatever.

Where you been at, she says.

Nowheres.

You want to smoke some.

All right yeah let's.

She is a true dope addict. She takes Bobby's hand and leads him toward her mother's car. It is a rice-burning shitbox. They sit in the back and his knees are jammed up against the back of the front seat. She reaches into her pocket and takes out a pipe and a small bag of weed. She steals it from her pa who apparently has the cancer growing high up in his ass. Bobby watches her stuff the bowl and work it with her little fingertips. Then she puts the plastic baggie into the front pocket of her jeans and comes out with some matches. She strikes one and it won't catch and she tries another and it catches and Bobby can smell the flint of it like a sharp sting and she puts the pipe in his mouth and holds the flame toward him and he can feel the small heat of it on his face and forehead.

He sucks on the pipe until he can taste the dope and he feels it in his lungs, burning in a nice way and he holds it. He closes his eyes and holds it and then he opens his eyes and lets it out and the car is filled with it. Carol laughs and she puts the pipe in her mouth and works it like an expert. Bobby takes another hit and she does too and then she looks him in his eyes. Hers are green and sometimes blue and green with gold specks.

You want more, she says.

I'm cool.

You look fried hey.

Yeah I'm cool.

Bobby laughs a little and she laughs, too. She takes one last hit off the pipe and then she puts it down. She puts both his hands in hers and gives them a squeeze. She smells soapy.

You still messing with that Doreen girl, she says.

I'm not messing with nobody, he says.

You always say that.

It's always true.

Heard you knocked her up.

You will hear shit if you listen hard enough.

You're saying she aint.

I'm saying I don't see how you can hear nothing when you're always talking.

Carol Ward kisses him hard and their front teeth knock together. She takes off her top and unzips his fly and uses her mouth on him. He undoes her bra and counts the pimples and other scars and scabs on the pale skin of her back. He looks out the window at the darkness as she finishes him and then cleans up with tissue from the glove box.

She puts her head against his chest.

I can hear your heart now, she says.

All right.

She listens more and he closes his eyes and it feels all right to just sit there and not do or say anything. He knows it won't last long because nothing good ever does.

He is starting to think about Doreen.

Well what should we do now, Carol says.

Just sit here for a while.

No I don't mean right this minute.

Bobby knows exactly what she means. He puts his hand in her hair and rests his chin on the top of her head. He opens his eyes and closes them and breathes out through his nose because they have had this talk many times before. She puts her hand inside his shirt. She counts his ribs and sticks a sharp fingernail in his naval and he jumps a bit.

So what we gone to do, she says again.

You do what you do, Bobby says. And I do what I do.

So that's it then.

Come on now.

She's not even your type, Carol says. That stuck-up bitch.

Shit.

I should be your girl and you fucking know it.

She's maybe right but Jesus. She sits up and gets some chewing gum from somewhere and it smells like peppermint. She balls up the little piece of foil wrapper and flicks it at Bobby and he almost smiles at her. He reaches down and picks up her shirt and hands it to her and she puts it on. She fixes her bra and snaps her gum with her tongue and reaches behind him for the door handle and the dome light comes on and she kisses him soft this time. Then she pulls away, a single tear on her cheek. He wipes at it with his thumb and holds her pretty face in his hand. So goddamn pretty it hurts. She looks away.

Bobby pulls himself out of the back seat and she climbs out, too. She closes the door and they walk back toward the party and she holds his hand just to get people talking and they will but he doesn't care right now. Her hand is small and warm in his. They don't speak and he listens to twigs snapping. Then somebody tells him that Fat Johnny is getting sick. Bobby finds him and he doesn't look too good. He's on his knees leaning over a puddle of his own rhubarb-colored guts. Bobby helps him stand up.

What you been doing there boy, Bobby says.

It's maybe what I aint did that's the problem.

Maybe should of ate something right.

Fat Johnny puts his arm around Bobby's shoulders and they walk like that until they find a rock he can sit on. Carol Ward has followed along and she offers Fat Johnny a stick of gum and he takes it and thanks her. His jaw moves as he works the gum and he puts his elbows on his knees and closes his eyes and shakes his head and moans. Carol Ward talks about him like he's not even there. That's a nasty habit she has.

Is he gone be all right you think, she says.

Yeah he will.

What makes you the big expert on everything, she says.

Acting the cunt is another of her bad habits.

Bobby throws her a look, recognizing the mood swings he has found typical.

Why you even ask me then, he says.

Always so sure about every goddamn thing.

She's not really talking about Fat Johnny being sick anymore and she's also taking a tone with Bobby and he throws her another look that says shut up and go away, and so she storms off in a hissy fit. Fat Johnny looks up at Bobby and shakes his head. Bobby doesn't say anything and Fat Johnny looks at the ground. He appears to study it.

Sorry, he says.

For what.

Getting sick and messing with your thing there.

He indicates the direction Carol had walked off in with a jerk of his head.

That's no thing.

Whatever.

You dying on me or what the fuck.

No I'm all right.

Well come on then.

Fat Johnny gets up straight and tests his legs.

You drive, he says.

Fat Johnny gives Bobby the key and they walk to the car and Carol Ward tries to make sure that Bobby sees that she's ignoring him. Fat Johnny gets in the backseat so he can lie down. On his back with his legs bent and his knees pointing up. Bobby gets in the driver seat and puts the key in the ignition and the engine starts on the first try but then stalls out when he takes his foot off the gas pedal so he pumps it three times and tries again. Bobby thinks there is some rust buildup in the fuel line. That's what it feels like to him at least. That will happen if you let the tank get too low. Then his mind turns to Uncle Thaddeus because he's the one taught him a little bit about cars. Uncle Thaddeus has taught Bobby many good things that maybe a father is supposed to pass on down.

He has also taught him many bad things best left unlearned.

Don't flood her, Fat Johnny says.

All right.

Bobby tries again, this time without the gas, and the engine starts and then he revs the idle a bit. He puts it in reverse and backs up and Fat Johnny moans. Bobby laughs and puts it in drive. As they pass the bonfire Carol Ward looks up and she waves and Bobby sure as shit does not wave back. He wonders about Doreen and what Carol said.

CHAPTER TWENTY-TWO

BOBBY DRIVES FAT JOHNNY'S BROTHER'S car through Stillwater and Bucktown and the hills of Indian Falls so they can sober up. Fat Johnny is passed out in the backseat and Bobby hears him groaning and rolling around. He turns off the radio and listens to the night sounds. He ends up on Sitterly Road and takes it to State Road and crosses 116 back into the center of Stillwater. He passes Doreen's house but her parents are home and they wouldn't appreciate him coming by at such a late hour. He parks in front of the Greek pizza place that is already closed, but you can still smell the pies—black olives and goat cheese and onions on thick, hard-baked crust. There's a good crowd at the Hot L. Bobby's old man's jeep is alongside another one in better condition. He turns off the ignition and opens the door and gets out and closes it. He opens the back door and shakes Fat Johnny by the shoulders until he opens his eyes and looks up at Bobby.

What the fuck, he says.

Wake up Sleeping Beauty.

Fuck.

He sits up or at least tries to sit up and Bobby helps him.

Come on fat boy.

Where we at, he says.

He looks around to get his bearings.

Oh shit.

You can crash upstairs, Bobby says.

I'm good.

What's a matter.

Don't want your old man poking no holes in me.

Fat Johnny puts his face in his hands. Bobby leans on the roof of the car. There is country western music coming from the bar and he can hear his old man's voice like a big dog barking in an abandoned junkyard. They can't make out his words. He must be holding court or preparing for a fistfight or very likely both. Fat Johnny takes the key from Bobby's hand and pulls himself out of the car and into a standing position.

Holy shit boy, Bobby says. You're fucked up.

Bobby laughs because Fat Johnny is so fucked up. Bobby has never seen him this fucked up before. Fat Johnny gives Bobby a shove and opens the front door and gets into the driver's seat. He starts the car with one try and winks at Bobby and nods his head. Bobby steps away from the vehicle and Fat Johnny puts it in reverse and backs into the street. Then he slips into drive and rolls slow north. Bobby watches his brake lights blink red for a beat at the train crossing and then his right turn signal flashes for two more and then he disappears past the lumber yard. He's going to take the back roads home.

Bobby walks around to the side of the Hot L and tries the door and it's open. There are a couple boys from Paciorek Electric crowding the small entrance, still in their blue uniforms and smelling like booze, but they know Bobby and they let him pass. One of them also named Bobby but at least ten years older claps him on the shoulder.

Hey wise guy, he says. What's doing.

Bobby nods at him and the others because they are all right but he doesn't say anything to them. Sue is at the bar and she sees him and motions for Bobby to come over. He turns sideways and makes his way through the bodies as quick as he can. When he gets to the bar Sue sets him up with a Jack and Coke on the house, heavy on the Jack. He sips it through a red straw that bends. It tastes good and strong. He digs a couple cubes of ice out of the glass with his fingers and sticks them into his mouth. He looks at Sue and she looks at him and she leans in so she can say something and be heard over the din.

Your father, she says.

Bobby cracks the ice between his teeth and spits what is left of it into his glass.

What about him.

He's in rare form.

Sounds like same old shit to me.

Sue grabs a wet cloth from under the sink and slaps it onto the bar and makes small circles with it, leaving smears and smudges and circles of crumbs, her best efforts failing against years of neglect. There are big glass jars with pickled eggs and cow tongues. Bobby tells her he's hungry and she twists the lid off a jar and spears an egg with a crusty fork. She drops the egg onto a thin paper napkin and slides it in front of his drink. He pops it into his mouth. Flypaper dangles like streamers from the ceiling in places and dead flies dot them like chocolate chips. Sue looks at Bobby.

Your uncle come looking for you.

Yeah when was that.

Other day.

Oh all right.

She looks him in the eyes, then she gets jumpy and changes the subject.

Where you been hiding at anyhow, she says.

At the hiding place.

Whatever, she says and snaps the rag at him playfully.

Then Bobby feels a hand on his shoulder. Sue seems to focus her eyes on a spot just over his head. Before he can turn around the hand squeezes harder and he feels his father's breath on the back of his neck. It is sick-warm and it gives him chills.

Boy, the old man says. What the fuck.

Bobby finishes his drink quickly and pushes the empty glass toward Sue and she takes it and drops it onto a tray behind her in one motion and without turning her head.

She smiles at his old man.

Just drinking a pop there Blackie, she says.

Pop my ass, he says.

He regards her briefly, coldly.

Bobby turns on his stool and faces Blackie and the old man clearly is fucked up. He has not removed his left hand from his son's shoulder even though he had to make an adjustment when the boy turned. He gets in close so his face is just a couple inches from the boy's and Bobby can see the white-capped pores in his nose. He can see the thin whiskers on his father's neck that he neglected when he shaved. He can see the star-shaped scar over his father's lip from when some stripper got fed up with his rough play.

What's that about your uncle, he says.

I was just telling him I heard Thaddeus been around, Sue says.

He pretends that he does not hear her as he digests this information.

Boy what the fuck you doing here anyhow, he says.

Nothing.

Where you been at.

Nowheres.

We been through this aint we.

I'm just heading up to bed and Sue gave me a Coke sir yes sir.

The old man processes this update slowly.

And where you been at till now, he says.

Just driving around.

What's that.

Sir.

He knows Bobby is lying and he wants to catch the boy in a lie but it does not really matter because he does not need an excuse to hit him. He stares into Bobby's eyes and his son looks around the bar for anybody else that his father can fight so he can use it all up on somebody besides him for once. There is Mongeon who'll square off with a man for no apparent reason. There is Skip Price who fired Blackie from the pickle shop after just three days of turning vats. There is Mugsy who stole the old man's girl one time. Sue is pouring beers for Oz from the tannery, he's another good candidate. But that would be an all-night job as he goes about three bills—have to pack a lunch for that one.

Look at me boy, the old man says, when I'm talking at you.

Bobby looks at his old man and he looks right back at Bobby.

If he knew it was Bobby cut the retard loose then he'd fix him good.

If he was even aware of it yet.

Bobby is surprised he hasn't mentioned it.

You been by Kat's, the old man says.

Fuck, Bobby thinks. Here it comes.

Nah sir, he says.

You think you're big enough now, the old man says.

Bobby does sometimes think he's big enough, but he's not yet ready to say it.

Nah sir, he says.

The old man laughs.

Bobby is trying to appease him in some small way and maybe avoid conflict.

Then Blackie puts his right hand on Bobby's other shoulder and to an observer it might have looked like the beginnings of a warm father-and-son embrace. Instead he squeezes both Bobby's shoulders and the boy's eyes well up but he does not want his father to know that he's hurting him, that he's capable of hurting him anymore; he does not want to give him the satisfaction. The old man squeezes and squeezes and squeezes. His eyes are dark and deep and empty.

He laughs.

All right then, he says like he done Bobby a favor by stopping.

He lets go Bobby's shoulders and the boy slumps forward a bit unintentionally.

Don't forget, he says. You're my boy.

Nobody will ever let Bobby forget that.

Not in this lifetime anyhow.

Stay away from Thaddeus, he says. If you know what's good for you.

I aint even seen him.

He might try and take you again.

Bobby looks at his feet and nods his head.

Now go on, Blackie says. This aint no place for you.

All right then.

The boy gets down off the stool and Blackie makes him walk around.

Bobby pushes through all the old drunks and gets to the stairs and he takes them two at a time. The door to their apartment is open and he goes inside and closes it. He goes into the bathroom and eats four aspirin and washes them down with warm tap water that tastes exactly like you'd expect from warm tap water traveling through rusted metal pipes. He sits on the windowsill and the window is propped open with a piece of rip-sawed two-by-four scrap. Bobby sits there until his eyes fall closed by themselves. Then he wishes the Staties or somebody would catch up to his old man right now this very fucking minute.

CHAPTER TWENTY-THREE

WHEN BOBBY OPENS HIS EYES the sun is leaking through the window and onto his face where he's lying on the couch. His old man is not around. He rubs the sleep from his eyes and stands up and goes into the bathroom. He splashes water on his face and looks in the mirror and runs his wet hands through his hair. He removes his t-shirt and drops it on the floor and he picks through a pile of others and settles on the one advertising Wolfie's that doesn't smell too gamey. Then he grabs his Fisher's Garage cap and puts it on backward. He drinks a warm beer and takes a pack of his old man's smokes and a book of matches from the Candlelight Restaurant and opens the front door and closes it behind him. Bobby does not lock it because the lock doesn't hardly work anymore. He walks down the stairs and there are two glasses with soggy ashes and dried-out cherries at the bottom. The bar is closed so he has to leave through the front door that leads to the street.

The day is bright and he turns his cap around the right way to shield his eyes from the sun. Bobby walks along the sidewalk past the Polish tailor's and Fortier's barber shop and the Olde Spirit Shoppe. Hebert's French Baked Goods. He crosses Main Street and enters the pharmacy and sits at the breakfast counter. Pat Crudo has a red pen in her mouth that she is chewing and she smiles at him and comes over to take his order. She has a stack of hair sprayed stiff on top of her head.

Hey, she says. What you want.

Eggs scrambled and some bacon.

Toast.

Rye.

Coffee, she says.

Black.

She takes the pen out of her mouth and writes it all down on a little pad that she keeps in her apron. As she walks away from Bobby she tears the slip of paper with his order on it from the pad and sticks it over the grill that Jenny is running today. There are several orders of eggs and pancakes and French toast already cooking. Sausage links and bacon strips. Cheese Danish cut in halves. Pat Crudo pours his coffee and puts it on the counter in front of him and the steam of it warms his face and he closes his eyes. He sips it until his food comes. Somebody has left part of a newspaper and he looks through the headlines. Bobby checks the police log to see if Blackie has earned himself another night at the drunk tank or worse, but there's nothing there except a bit on some dude from Athol who got beat down and is in a coma over at Cooley Dick. Then Pat brings his plate with extra bacon. He mows her lawn sometimes. She refills his coffee.

So what's doing, she says.

Nothing.

You keeping clear of trouble.

When I can.

She snorts and he loads some egg onto his fork and shoves it into his mouth.

I want to ask you, she says.

Bobby chews and chews and swallows.

Can you cut my grass, she says.

He looks up at her.

When.

Today or tomorrow, she says. Maybe once the sun dries everything.

He scratches his head.

All right hey, he says.

Let me pay you now because I might won't be home.

All right.

Gone to the lake.

All right.

You know where everything is in the barn.

Yeah.

See me before you leave then.

All right, he says.

She walks away with the glass coffee pot against her hip. The butter has melted on Bobby's toast and he smears strawberry preserves on top of it. He uses the last bit of bread to wipe the plate clean and he finishes his coffee and stands up. He folds the newspaper in half and sets it down. Pat Crudo brings his bill and he pays her and she goes to the register and comes back and gives him change and he leaves a dollar tip under the plate. Then she gives him a ten spot that she produces from the pocket in her apron.

All right, she says. Here's this.

Bobby takes the cash and puts it in his back pocket.

He needs all the money he can get.

Later today would be better, she says. Because it might rain again.

All right.

Front and back and up to the treeline on the sides.

I remember.

She smiles a little.

Course you do, she says.

She puts her hand in his hair like maybe a mother would do. He steps back and she leaves her hand in the air for a moment and he thanks her and exits through the front door. Westy and LaPinta are crossing the street toward him. He acts like he does not see them but Westy calls his name several times until he looks in their direction. He stops and they walk up to him. He looks at Westy and he looks at LaPinta and then he looks at his feet and jams his hands into his back pockets to appear carefree. They stand in front of him for a couple beats. He adjusts the cap on his head and spits over his shoulder.

What, Westy says. You didn't hear us.

Nah.

Going deaf then.

I was just thinking and stuff.

LaPinta laughs and grabs the hat off his head, holds it up high so he can't reach.

This must be your thinking cap then, he says, the fucking prick.

Give it back, Bobby says.

LaPinta laughs until Westy tells him to give it back and then the prick drops it on the ground and Bobby looks at him, and then he picks it up and puts it on backward. Westy tells LaPinta to go inside and get a couple coffees for the road. He gives him the money. LaPinta gets all sore like somebody rained on his parade once again.

We're looking for your father, Westy says.

Aint seen him.

Since when.

Last call at the Hot L.

They serving you in there already, he says.

I was just like going home and he was in there.

Westy looks at Bobby and doesn't say anything for a few seconds.

Shakes his head.

Tsk, tsk, tsk, he says.

Bobby grunts.

All right, Westy says.

Bobby spits over his shoulder into the street. Westy doesn't say anything.

Is that it then, Bobby says.

He still with that gal over to the Shutesbury AC, he says.

You mean the human punching bag.

Westy grunts. He's heard something about that.

That what you call her, he says.

That's what she is never mind what I call her.

Well, he says. Is he.

He doesn't tell me his business and I don't tell him mine.

Aint that a sweet deal.

Yeah for me I think it is.

You see him, Westy says. Tell him come see me.

LaPinta returns with the coffees and he tries to stare Bobby down and Bobby smiles at him and spits a long stream of saliva over his shoulder into the street. LaPinta hands one coffee to Westy and he takes a sip from the other one and he burns his tongue and he curses and spills some coffee on his nice pressed shirt. Bobby laughs at him and Westy laughs, too, and LaPinta goes back into the pharmacy to get a few napkins.

Motherfucker, he says under his breath as he crosses the street.

Is that it then, Bobby says to Westy. Can I go.

Where you rushing off to boy.

I got work.

Pumping gas today.

Nah.

What then.

Cutting some grass.

That's good for you.

Bobby doesn't say anything back and he turns to leave and Westy tells Bobby to stay out of trouble. Westy knows that trouble will find Bobby whether or not he stays away from it.

Hey, he says. I heard your uncle been around.

Drops it on him all casual like. That's how Westy will catch you off guard.

Bobby stops and turns back around and looks at him and spits.

Tell him I said hey.

Westy holds Bobby in his eyes for a few heartbeats.

I aint seen him, Bobby says.

Well, Westy says. Call me when you do see him.

All right.

If you see him and don't contact me, he says. They got a term for that.

Really, Bobby says. They got a term for everything now.

Westy laughs and tells Bobby to go on and so he does.

CHAPTER TWENTY-FOUR

THE PHONE RINGS THREE TIMES before Gidget picks it up. She's a retired schoolteacher who volunteers at the tri-town police station—filing reports, cleaning up, answering the phones. Before teaching she managed the president's office at Capp Valve in Indian Falls. Her late husband was a cop in Stillwater for thirty years and she's still living off his pension so she feels obligated. The woman on the other end of the line won't identify herself.

And she's crying hysterical.

I can't write it down if you don't give me your name, Gidget says.

That's the rule. The chief says anonymous tips lead to wild goose chases and they just don't have the manpower for that. Gidget is getting ready to hang up on this crazy bawling woman. But there's something that keeps her holding on that she can't explain.

I'm gone to hang up, she says but she doesn't really mean it yet.

He's here, the woman says. That soft brain.

Gidget stops. Shifts in her seat. Gets a pen and paper off the desk.

Who's that now, she says.

That soft brain you looking for.

Gidget catches her breath.

You talking about the Redwine boy, she says.

That's him.

Gidget writes the boy's name down in her secretary's shorthand scrawl.

What you mean he's here, she says. Where's here.

He took him from the street, the woman says.

Who's that now.

The boy or somebody tried to save him but he found him in the yard.

Who done that now, Gidget says. Hold on and let me get this straight.

He was hiding in the bushes.

Uh huh.

More crying. Gidget is very patient, the chief refers to that trait as her gift and she believes it to be true. She tells the woman to be calm and that everything is all right. Tries to get her to spill the beans on the alleged perpetrator but the poor girl is awful scared.

It's all right, she says.

The woman laughs now and her tone changes.

Oh nah it aint all right hey, she says. It aint never all right.

Gidget writes something down.

Not by a longshot, the woman says.

Gidget changes her tone, too, going with strict schoolmarm now.

All right, she says. We'll get to that later.

She listens to the woman blowing her nose.

Where is Raymont right now this very minute, Gidget says.

The woman gives her an address that Gidget recognizes—Chet Kosloski's rented-out duplex. Right down the street from where the Redwine family lives. Right under their nose the whole time, within a mile, in fact. The chief is going to be pissed. Gidget tries to get the woman to stay on the line but there is some noise on the other end and then the woman disconnects and so Gidget takes a moment to collect her thoughts, something else the chief always appreciates, and then she tries to get him or Westy on the walkie-talkie.

KAT DIDN'T KNOW HE WAS home but she figured he'd know she made the call anyhow. She had never been able to keep a secret from him. So she isn't surprised that he has discovered her but what she did not expect is how calm he is. He seems more resigned than angry. She braces herself for an outburst regardless. He stands there looking at her.

The telephone is in a million pieces on the floor at her feet.

Why'd you have to go and do that, he says.

Shit I don't know Black.

You don't know.

It just seemed a shame I guess.

A shame you say.

What you're doing to that boy.

Uh huh.

It had to end, she says. This whole thing did.

He lets that sink in for a couple three heartbeats.

Everything got to end, he says.

She has a bowl of cereal in her hands, half eaten.

He takes it from her and puts it on the counter.

You had to call the fucking cops, he says.

Oh Black.

Stay calm now, he says.

Please don't.

What did you expect, he says.

Black.

Hold still now woman.

He puts his hard-knuckled hands on her chest, shoulders and then neck. Her windpipe is beneath his thumbs. He can feel it. He can feel her try to swallow her last spoonful of cereal but she can't now. He closes the narrow passage even more and her eyes look about ready to pop out of her head like one of those silly squeeze toys you might buy for a baby. She won't even fight him. She's never been much of a fighter.

CHAPTER TWENTY-FIVE

FAT JOHNNY PICKS UP BOBBY. Bobby tells him about the grass at Pat Crudo's and they drive down there. They cross the blue-painted bridge over the Swift River into Indian Falls. She lives past the auction house and Skibiski Insurance. Fat Johnny parks behind her house in the shade. They drink a couple beers and listen to some music. Pat Crudo lives alone, no kids. They decide that if the door is locked then Fat Johnny can slip through the kitchen window that is typically partially open while Bobby is mowing the lawn, which should take about an hour, and look for some cash or stuff they can hock.

Not a total raid, not enough so she'd even notice.

Don't go nuts, Bobby says.

Fat Johnny grabs his nuts to be funny.

She's good people, Bobby says.

We're good people, Fat Johnny says.

Bobby gets out of the car and walks to the barn where she keeps her garden tools and gas-powered lawnmower. He stops in the doorway and looks back and Fat Johnny hops up onto the porch and checks the door and then he shoves the window all the way open. He disappears inside. There is a block of wood jammed into the double doors of the barn and Bobby kicks it aside and opens them. There is a rusted and cobwebby antique Studebaker inside, dust on the windshield an inch thick. Then he finds the old red lawnmower and checks the oil. It is fine but the gas is low. There is a plastic container that is half full of unleaded. He fuels the mower and pushes it outside and hits the primer button three times with his thumb and he can hear the fuel squirt and he gives the rope a tug. His shoulder pops and he lets go the rope and works it out and tries again and it fires up. Bobby starts out front. It is getting hot so he takes off his t-shirt and puts it in his back pocket. He adjusts his wet hair under his cap. He cuts straight lines across the lawn that is sparse and dried out in places and stones and twigs get caught in the blades and shoot out and sometimes hit his legs like a million bee stings. She has a big black metal mailbox that is misshapen from being blown up by M80s and beaten down with baseball bats. He cuts around the white pail that is filled with cement and now serves as the foundation of it. He makes it around to the east side of the house and then there is a knock and he looks up at one of the upstairs windows and Fat Johnny is smiling. He opens the window and sticks his head out. Bobby kills the gas by releasing the throttle bar so he can hear him.

Boy we hit the fucking jackpot, Fat Johnny says.

He's excited about something but he wants to leave Bobby hanging. Bobby resists the urge to probe his friend for full disclosure and he takes the t-shirt out of his back pocket and wipes his face with it. He stands there and looks up at Fat Johnny and he smiles some more. Then Bobby puts the t-shirt back into his pocket. Cracks his neck side to side. There are a couple three pops and he feels better, looser, already.

The front door is open, Fat Johnny says.

All right.

You coming or what.

Bobby gestures at the unfinished yard with both his hands.

I should finish this up first hey, he says.

Suit yourself Mr. Responsible.

She paid me up front.

All right.

After a few beats Bobby couldn't hold back anymore, his curiosity piqued.

Why what the fuck you got up there, he says.

Funny you should ask.

Then Fat Johnny just shakes his head at Bobby and disappears back inside. Bobby doesn't feel like playing games so he fires up the mower and makes a few more passes in the front yard. A car drives by and honks at him and he waves. It looks like Carol Ward and Dee Dee Zewski and maybe some other girls from town. Probably going for a swim by the rope swing. He watches them slow down by the Creamy but then they accelerate and round the corner. It occurs to Bobby again that he hasn't seen Doreen in a few days.

He parks the mower in the shade of an old elm tree and shuts her down. There is a garden hose wrapped around an old truck wheel bolted to the side of the barn and he wipes away some cobwebs and drinks from it. The water tastes like the rubber hose but it is cold and all right. He wets his hands and runs them through the hair under his cap and he wets his t-shirt, too, and puts it on his face. The screen door opens and closes and it sounds like old bedsprings. Fat Johnny comes out and sits on a rusty metal chair. He's smoking something. He smiles at Bobby through the smoke and Bobby looks at him.

What you got there you fat fuck, Bobby says.

Fat Johnny shows him a thick blunt.

Seems Pat has a eye condition, he says. And this is her prescription.

Fuck me.

Bobby has heard about that; folks using dope for their eyesight. He walks over to the porch and the three wooden steps need some fixing and he can smell it now. He stands over Fat Johnny until he hands him the joint. Bobby smokes it and closes his eyes. After a while he opens his eyes and exhales and Fat Johnny is leaning way back in the chair. The dope is stronger than anything Tyrone Mayfield has ever sold them. That's for sure.

Oh shit hey, Bobby says.

Yeah there's a whole pile of it up there.

A whole pile.

Yeah that's right boy.

Well shit.

Bobby coughs and pulls a rusty metal chair alongside Fat Johnny and they smoke the rest of it. There's a breeze that smells like the top layer of green scum that builds up on the manmade pond this time of year. Eventually they go inside the house to look for food. There are three stuffed bell peppers wrapped in aluminum foil and half a shoo-fly pie in a round tin and some kielbasa links. They put it all on the small foldout table in the kitchen and Fat Johnny gets a wooden spoon from the bowl over the stove and Bobby uses his hands. They eat without speaking or even looking up. There's a quart of milk and Fat Johnny drinks it and belches. Bobby laughs at him and he laughs back at Bobby. A breeze is leaking in through the open windows, whispering promises of a cooler dusk.

When she coming back from Lake Wyola, Fat Johnny says.

I don't know.

She didn't say.

Today or tomorrow but I fucking forget.

Fat Johnny surveys the mess they have made and he laughs.

Better be tomorrow boy, he says.

Bobby laughs, too. They're at that point where everything is funny.

Pat has some cash and coins in a pickle jar on a shelf in the living room. Bobby counts out twenty three dollars and some change and he stuffs it in his pocket. Fat Johnny takes some jewelry from the bedroom. A necklace that might be gold and a ring with a blue stone. Then they sit on the couch in front of the television that only gets three channels. They watch baseball. The Red Sox are losing in the eighth. Somebody hits a dinger. Neither of them gives a shit. Bobby closes his eyes and when he opens them it's dark. Fat Johnny is asleep on the floor. The baseball game is over and there's a news program on.

The sound of gravel under tires startles him and Bobby gets up and looks out the window. A car with one headlight aiming lazily up at the trees is pulling into the driveway slowly. He shakes Fat Johnny awake. Fat Johnny rolls onto his back and looks at Bobby and he appears lost, unsure of his surroundings, completely disoriented.

What the fuck, he says.

Pat's here.

Oh fuck.

Fat Johnny snaps to and gets up quick and Bobby turns off the television. The car door closes and then they hear her footsteps on the porch stairs. They slip out the front door just as she is coming in through the side door that leads into the kitchen. Fat Johnny had parked his car alongside the treeline on the north side of her property so likely she didn't see it. They get to the car and open the driver side door quietly and Bobby gets in and slides over and Fat Johnny gets in and shuts the door with barely a sound. He puts the key in the ignition and looks at Bobby before he turns it and Bobby looks at him.

If he starts the engine, she will hear them.

Shit, Fat Johnny says.

Got to wait.

For what.

Till she's asleep or something.

She'll see our mess in there.

The mess they made in the kitchen is a sure sign that they have been there, all the crumbs and dirty dishes and whatnot, inside her place that is supposedly off-limits. Then Pat will see the mower under the tree in the morning and put two and two together.

Fuck, Bobby says.

We're fucked hey.

I am anyhow.

Well if you are then I am too.

Nobody would know for a fact it was him with Bobby. But everybody would figure it was so and they both recognize that. Fat Johnny slouches in his seat and pulls his cap low on his head so he can barely see under the rim. They watch the house for signs.

She'll call the cops, he says.

I guess anybody in their right mind would.

Lights come on in windows as she moves through her house. Kitchen light, living room light, hall light, upstairs bedroom, upstairs bathroom. They track her that way. She is following their footsteps. She is measuring the damage done, taking it all in, maybe figuring an intruder is hiding in a closet, some cokehead nigger or spic from Holyoke, probably already thinking 911 or worse. They know she can shoot a gun.

There was an old Colt rifle they had seen under the bed.

Fat Johnny sits up straight and looks at Bobby.

We should make a break for it while she's up there, he says.

Yeah that might be the thing hey.

He turns the key and the engine catches and then falters and then catches again. He looks up at the house, at the windows upstairs, as he slips the transmission into drive. Bobby looks over Fat Johnny's arm that is a straight line from his shoulder to the steering wheel. They roll across her lawn and over the curb onto the street and when all four tires are on the blacktop Fat Johnny punches the pedal with his right foot and they fishtail and rubber burns and surely leaves behind a tarry patch. They get up to around sixty miles per hour and then he takes it easy when they get to the intersection at Route 47 because Indian Falls cops are real shitheads about speeding or maybe just in general. They sit at the red light and Bobby is stone sober now. Fat Johnny takes off his cap and puts it in his lap. His forehead is sweaty. He uses the back of his hand on it, looks over at Bobby.

Well what now then, he says.

As though Bobby will have an answer.

Yeah, Bobby says. What now.

If Pat doesn't call the cops right away, she will certainly tell them in the morning when she is working her shift at the pharmacy and they come in for a dose of caffeine and smoked meat. She will tell Westy and LaPinta and they will be all over Bobby's shit. Now they'll be wanting to talk to him and his old man. And his uncle. Bobby is truly fucked.

The light turns green and there are no other cars around and they cross the blue bridge carefully. Sunsick Mountain is a looming granite shadow. Boho's Appliance Repair and Schuster's Funeral Home and the U.S. Post Office. The street is dark because most of the lamps have been shot out with a twenty-two. A canopy of elm and maple and white birch. They stop at the town common, but that is too obvious so Fat Johnny pulls around and they park behind Rogers & Brooks. Bobby's old man's jeep is in its usual spot in front of the Hot L. Bobby doesn't know why Westy can't seem to find him.

He laughs to himself.

If any person was predictable in his habits it would be his old man. He used to say he could never be a U.S. president on account of he'd be too easy to assassinate because of his predictability. He said it like it was the only thing keeping him from making it.

Bobby has always been amused by the thought.

And then he sees the cruiser in the alley. Well, goddamn, somebody finally did some detective work after all, Bobby thinks. The passenger door of the cop car is open and a leg is sticking out. It looks like LaPinta is sitting in there. Probably Westy put him on time out again and he's sulking. The cruiser's lights are off, but there are gray puffs jumping like rabbits from the small opening of the exhaust pipe. Bobby points so Fat Johnny will look up. He sees what Bobby sees and makes a noise with his tongue.

I smell bacon, Bobby says.

It's another joke that never gets old with them.

Fat Johnny looks at the cop car and he looks at Bobby and he laughs a nervous laugh. He takes his palms off the steering wheel and puts them behind his head.

Shit what they working on over there, he says.

My old man I suppose.

PART III:

"Right and wrong don't mean shit round here."
—Thaddeus DuBois

CHAPTER TWENTY-SIX

A WHITETAIL DEER WITH A red-brown coat noses the lid off of a metal trash can. Bobby and Fat Johnny watch the cop car and wait and then the music from the bar spills into the street. Loud voices. Laughter. Billiards. It is a strange symphony. A lullaby. Bobby slouches like Fat Johnny and feels as though he's in a trance. Then all of a sudden LaPinta gets out of the cruiser with a sense of urgency and with his right hand on his hip he takes the front steps to the Hot L two at a time and goes inside. Fat Johnny hits Bobby with the back of his hand. Bobby sits up straight. After a few minutes the music stops and the loud voices stop and pool game stops. It is an eerie hush that permeates the scene.

The doe bleats and skitters away, sensing danger.

Some shit is going down, Fat Johnny says.

Fuck me.

Then LaPinta comes flying horizontally out the front door obviously not of his own accord and a wood chair is in his wake. He lands in a pile of blue uniform on the sidewalk and the chair touches down a few feet away and breaks apart. He appears to be unconscious. Then Westy and Bobby's old man emerge as a two-headed beasty. The sounds it is making are not human. It pounds four-footed and clumsy down the stairs and patrons are hesitant to follow but they do, keeping a distance and with drinks in hand. Sue is there with a rag on her shoulder. And Whitey and

Mugsy and the men from Double D's. The beasty finally breaks apart and Blackie is holding Westy's sidearm pistol uncomfortably as though it is a new body part. Westy is on his knees and there is a thick, bright red stripe on his cheek from his ear to his nose. Blackie is facing him now maybe five feet away in a crouching position and considering that bad thing in his hand. Time stops for a beat. The crowd is quiet as it can be until there is a shaky voice and it is Sue.

All right now boys, she says. Hold up.

Breaking Blackie from his spell.

Then she steps from the throng and makes her way down the stairs very carefully as though the planks are made of hot coals. Westy looks at her but does not really look away from Blackie either. Blackie stares at the gun in his hand. LaPinta doesn't move.

Put that thing down now Blackie, Westy says.

Sue holds one of her hands out in front of her chest toward Blackie like you would to a rabid dog. With her other hand she holds a corner of the bar rag that is still on her shoulder. She is rubbing it between her thumb and her forefinger in a nervous fashion. Sue asks Blackie to give her the nine millimeter. Westy stands up to his full height and seems to want to regain control of the situation. He clears his throat.

Sue, he says. Step on back now.

She stops in her tracks and looks at Westy and then back at Blackie who has not moved. He is still as a statue. Bobby has seen that posture before. It's not a good sign.

He won't do nothing to me, she says.

No he won't do nothing to nobody, Westy says.

Come on Blackie, Sue says. Put that down now.

Then Blackie looks at her and she has a change of heart and gets back up there with the rest of them like she was originally told. Westy's voice is hard and measured now that Sue is out of harm's way. LaPinta stirs, but just a little bit. Bobby's old man does not move except his head so he can look Westy in the eye.

Well all right what now then, Blackie says.

Put that down and let's talk.

But I'm all done talking.

Maybe it was a case where you lost your marbles for a minute.

I got nothing to say to you.

I could get somebody down here to talk, Westy says. Maybe a preacher.

Blackie laughs.

Nah, he says. I don't need that.

All right then just put it down there Black.

Then LaPinta awakens and picks his head up and Bobby guesses he sees Blackie standing there with that gun because he reaches for his own belt and before he can even unclip it and retrieve his piece Blackie moves exactly enough and there is a single crack and LaPinta slumps back over again as though returning to sleep. And again the silence and then an animal wail as Bobby's old man fully recognizes the weight of the culmination of his transgressions and he drops the gun and there is a sick metallic clank when it lands near his feet. He hits his knees where he was standing and his mouth is open and his eyes are closed. Mugsy steps in and kicks the gun away from Blackie and it skips across the cement leaving a trail of white sparks and stops at the base of the pay phone in front of the coin-operated laundromat. Then Westy attends to LaPinta and Whitey runs toward the firehouse to sound the town horn for an emergency. Sue is alongside Westy and she hands him her rag and he uses it to try to plug the perfect hole in LaPinta's neck. He is talking to his partner calmly but it is too late for that, even Bobby can tell from where he is sitting. Fat Johnny looks at Bobby and Bobby looks at him.

Fuck me, Bobby says.

This is some shit, Fat Johnny says.

Bobby gets out of the car and walks slowly and deliberately toward the scene. He thinks he can hear Fat Johnny behind him but he's not positive about that. Sue sees them first and she cries and Westy looks up and shakes his head at Bobby and Fat Johnny.

Fuck you doing here, he says.

The boys stop walking but they don't turn back. They don't say anything.

Go on now, Westy says.

The rag that Sue had given to Westy is dark and moist now and LaPinta looks like a fucking ghost of himself. And he is leaking motor oil. Westy has LaPinta's head in his hands that are wet and red. Sue is crying and she crosses her arms over her stomach. Then Fat Johnny is next to Bobby and Bobby can feel him there he is so close and his old man opens his eyes and closes his mouth and sees his son. He does not recognize him at first. He does not recognize the entire situation perhaps. Then he smiles and he speaks.

See what happens, he says.

He says it like somehow Bobby will understand.

See how things go, he says.

As though he's trying to impart some kind of lesson.

Bobby nods his head at his father and his father looks at him and he looks back.

Go on now like he done told you, Blackie says. We'll settle up later.

Sue is crying harder and Fat Johnny takes Bobby by the elbow. They sit on the chipped curb across the street. Bobby hears the town horn. Volunteers shake off sleep and arrive within minutes in cars and pickups and somebody has a red and white toolbox with gauze and tape and scissors. Somebody else has a stretcher and a blanket. There's a certain amount of confusion and they roll LaPinta onto the stretcher after they try to dress his wound and Westy rips open his partner's shirt and tries chest compressions. Bobby's old man is on his back in the middle of the street, still unrestrained other than by his own dim conscience and alcohol-induced fatigue. Sue puts her hand in Westy's hair. He's straddling LaPinta and pushing and counting ten. With each push blood spurts from the bullet hole and through the thin bandage like a miniature human volcano.

He's gone, Sue says.

Westy counts to ten.

He's gone now, she repeats.

Westy pushes and pushes and pushes.

Let him go, Sue says.

Westy stops and looks up at Sue and then he looks at Blackie and he has a look on his face like he has forgotten that the shooter was even there. Like he wasn't the cause of this. Like it was just an accident that they were all witness to and not an act of violence. Westy stands up and

Sue helps him. A blanket is thrown over LaPinta's face. Westy walks over to where Blackie is on his back and Westy stands over him. Westy puts his hands at his side with his fingers outstretched. Sue stays back a careful step.

She makes the sign of the cross that ends at her lips.

Get up Blackie, Westy says.

There isn't even the hint of anger in his voice.

Blackie lifts his head and struggles into a sitting position. He considers Westy and resigned he holds his palm up and Westy helps him stand by holding his fingers in one hand and his elbow in the other. It is a gentle human transaction. Then Blackie turns and Westy produces handcuffs from his belt. They walk together and Blackie is limping, he hurt his leg during the struggle in the bar, and then he's stuffed into the backseat of the cruiser that's still running, has been running this entire time. Bobby closes his eyes and Fat Johnny drapes an arm across his shoulder. When Bobby opens his eyes the cruiser is backing into Main Street and LaPinta is on his way to Cooley Dick in the back of Mugsy's pickup and Sue is ushering everybody back inside for a drink on the house. The crowd is recapping what just took place and making hushed predictions.

Come on you redneck motherfuckers, Sue says. Drinks on the house.

Even with the somber mood that has settled on the mob, her guarantee elicits crude whoops of pleasure. Fat Johnny gets up from the curb and Bobby gets up, too. They walk to the car and get inside and sit there. Bobby closes his eyes and Fat Johnny looks at him.

Fuck, Bobby says. He shot that boy dead.

Fat Johnny turns the key in the ignition.

A fucking cop killer, Bobby says.

Guess your uncle be coming real soon now.

Fat Johnny is looking at Bobby and Bobby is now looking out the window at the side of the building and the maggoty dumpster that is always overstuffed. Even weekly runs to the public landfill can't keep the trash at bay. There is a smell like linseed oil.

CHAPTER TWENTY-SEVEN

IT'S UNSEASONABLY CHILLY AND THERE'S a bit of weather outside and Bobby pulls an early morning shift at Frontier Service Station. Festus manages the place for Eugene. He says it's colder than a witch's tit. He tells Bobby that Paciorek brought his fleet of vans in for oil changes and grease jobs. He shows him Karl Wysocki's old Malibu that needs a new radiator. Hawk delivers ham and egg sandwiches from the pharmacy and Festus gives him a couple bucks from the register. Hawk licks his lips, which is not a pleasant sight.

Don't drink it all in one place, Festus says.

Hawk tells him to fuck off and then camps out under the heater hanging above the front door for a minute. The stink coming off the old drunk is amplified by the machine.

Jesus Christ man, Bobby says. Can't you stand nowhere else.

Hawk looks at him.

Bobby unwraps his sandwich on the countertop and cuts it in half with a white plastic knife. Festus follows suit. Hawk watches them eat but it's not food that he craves. Then he exits the facility just as the mud-splattered cruiser pulls alongside the gas pumps. The bell inside the near bay sounds to indicate that a new customer has arrived.

Fuck me, Bobby says.

Festus eyeballs the squad car.

What'd you do now, he says.

Aint what I did.

Well what then.

Festus hadn't seen the paper yet or been in the pharmacy to get the latest news. Bobby fills him in while Westy waits patiently in his car with the engine turned off.

Oh shit, Festus says.

Right.

On top of everything else.

Festus takes the last bite of his sandwich and egg yolk leaks down his chin.

So after today I don't know, Bobby says.

All right.

Like where I might end up or whatever.

Right.

So if we can square up at the end of my shift.

Sure okay kid.

Westy taps his horn lightly outside.

Bobby finishes his sandwich, too.

Guess you best see about that, Festus says.

Bobby pushes the front door open with his foot and steps over the threshold. He approaches the driver's side of the cruiser. Westy rolls down his window and looks at him.

How you doing kid, Westy says.

All right.

All right you say.

Yeah.

Well that was some shit last night with your old man.

Bobby doesn't know what to say.

It'll be a while before you can see him.

Bobby shakes his head.

Will you be okay while I try to figure something out.

Figure what out.

Well, Westy says. You can't live on your own.

Bobby doesn't say anything.

Fill her up with unleaded will you.

The twenty-gallon tank is behind the license plate so Bobby goes back there dragging the heavy black hose and he twists off the cap and inserts the nozzle. He activates the pump and watches the numbers roll over. When he's done Bobby ducks inside the office to get a slip for Westy to sign because the police have an account.

Westy signs the slip.

Hit them windows for me, he says. They're awful muddy.

Bobby washes the front and back windows with a squeegee.

Thanks kid, Westy says when he's finished.

All right.

So we'll talk later.

Sure.

Don't go nowhere, he says. You know.

All right.

Festus wants to know what Westy said and Bobby tells him.

No shit, Festus says. Playing it like that.

Then he tells Bobby to go ahead and take care of Paciorek's vans first. He brings the maroon one into the bay and parks it over the lift. Bobby gets on his knees and adjusts the metal tabs beneath the frame. Then he operates the hydraulic switch against the wall with one hand and guides the vehicle's bumper with the other and you can hear a sputter and hiss and it takes less than a full minute before the lift is completely extended and Bobby can stand under the van at his full height. He drags over a red cart with standard wrenches and ratchet sets laid out in an organized fashion. There's a large funnel attached to a labyrinth of pipes and elbow connectors that ultimately disappears into a threaded hole cut into the cement floor. Bobby unscrews the plug to the oil pan and the stream of black juice arcs and he adjusts the funnel accordingly. He maneuvers a red-handled lasso wrench to remove the old oil filter and then hand-tightens the new one into place.

He uses a pink rag to wipe the nipples of the various tie rods just before he hits them with the grease gun, linked by a thin rubber tube to a bucket standing on a square of plywood set on wheels that's typically stored in the corner. Then he puts the plug back in the pan and tops off the air pressure in the tires. Bobby drops the van back down to the ground, where he replaces the four quarts of thirty weight oil he had drained as well as checks the radiator, transmission, brake, power steering, and windshield wiper fluid levels. He starts the engine and lets it run for two minutes and then regards the dipstick.

Bobby repeats the same procedure with the other two vans, one silver and one black, and the monotony of the task allows him to keep his mind off the situation with his old man for the most part. It's almost noon by the time he's parking the black van in the dirt lot out back and he wants to get started on the Malibu's radiator before lunch. Just as he's popping the hood to the Malibu he hears Festus talking to somebody in the office.

Then Festus pokes his head into the work area.

Hey kid, he says.

Yeah.

You got a visitor.

Bobby cleans his hands with goop and water as best he can and dries them on the rag he then sticks in his back pocket. Doreen is there sitting on the bench seat ripped out of a Dodge Ram and bolted to the cement floor. Her legs are crossed. Bobby sits next to her and Festus pretends to take a phone call and he closes the door to his office so they can have some privacy. Doreen stays quiet and looks out the big window for a while.

Then she looks at Bobby.

Hey, she says.

Hey.

What you doing.

Same shit different day.

They sit in silence for a little while longer and then she puts her hand on his knee. Bobby tells her about his old man shooting John LaPinta dead. But she already knew. Her father had read about the incident in the paper and couldn't wait to throw it in her face.

So what's it all mean for you, she says. For us.

Damn if I know.

I mean where you gone to stay now.

Bobby shrugs his shoulders.

My father says you'll have to go away.

I don't know.

Then it's lunchtime and Hawk shows up with cheeseburgers and French fries and strawberry frappes. Festus comes out of the office to pay him more booze money and then he goes back inside his office to eat. Bobby is eating, too, when Doreen tells him about getting jumped by the boys in Bucktown. He stops chewing when she says it.

Jumped how, he says.

You know.

No I don't.

Please don't make me say it.

They better not have.

Jesus, she says. Bobby.

You better fucking tell me.

She tells him.

He gets up and puts his fist through the plaster just above the cigarillo machine.

Hawk jumps back when he does it and then disappears out the front door.

Doreen cries and describes in detail the full extent of their trespass and Bobby can't finish his lunch and he can't stand to look at Doreen and he wants to hit somebody, anybody, in the worst way. His old man is going to get locked up for forever and a day and now this. It's too much. He stuffs the rest of his lunch back into the bag and tosses it into the trash can. He stands up and Festus pops his head out nervously and tells Bobby to get going on the radiator job and Bobby welcomes the distraction. But he goes into the garage bay and flips over the red tool tray and kicks over an empty oil drum until Festus has to tackle him to get him to stop and Doreen tries to stop crying, but she cannot.

CHAPTER TWENTY-EIGHT

SUE TELLS BOBBY THAT UNCLE Thaddeus has been looking for him again. They don't talk about his father or what happened the other night. There's nothing really to say about that now, but she's concerned about his future situation. She lets him eat half of her chicken grinder with grilled onions and pickled red bell peppers and he sits at the bar.

She smiles at him from time to time.

Thaddeus went up there again, she says. Looking for you.

Bobby glances toward the door that leads up to their room.

I tried to stop him but you know how he does, she says. How they all do.

Well where's he at now.

He says when I see you that I'm to call him over to Billy Tucker's.

Bobby takes the last bite of the sandwich and runs a napkin across his mouth.

Call him up then, Bobby says. I guess I'm ready.

Are you now.

Shit.

Sue rolls her eyes at him for cursing like a man. Like he's not man enough already after what he has seen and been through.

I don't think it's a good idea, she says.

You got a better one then, he says. Cause they won't let me stay on my own.

Why not let Westy work things out with that judge.

Bobby shakes his head and balls up the napkin and drops it on the plate. Westy has promised to go to bat for him and he believes the man's heart is in the right place but he also believes that a well-intentioned heart will never be enough. Not in this bad world.

Fuck them fag judges in Bucktown or wherever, Bobby says.

Watch your mouth now.

They'll stick me somewhere I don't fucking belong, he says. Excuse my French.

You don't know that.

Then he looks at Sue and in her eyes Bobby can see that she accepts that he does actually know a thing or two for sure. Bobby looks at her and she looks at him and then she turns and picks up the phone. She dials a number and waits. Bobby pokes at some of the steak-cut fries that are left over and soggy from soaking in hot oil and then ketchup.

Thaddeus there, she says into the phone.

She listens and waits.

Hey, she says. The kid is here now.

She listens and waits some more.

All right, she says. I'll tell him.

She hangs up the phone and looks at Bobby.

You boys sure have a way with words, she says.

Bobby laughs.

He said to wait right fucking here, she says.

BOBBY SITS OUT FRONT UNTIL Thaddeus rolls up in an old Buick Skylark he just stole. Bobby barely recognizes him behind the dead-bug-splattered windshield and he waves his hand and his uncle nods his head and smiles. Bobby almost smiles, too. Thaddeus goes to park out back because the car is hot. Taking automobiles has always been a specialty of his. Bobby gets up and walks along the side of the building to the back and his uncle kills the engine and gets out of the Buick. Uncle Thaddeus is a big-boned man and when he unfolds himself from the driver seat and stands in the dirt of the parking area he makes everything around him seem smaller—the car, the chain-link fence, the back of the building, the purpling Franklin County sky. He stretches his lower back and looks at Bobby and smiles. This boy sure looks like a DuBois, he thinks. Square chin and all.

Look at you boy, he says. Goddamn.

His hair reminds Bobby of a basket of yellow yarn that a cat got into.

Bobby walks over to him and they stand there looking at each other, sizing each other up, and the large man puts his hand in his nephew's hair. Then he pulls him in and squeezes him tight with his arms and Bobby lets him for a few moments until he releases.

So I got some your stuff there, Uncle Thaddeus says.

He indicates the car with his thumb and Bobby nods his head.

What, Uncle Thaddeus says. Cat got your tongue.

Nah sir.

All right then, he says. That's better.

Bobby spits.

So your pappy got himself deep in it now, Uncle Thaddeus says.

Yes sir.

That was some shit the other night I heard.

Uh huh.

All right, he says. Now down to brass tacks.

Bobby spits again.

I figure they're trying to place you, Uncle Thaddeus says.

Yeah.

Westy and them others, he says. Social workers and judges and whatnot.

They been sniffing around.

I know what that's like, Thaddeus says. So you'll come with me instead.

All right then.

Which was my intention all along anyhow.

Bobby spits.

Well shit, Uncle Thaddeus says. Let's go then boy.

Just then Sue pokes her head out the back window and calls their names.

They both stop and look at her.

You take care that boy now, she says to Thaddeus.

Uncle Thaddeus looks at her and then he looks at Bobby.

Yes ma'am, he says.

And what should I tell Westy and them, she says.

Don't tell them nothing.

Oh that's priceless.

Uncle Thaddeus looks at Bobby again and makes a funny face at her nagging and the boy laughs. Then Thaddeus looks back at Sue. She's chewing on the end of the ring finger on her right hand. Bobby notices a ring where there hadn't been one before—two slender hands clasping a heart surmounted by a crown. They call it an Irish engagement ring, Bobby thinks. It's upside down, with the point of the heart toward Sue's fingertips.

Bobby can't recall the significance of wearing it like that.

Then Uncle Thaddeus speaks, snapping Bobby back to the present.

Just tell them you don't know where he's at, Uncle Thaddeus says.

All right then, Sue says. I guess that is the truth since you won't tell me.

Best you don't know.

She spits a cuticle and smiles unconvincingly at Bobby and pulls herself back inside and closes the window. It doesn't close easy and they listen to her cursing at it.

Uncle Thaddeus gets in the car and Bobby does, too. He starts the engine and taps the gas pedal. He tells the boy he borrowed it from somebody at the Hollywood in Bucktown. He puts it in gear and pulls around. Bobby asks him where they're going and Uncle Thaddeus shrugs his shoulders. He actually have a specific place in mind yet.

We'll just lay low for a bit, he says.

You know I got me a girl.

Thaddeus looks at Bobby and brakes and looks up and down South Main Street.

Yeah I seen her the other day, he says.

That's right.

She's a real tomato.

Yeah she's all right.

Bobby tells him about how Doreen got attacked and Uncle Thaddeus agrees that payback can be a bitch. He ascertains that Bobby knows the identity of the attackers.

Let's take a ride up there then, he says.

Bobby likes the way that sounds.

See about that before we go, Uncle Thaddeus says.

I suppose we could.

But regardless you'll have to quit her for a while, Thaddeus says.

Bobby doesn't say anything and his uncle is definitely waiting for him to respond somehow. Uncle Thaddeus wants to be sure that Bobby is prepared to make sacrifices.

Can you do that now, Uncle Thaddeus says. Quit her for a while.

Bobby looks at his uncle and then out the window.

Especially in light of what just happened to her, he says. Your girl.

Uh huh.

Because I got to know, he says. If you're up to it.

Bobby thinks about it and he isn't convinced he can do it, but he doesn't say so.

All right, he finally says.

Bobby doesn't yet mean it and Uncle Thaddeus knows that to be the case. But he turns the Buick left and they drive along in silence. Thaddeus tells Bobby he's got a girl, too, and they can shack up with her for a minute or two. He tells his nephew that he can fix him up with some female tenderness so the separation from Doreen won't seem as difficult. He laughs when he says it and reaches over and puts his hand in the boy's hair.

THEY MAKE A FEW DELIBERATE passes up and down the main road that cuts through the center of Bucktown. Their heads swivel slowly and their dark eyes scan the faces of pedestrians and fellow motorists alike. The Skylark's exhaust system is equipped with a rudimentary glasspack and so the car appears to hiss and growl at onlookers curious about the purpose of this determined search party. Bobby and Uncle Thaddeus stop for fuel at a filling station off of Route 5 and that's when Bobby sees those cocksuckers that attacked Doreen, eating Slim Jims and getting soda pops from a red Coke machine.

Bobby points them out to Uncle Thaddeus.

Thaddeus grinds his teeth together and Bobby can hear them, see his jaw working.

Stars lining up for us already then, Thaddeus says.

Bobby flexes his neck, stretching the chords of it.

It's a nice day for comeuppance, Thaddeus says.

They wait outside near where a Ford Pinto is parked alongside the box-shaped building and nearby a weathered wood picnic table that's falling apart. The Bucktown boys come around the corner laughing and then they see Bobby and Thaddeus and then they are not laughing anymore. Thaddeus lets Bobby take the lead because he wants to see what he's made of. Bobby doesn't say shit because that's not his style and truth be told he is too angry to muster any words. He puts the hardest part of his skull into the bigger one until his orbit bone below his left eye is smashed in and he'll never look the same again. Then Bobby achieves an understanding of what they mean when they say you see red and things get blurry. When he's done the dude is in a puddle of himself and Thaddeus is stuffing the other one who's also a fucking mess into the trunk of the Pinto.

CHAPTER TWENTY-NINE

TWO DAYS LATER UNCLE THADDEUS knocks the TV off the stand and it breaks into pieces on the floor. His girlfriend tells Bobby to watch his step. Thaddeus calls her Darling Nikki.

And go put on some shoes, she says to Bobby.

His uncle does not clean it up and he goes and sits in the barn in the yard with the beer he gets from the back of the Buick. His girlfriend says he's mad because of her ex the Shelburne undertaker who called on the phone. Her nose is still crooked from the last time. She cleans up the television with a broom and a pan and Bobby helps some. She cooks dinner and the kitchen is warm from the stove and she tells Bobby to go get him.

Go get your fucking no-good uncle, she says and coughs into her hand.

Bobby gets up from the hardwood chair where he's sitting and looks at her.

Tell him his dinner's on the fucking table, she says.

Bobby opens the door and she's still talking as though there aren't enough words in the world to accommodate her thoughts. He is slightly amused by her behavior.

Tell him his dinner's getting fucking cold, she says.

Brown sugar pot roast so tender it dissolves on your tongue and mashed potatoes and carrots. The barn leans north and east. Uncle Thaddeus says he's still mad, but Bobby cannot tell. He's sitting on studded snow tires near the sagging expanse of the back door frame that is dark and cobwebby and held together with a metal bar hastily wedged into place. He says he is not hungry. He says he wants to be left alone. He tells Bobby that there's no way in hell he is going to eat in that house. He has a real temper. There's a temper present in DuBois men sure as the black blood coursing through their veins.

Never again, he says.

Bobby chuckles.

Not with her in there, Thaddeus says. No fucking way.

Bobby sits on the part of the floor that is cemented over and he smokes a cigarillo.

He knows that Thaddeus doesn't expect him to respond.

No way in hell, Uncle Thaddeus repeats like a mantra.

Bobby stays in the barn and smokes with him until Nikki calls his name.

Uncle Thaddeus tells him to go on and get his chow.

Whatever.

Bobby stamps his butt out in the dirt.

Go on ahead now boy, Uncle Thaddeus says.

All right.

He touches Bobby's leg and four red-back chickens suddenly squawk and scatter from a stall that harbors many things and the activity startles them both. Thaddeus laughs at the chickens and Bobby laughs at him laughing. It's a real moment that they share.

Go on now, Uncle Thaddeus says. Like I said.

Bobby stops in the doorway and looks back at him.

Westy and them others coming for us, Bobby says.

They coming all right.

Is my old man locked up already, Bobby says. At the Junction.

Thaddeus doesn't say anything about that.

It's difficult for him to imagine a cage that could truly hold Blackie.

Then Bobby eats dinner with his uncle's girlfriend and she talks his ear off about everything and nothing in particular. Then he brings Uncle Thaddeus a plate she has kept warm under a sheet of tinfoil in

the oven. He stays in his shadowy spot without saying anything. There
are birds in the barn that have a nest by the busted window near the
ceiling beams and gunstock posts made of chestnut. They appear to be
swallows. Bobby hears their wings flapping, but he does not see them.
He hears Uncle Thaddeus eating his biscuits and meat and drinking his
beer, but he does not see him anymore either because it's dark and he
is brooding now in the buckled corner where they'd used a chain and
come-along to cinch it back into place earlier in the day. It was the least
they could do as it was their drunk driving that had convinced the wall
to fall in on itself in the first place.

Smashed that Buick smack into the barn upon arrival.

Still drinking in there is she, Uncle Thaddeus says.

She's hitting that whiskey bottle pretty good.

And talking on the fucking phone I guess. That's her other specialty.

Mostly to me and just drinking and crying and eating her dinner.

Thaddeus nods his head and seems happy to hear this report. Bobby
surveys the inside of the structure. Tenons that connect posts and
beams are big as corncobs, light-colored as if jammed and hammered
into place yesterday, and hand-cut timbers that support the structure
are blond and wide at the top and tapered down at the bottom.

Then back in the house Darling Nikki says Thaddeus can stay in
there forever if he wants. She's drinking a Jack and Coke now and her
eyes are red from crying. Bobby asks her if they can visit the horses
in the morning and she says to get up early because she has to work
first shift at the plastic shop. She calls that her bread and butter and
stripping weekends for Jimmy the Greek at the Castaway Lounge gives
her the frosting on the cake. She says funny things like that all the time.
She gives Bobby a curious look.

So tell me, she says. Since when you give a fuck about a horse.

He doesn't really want to ride but Doreen will meet him there at
dawn. Bobby doesn't tell Nikki about Doreen because Uncle Thaddeus
is sure she'll lead the cops or some others to them. So he doesn't say
anything and she looks at Bobby and sticks her thumb in her drink.
Puts her thumb in her mouth. She lets it pass because her mind is on
other things. Then Bobby goes to bed and falls asleep right away. Then

he hears something and wakes up and listens. It's still nighttime and maybe it was a dream and there's nothing and a minute later he kneels by the window but that's it. He closes his eyes and breathes deep the lanolin and hay and manure. Then the black of the sky spills into other parts of the yard, too, and he closes his eyes and that old barn on the edge of the property seems to vanish. Bobby sleeps until he smells his uncle's breath very close.

Come on boy, he says. I got something for you.

UNCLE THADDEUS TELLS HIS GIRLFRIEND to get undressed and dance. Bobby is sitting on the couch now. The radio is playing Aerosmith's "Walking in the Sand." Darling Nikki leaves her clothes in a pile on the floor and smiles at the boy and gyrates half-heartedly in front of him. Then she stands him up and removes his pants and shorts and sits him back down. Uncle Thaddeus is drinking a can of beer and watching them. It's the dark part of morning and candles are still burning and dripping wax and you can smell them.

Go ahead now and make him a man, he says.

Bobby told him he'd already done it plenty, but Thaddeus said girls his own age don't count. He said it doesn't count until you stick your dick in a woman with miles.

Nikki looks at Thaddeus over her shoulder and then she looks back at Bobby.

Come on now, Thaddeus says. Get you some.

He's got his hand jammed into the front of his jeans.

They are not mad at each other anymore, Uncle Thaddeus and Darling Nikki. Fucked all the anger out of each other is how he put it to Bobby. The boy has heard them going at it like wild horses kicking, trying to bust loose from a stall that holds them.

Fucking is one thing but some folks just aren't fit to live together.

You ready there, she says nicely to Bobby.

She's got a sweet side to her and he bets she makes good money for the Greek.

All right, he says.

Then Bobby nods his head and she reaches down and takes him in her warm grip, puts a condom in her mouth and sheaths him with it like that. She does most of the work and occasionally whispers instructions in the boy's ear. It's different than when he does it with girls his own age, even Doreen; much less urgent. His uncle watches the whole thing. Afterward he fixes his pants and Thaddeus has to fix his pants, too. Bobby smells her on him and he can smell the sticky parts of his uncle that she hadn't washed off from earlier, too. Then she puts on her soiled white t-shirt with its yellow pit stains and she lights a cigarillo and blows smoke upward and it gets caught in the slow-turning ceiling fan. Bobby watches it get caught up there. Then she goes to the bathroom and Bobby can hear her running water and doing her business and then after a while the toilet flushes and he listens to dirty water rushing through the pipes behind the thin walls of the house.

CHAPTER THIRTY

THEN HE'S NOT SURE IF it's a dream or a memory. In it, the man puts the young boy on his shoulders and walks along the side of the mountain road like that. It could be his uncle or his old man. A creek runs alongside the road, too, and you can hear the nice sounds of it. The man is walking fast and with purpose like he is trying to get away from something. The boy seems oblivious to their plight, at least for the moment. He is focused on a small and silent black bird that is just ahead of them and darting in and out of the thick foliage.

Fucking cunt, the man says.

The man's gruff voice breaks the boy from his distraction.

Watch out for that, the man says.

The bird disappears and the boy listens to the man.

Watch yourself, he says. Cause they are poison.

The man spits and keeps walking and the boy stares straight ahead.

They poison your soul boy, the man says. And rot you inside.

The sound of a vehicle coming up from behind gives the man pause and he steps off the road with the boy and into the trees. They duck beneath the branches and hop the creek. The man tells the boy to shut up and they stand there and wait. Watch the curving road from their hiding place. Then the man lifts the boy down and they kneel beside each other on a carpet of leaves. The soil beneath them is dark and moist. The man is breathing fast and he can feel his heart in his chest. He can hear the creek water running fast. Then it is a rusted red pickup truck driving slow and thoughtful. Two fat rednecks in the cab and a chocolate Labrador standing in the back sniffing the wild air. The man is relieved and he puts his hand in the boy's hair and smiles at him. The truck goes around the bend. Then they cannot hear it anymore. The boy throws a stone into the water.

Come on, the man says.

He stands up and the boy stands up, too. There are stains on their knees from the good earth. They hop the skinniest part of the creek again and lower their shoulders through the shrubs and back onto the weather-cracked road. The man slows his gait so the boy can keep up and the boy takes longer strides to match those of the man. They are an odd pairing these two. They walk side by side as the morning sun dapples shadows.

CHAPTER THIRTY-ONE

DOREEN'S GREAT-AUNT IS GETTING ON in years and even though she denies it she needs help on her spread from time to time. She has a pack of stray dogs and feral cats that roam her property freely. There are always weeds to cut back and farm animals to tend to, as well as miscellaneous projects that seem to crop up regularly and are perhaps indicative of what some people refer to as her aunt's harmlessly eccentric nature. This particular evening Doreen's aunt is busy on a borrowed front-loader digging out a catfish pond.

Doreen stops by for a visit and to see if she can help with any chores and so her aunt gives her a list. Doreen fills two five-gallon pails with warm water from the tub. She rolls her shoulders back and carries them through the kitchen and out the side door, one in each hand, spilling a bit along the way. Toward the back of the parcel her aunt keeps a horse and a pony. Doreen follows the uneven stone path to the end and puts the pails down and throws open the barn door. She slices the string on a bale of hay and breaks it open inside Jennifer's stall, waters it down—water cuts the dust and makes the dry grass more palatable. Then she does the same thing for Sydney. Doreen calls to them and Jennifer appears gracefully until Sydney bites her rump and she bucks. Doreen manages to separate them without much trouble and she leads them each to their respective stalls, where they can still nudge each other through the wide gaps between the boards.

Behave now, she says. I don't want no trouble.

While they eat she puts a new salt lick near the half-full grain barrel in the small pasture that is mostly ankle-deep mud and shit. There is another closed-off section with a few scant green patches that will need to be opened soon to allow for some grazing. Then she combs Jennifer and lets her loose to run and then she tends to Sydney's coat, as well.

How's my fat boy, she says in his ear.

She gives him a couple cubes of sugar from her jean jacket pocket and he pushes his wet nose against her arm. When they walk outside together Jennifer is nowhere in sight. Doreen calls for her and searches for a break in the fence where maybe the horse got sprung and wandered off, but there's no indication that that's what happened.

Where's she at, Doreen whispers to the pony.

They walk the perimeter until eventually Doreen hears a loud snort followed by heavy breathing. Sydney leads her to a clump of tall grass growing on the top of a short mound and from it she sees that Jennifer has fallen into an underground creek and landed upside down. Doreen says shit and can see that her aunt has disappeared over the piney knoll to deposit another load of dark dirt and so she hurries to get her aunt's neighbor to pull Jennifer out with his John Deere tractor and some rope before her lungs cave in.

Luckily the neighbor is putting around in his garage and he comes along straight away as she explains the situation to him. He's of a previous generation and he moves with a bow-legged amble. Then it becomes clear that he's the kind of man who likes to talk as he works. Doreen only half listens and kneels and keeps Jennifer calm with her own voice. Sydney watches the efforts curiously, dispassionately, and munches his oats.

Thing about underground creeks, the neighbor says. Is you can't see the danger.

Doreen thinks of Bobby.

They flow just below the surface, he says. Never know where till it's too late.

He says this last bit over the chortle and hum of the tractor's old engine as he manipulates it back and forth for traction and then he un-gently guides Jennifer out of the hole and she scrambles to her hooves, kicking clods of dirt with her powerful legs. Doreen undoes the ropes with some precision and rubs the horse's neck and Sydney stands a few feet away attempting to bray and showing teeth. The neighbor collects his ropes and gear and Doreen thanks him. Then for some reason she looks up, and across the way at her aunt's house a curtain is caught in a breeze and waving from a partially open upstairs bedroom window like a white flag signaling sure defeat in some timeless battle.

She puts both her hands on her belly.

At that moment she yearns to see Bobby more than ever before.

She wants him to come home.

CHAPTER THIRTY-TWO

AT DAWN THE SUN IS staining clouds various shades of purple and pink and Doreen is sitting by the aluminum deer stand like Bobby told her to. There's a white dog there with her as well. Doreen does not see Bobby at first because of her angle but when the dog barks and wags its tail she stands up and smiles. Bobby walks over to her and she puts his face in her hands. They kiss hard and her tongue is in his mouth and then she starts to cry.

The dog sits.

I brought this for you, she says.

He looks at the dog.

To keep you company, she says.

Oh.

It's from Malek's, she says.

Malek is the dogcatcher. He shoots them after ten days and the crazies even sooner. Bobby puts his hand down to the dog and she sniffs at his fingers and palms.

My aunt rescued it, Doreen says.

What I'm gone do with a dog, Bobby says.

Give it a name for one thing, she says.

Is it one of those crazy fuckers, Bobby says.

Why would that trouble you, she says. This whole situation is crazy.

Uh huh.

You on the run like you done something wrong, she says.

Right.

You oughtn' pay for your father's sins.

Well that's what you say.

She stands back and looks at him, sizing him up.

Well at least you look all right.

Yeah.

You got a place.

We had a place.

She looks surprised and then disappointed.

I thought your uncle had a girl or something, she says. With a place.

I guess he did but that didn't work out so great.

Why not.

I'm thinking my uncle is not really the girlfriend type.

Doreen shakes her head.

They climb the wood ladder up to the elevated metal shack and the dog barks as they do so. The door hangs on a single hinge and Bobby pulls it aside with one hand and knocks cobwebs down with the other. She follows him inside. It's just an old mattress in there and it's dusty and they sit on it and she makes a face and sneezes. She has healed up nicely from the attack. They lie back and touch each other and she feels better.

The dog is barking like crazy down below.

How long we gone to do this, she says.

I'm almost done.

She laughs and looks at Bobby.

I don't mean this right now, she says.

Bobby knows what she means. He doesn't say anything for a little while and she goes back to work on him. Then he's finished and she kisses him fast on his mouth and pulls away. He closes his eyes. It is a rare moment of comfort that he'd like to stretch out.

So, she says.

So what.

So you can't just live in the woods forever like some hermit.

All right then.

Got half a mind to bring Westy next time.

Bobby gives her a look and she knows he means business.

He pushes her off his lap and stands up.

Take it back, he says

I do take it back, she says.

She reaches up and takes hold of Bobby's hips.

I said I didn't mean it, she says.

You can't even play like that or we're through doing even just this.

Don't say that, she says. Don't ever say that.

She cries. It seems to Bobby like she is always crying about one thing or another. She stands up, too, and he gets her to calm down a little bit but she is shaking now like some kid. Jesus fucking Christ. Maybe Uncle Thaddeus is right about females, he thinks.

Come on now stop it, Bobby says.

I'm sorry.

Don't be sorry, he says. You just can't do like you said.

I know.

This is some serious shit, he says.

I know it.

All right then.

But the damage is done. Bobby sees trust as a length of firewood and when Doreen threatened to bring the police it was like she chopped off a piece of it with an axe. She doesn't say anything else and they hold each other for a while but he has to get back so that his uncle doesn't get suspicious. Behind an electric fence a cow is switching its coarse tail at flies. He watches the cow over the top of Doreen's head until she speaks.

Well maybe I can run with you then, she says.

Bobby laughs.

He can picture how that would sit with his uncle.

Then he looks out the rectangular plastic window and there in the near distance is a cool-eyed timber wolf already with its thick winter pelage. Gray brown and stiff-legged and tall. Looking at the barking dog with ears erect and forward. Bobby watches it and he runs his fingers along the new scabs on Doreen's arm where she has scratched his name into her flesh with a beer bottle cap so that everybody in the fucking world can see it.

CHAPTER THIRTY-THREE

UNCLE THADDEUS HEATS RIVER WATER in a metal can that is balanced on some rocks over an open fire. He sits on his haunches and watches it start to boil. He pokes at the fire with a stick. There is a frying pan off to the side so he can cook up the half-dozen eggs they stole from Len Boulanger's hen house by the apple orchard. He has not looked at Bobby for a long time and he will sure as shit not look at Doreen. She is next to Bobby, wrapped in an old wool blanket. Then he pulls the sleeve of his flannel shirt down a little so it covers his hand and he takes the metal can from over the fire and rations out the boiling water into three chipped cups. Now the coffee smell is up. He rests the metal can in the dirt where he cleared it with some hemlock branches.

Come on now and get you some, Thaddeus says.

Spitting into a pile of sawlogs he indicates Doreen with a wave.

I won't say much on the topic but I will say this, he says.

Bobby and Doreen look at him.

She shouldn't be here, he says.

Doreen looks at Bobby and he looks at the fire.

Not happy about the dog either, Uncle Thaddeus says.

The dog barks.

For the record, Thaddeus says.

Bobby kicks dirt at the fire with the toe of his boot.

But at least we could eat the mutt if it came to that, Uncle Thaddeus says.

He doesn't look up when he says it. Then he puts his cup to his mouth and stands and blows a little and takes a sip and closes his eyes standing there. Bobby gets up, too, and walks over to get his and Doreen's. The cups are hot and he can feel it on his hands. Doreen pulls her sleeves down and holds hers like that and she lets the steam rise up into her face. Bobby stands next to where she is sitting and puts his hand in her hair.

Uncle Thaddeus speaks.

This aint no life for a pretty little thing, he says.

He looks at her and then he looks at Bobby and Bobby looks at his coffee.

That's all I got to say on the matter, Uncle Thaddeus says.

Then he turns to fixing the eggs.

Well that and also that she might've been followed, he says.

He looks straight at Bobby when he says it.

Which I warned you about, he says.

He puts the pan over the fire, resting on the same two rocks, and after a couple minutes he spits into it. Then he cracks the eggs two at a time into the pan and chucks the shells over his shoulder. He stirs them up with a stick and puts them over the flames until they thicken up just enough and you can hear them pop yellow and white. Then he lifts the pan out and puts it in the dirt to cool. The damn dog sniffing at his legs the whole time. They eat together and rest atop a carpet of leaves under a blue-lavender sky.

Uncle Thaddeus lets Doreen puff on his cigarillo and she coughs. The boy has slipped off with the mutt to catch lunch from the river. There are twigs in her hair from when she was napping. She gives the cigarillo back to Uncle Thaddeus and he smiles at her and he sits down next to her on the blanket that is spread out on the cold hard-clay ground. She is sitting with her knees pulled up against her chest and she rocks back and forth a little.

I don't mean, he says. To make you feel unwelcome.

I know.

You just complicate matters.

Sure.

He doesn't say anything else for a spell and neither does she.

You sure are a pretty little thing, he finally says.

She smiles until she looks at him and recognizes the look in his eyes. It makes her nervous. Her whole body shivers. He finishes his smoke and drops what's left in the dirt.

I heard what them others done to you, he says.

Yeah.

That's an unfortunate thing.

Uh huh.

A girl like you can never be too careful with menfolk.

A thing I'm learning.

He slides a little closer to her.

She wonders about Bobby, if he'll be back soon.

CHAPTER THIRTY-FOUR

THE KID DRIVING THE TRANSPORT van has been drinking all night. He is still half in the bag. Blackie convinces the kid to unhitch him just long enough to take a leak. Then he's easy to overpower, doesn't even fight back. Blackie leaves him in the shrubs and takes the van with the others in the back hollering at him. These boys might come in handy, he thinks.

CHAPTER THIRTY-FIVE

WESTY IS SITTING AT A desk across from Doreen and her father. She is dirty and her face is bruised and she has been crying. Her father is beside himself with anger. Westy has some forms spread out across the desk and a yellow pad of paper and a pen. He is writing something and then he takes a break from writing and he looks at Doreen.

What happened to your face, Westy says.

She fell down, her father says.

Westy looks at him and shakes his head, and then he turns to Doreen.

All right so you seen them out there, he says.

Uh huh.

I mean Thaddeus and Bobby.

She nods her head. Her father can barely look at her.

And where was this exactly, Westy says.

And what the hell were you thinking, her father says.

Please, Westy says to the father.

Doreen has a coughing fit and Westy stands up and crosses the room to the water cooler and he gets a small paper cone and fills it with cold water and hands it to her. She takes it and thanks him and drinks it. Then she puts the cone in her lap and smoothes it out flat with her hands. She is clearly very nervous. She cannot look at her father either.

Westy sure wishes he had a female on the staff today.

He can't even imagine having a daughter.

Take your time, he says.

I can't tell you where.

Her father shifts in his seat.

Westy looks up at her.

Why not, he says.

He'll do something, she says. To Bobby.

You mean his uncle, Westy says. Thaddeus.

Right.

Westy is looking at her. He can see that she is pregnant.

Is that baby his, he says. I mean Bobby's.

Her father looks at Westy and Doreen nods her head and she looks away.

Yeah, she says.

What you gone to do about this W, her father says after a few heartbeats.

Well.

That boy, he says. Put her in that condition.

We're out there looking for them both, Westy says.

My cousins and me are fixing to help in that regard.

I don't recommend it, Westy says.

No I guess you wouldn't.

CHAPTER THIRTY-SIX

WESTY PUTS THE CRUISER IN park and leaves the engine running and opens the door and looks over his shoulder at Cap Warger. He tells him to wait in the car. Cap is half asleep and he could give a rat's ass about that. He is sipping at a cup of coffee. Westy gets out and shuts the door and goes inside the Hot L. It is the middle of the day and only Hawk is sitting at the bar and he doesn't even look up when the door opens and throws some sunlight on him. The place smells like peanut shells and piss. Westy stands next to where Hawk is sitting and looks long at the infamous old drunk.

What's doing, he says.

Hawk looks up now at the sound of a human voice. He looks at Westy in the face and tries to focus as best he can. His eyes are just thin slits like somebody made them with a knife. Then he smiles, if you can call it that without teeth.

You all right, Westy says.

Yeah sure.

Folks treating you good.

Shit, he says. Good as they ought to.

You'd let me know.

Sure.

Westy remembers when Hawk used to work for the Plastics and his mind was sharp. Even today, as pickled as he is, he can still recite the capital cities of all fifty states. Local boys have been known to use this capacity of the old drunk as the central prop of a bar trick, the essence of which is to awaken the slumped-over inebriant and get him to display the signs of raw intelligence. Responding correctly earns him a drink.

Hawk has been in a funk ever since the news about Raymont Redwine. It would be a stretch to call them friends but over the years the town drunk and the local retard had formed a quiet alliance perhaps unique to society's misfits and certainly more obvious in a small community. He reaches up and tries to put his hand on the cop's shoulder but he misses after two tries and both times his hand is like a broken bird falling slowly. He gives up and rests. Westy smiles at him because the gesture did not go unregistered.

All right, he says.

He pats Hawk on the back and dust comes off the old drunk's jacket. It makes Westy cough. He coughs and coughs and Hawk puts the short fat glass to his dry lips until the brown liquid is gone. His hands are better now. Then Westy finishes coughing.

Where's Sue at.

Hawk shakes his head and rubs his mouth on his sleeve, leaving a filmy circle.

She out back, Westy guesses. Having her a smoke then.

Uh huh.

Oh by the way, Westy says. Colorado.

Denver.

Westy laughs.

You still got it, he says.

Hawk shakes his head and looks at Westy and his eyes are watery and full of something. Westy gets up and goes behind the bar and gets the bottle of Old Crow. He pours the old drunk a full drink. He puts the bottle back where it goes, lined up with all the other toxic soldiers, and then he comes back around to the other side of the bar again. Puts some money on the counter. Hawk stares at his sickness. He sits very still like that and Westy watches him for a good couple minutes. Then he hears a screen door creak and bang and Sue comes into the room fanning the air in front of her. She sees Westy and smiles. She runs a hand through her thin blond hair that won't take a perm no matter how many times she tries. Westy straightens up some and smiles right back at her.

Having you a smoke, he says.

I'm trying to quit hey.

We all got our vices.

Do we, she says.

Some more than others.

He nods his head toward Hawk and Sue laughs a little bit. She takes her post behind the bar. Asks Westy if he wants anything and he tells her he's on duty but thanks.

So you're here on business then, she says.

That's right.

She looks disappointed.

Well, he says. Where's that boy then.

Damn.

It's been a while since I seen him, he says. Thaddeus gone too.

Well.

Well what.

Sue looks away and then down at her feet and then back at him before she answers. She doesn't want to lie to Westy but she doesn't want to do the boy wrong.

And she doesn't want to get on the bad side of the DuBois clan.

Aint seen him since that night, she says.

No.

Nope.

He doesn't believe her.

I know he's out in them woods, he says. The both of them are.

Then you know more than me already.

But it'd be nice, he says. If I could narrow it down some.

Then he tells her about his visit with Doreen and her current condition.

Oh shit them boys, she says. Why can't they wear a rubber.

Westy laughs and shakes his head.

Does he even know, she says. Bobby that is.

Westy shrugs his shoulders.

She thinks about holding Westy's hand the night LaPinta was shot.

You remember that night, she says. Don't you.

Yeah what you think hey, he says. Of course I remember all right.

I don't mean him getting shot.

I know what you mean.

Well I was wondering because you haven't called or nothing.

I been busy hey.

She waits for him to say more and he doesn't and she looks hurt, but she keeps her mouth shut and fidgets with a cocktail napkin that has dumb jokes printed on it.

All right, she says. So babies having babies.

There's that and another thing now too.

Another thing.

The little fucker stole some shit this summer.

Sue shakes her head and repeats what he just told her.

He stole some shit, she echoes flatly.

Him and that running buddy of his.

What exactly.

Jewelry and money and stuff from Pat Crudo's house.

So now that on top of everything else.

Pat says he can just return it and she'll let it pass.

Shit.

She was waiting to see if he come back around, he says. But since he aint.

Sue puts her elbows on the bar and she rests her chin in the V-shape of her hands. Hawk has closed his eyes now and appears to be asleep. He is breathing deep anyhow.

Well shit, she says. That boy.

The apple maybe doesn't fall far from the tree.

So what's that mean then in terms of where he goes and what happens.

If the judge gets wind it could mean a lot, he says. It could mean everything.

If the judge gets wind.

If Pat doesn't get her shit back she's gone to report it official.

But if she gets her shit back.

He shrugs his shoulders.

Sue is conflicted and he can read it in her face. He lets her think. Then Hawk starts and his eyes open as much as they ever do. Sue looks at him and puts her hand on his forearm. The old drunk settles back down. Westy recognizes the tenderness in her touch. He thinks that she would make a good mother and a good wife and he wonders why nobody has snatched her up just yet. She sees him staring at her and she blushes.

And that's not all, he says.

She leans toward him and says she's all ears.

Blackie slipped out during his transfer out to Cedar Junction, Westy says.

You mean fucking escaped.

Yeah.

Oh shit.

Oh shit is right.

CHAPTER THIRTY-SEVEN

BLACKIE COULD HAVE BEEN A salesman in another life, the way he had pitched it to his shackled van-mates: promise to help me get my boy and you can live or else I'll slit your throats here and now. It was truly an offer they couldn't refuse and they each swore on the pocket-sized bible he procured from the horrified clerk at Streeter's Market.

CHAPTER THIRTY-EIGHT

BOBBY SECRETLY MEETS LIZ UNDER Stillwater Bridge and she gives him a paper bag with food. He starts to go through it right away. He looks too skinny to her. And there is a strange dog sitting at his feet—equally starved and impatient, and equally mean.

When you eat last, she says.

I don't know.

Ah that's no good then.

And so how's my grandpa.

Liz laughs once through her nose.

Oh shit, she says. How he always is.

Bobby looks up at her and then continues rummaging. He comes out with a peach and he takes a bite and the juice of it leaks down his chin. He drops some venison jerky for the mutt. Liz shakes her head at him, at them both really. He finishes the peach and tosses the pit off to the side. There's a small plastic jug of chocolate milk and he twists off the top and swallows about half of it right away. He holds the jug at his side.

The dog stretches its neck and licks at the lip of it.

Bobby tilts the jug so the dog can take a proper drink.

He taking good care you out there, she says. Your uncle.

Bobby doesn't say anything and won't meet her eyes with his.

Maybe there's another way, she says. Have you thought of that.

Bobby can't think of another way. There are some graham crackers that he goes through and he drops the translucent wrappers where he stands. The dog chews the wrappers, too. Bobby is so gaunt and pale. It troubles her greatly to see him like this.

More than ever he seems just a boy to her now.

She indicates the dog.

And so who's this now, she says.

Bobby puts his hand under the dog's chin.

Then Liz tells Bobby that Blackie got loose.

He'll come for you, she says. He don't want you with nobody else.

Uh huh.

His son and all, she says. More than anything that's what he wants now.

You mean what he don't want.

Right.

I say come on then.

Liz is troubled by the echoes of Thaddeus and Blackie she now hears in Bobby's voice. Over the ridge past the patchwork fields a black cloud is blocking half the sun.

CHAPTER THIRTY-NINE

THE WATER UNDER STILLWATER BRIDGE is high and fast and the sound of it rushing fills the ravine. Uncle Thaddeus is sitting on a red rock out in the middle of the current. He's in cutoff jeans and his skin is mostly white and red in splotches and covered in hair and Bobby thinks he looks like a fucking bear. Thaddeus calls to the boy but his voice goes unheard. He beckons with his long strong arms. Bobby watches his uncle for a minute and then he takes off his t-shirt and his cap, too. He drops them in the dirt and with the dog on his heels he hops skinny-shanked down the short embankment and steps into the soft black mud that stinks. He sinks in it to his ankles and pulls his feet out and he has to pick up the dog and he walks on large stones and when the water is deep enough he falls into it and swims and the current pushes him and the dog to the rock and Uncle Thaddeus reaches down and scoops them out of that dark and white swirling cauldron.

Shit boy, Uncle Thaddeus says. You can't beat that.

He's invigorated.

The dog shakes.

We spent a lot of time here as kids, Uncle Thaddeus says. Your father and me.

All right.

That's why I brought you here.

I seen it before, Bobby says. This place.

Have you now.

It's nothing special to me, he says. Just another place.

The dog barks.

Bobby stands up, dwarfed next to his uncle, who is laughing and looking at the sky. Bobby looks at the sky, too, and the sun. The man puts his hand in the boy's hair. They sit and sleep on the red rock for hours, swimming in the river when it gets too hot. Then a mechanical sound in the distance is getting nearer and Bobby knows too well what it is. Something he has expected. Been waiting for. Sure as the sun will rise at dawn.

The engine on his old man's Willys sounds like the roar of a mountain lion.

He's coming now, Bobby says. How'd you know he would.

I know a thing or two.

Uncle Thaddeus looks his nephew in the eye.

We did what we could until now, he says.

Bobby nods his head.

Tried to lay low and avoid a conflict I mean.

Right.

This here is between me and your father, Uncle Thaddeus says.

Seems like I got a sizable part in it.

No you don't either, Uncle Thaddeus says. You just keep out of it.

But if he tells me to come on.

Oh he will tell you that.

And what then.

You turn a deaf ear to that nonsense.

The boy understands. He sits down on a cool part of the red rock and it's very peaceful to him at that moment. Mapleseed helicopters are descending into calm pockets of water. Some strange daddy longlegs is doing its dance on the surface. The sound of a carpenter's hammer echoing in the valley. The engine grunts when it is killed. Heavy doors slam. Then he hears pieces of loud shouting voices. Uncle Thaddeus stands tall as possible and watches the path coming down the water's edge from the logging road. Then from the trees bursts Blackie and his newly collected cadre of rough fools in orange jumpsuits issued by the state of Massachusetts.

Bobby is expecting this but yet he is still surprised to see his old man. He looks the same but more malevolent if that is even possible. The old man is shouting but they cannot decipher his words for the river. Blackie is looking at Thaddeus and not at his son. He looks at him a long fucking time.

The dog barks and growls, showing its yellow teeth.

Well, Bobby says. What we gone do.

The boy looks at his uncle.

Thaddeus stays looking at Blackie when he speaks.

Let him holler all he fucking wants.

Damn look at him, Bobby says. He's going nuts.

Loud words is still just words.

Then Blackie is done hollering and he turns to the three men cut from the same cloth that have joined him. He is giving orders, you can tell that for sure. Two of them undress down to their undershorts and get to the water and test it. The redhead picks up a jagged stone that is just bigger than his hand and the other one fishes a thick wet stick draped with green; crude weaponry to match the nature of their assignment. These are not water men, Bobby can tell that. And he's prepared to fight these men, too, if his uncle asks. The current is stronger now as the dam over to Old Squaw Reservoir must have been lifted again. After some discussion the strangers hold hands to try to challenge the rapids that way and they get up to their waists before the redhead loses his footing and panics and drags the other one down with him. The redhead disappears and the other one is just a face, all chaos and desperation. Bobby and Thaddeus watch calmly as the other one is swept away, too. They'll probably wash up down to Cheapside Bridge or farther along or get snagged in some low branches or get stuck on a beaver hut. Uncle Thaddeus laughs a mean sort of laugh and looks toward Blackie across the way.

Look what he's got now, he says to his nephew.

Bobby looks toward solid ground toward his old man who is holding a bone-handle pistola that Bobby recognizes even from a distance. It belongs to his grandfather, who got it in a foreign land. There is a story behind it he now recalls—Earl Ran got it off a dead soldier. Blackie is now pointing it at him and his uncle and the rock.

Not from there he can't, Uncle Thaddeus says.

Then smoke comes from the barrel and the old man's arm kicks back and there is a soft muffled pop. Bobby flinches and closes his eyes instinctively and then he opens them again. The old man fires again a couple more times. Blackie is pissed that they are clearly out of range. He yells at the trees and then he yells at the pistola in his hand. Then he yells at the small man left with him and sticks the pistola into the waistband of his pants. The small man nods his head up and down and strips down to his shorts and he takes the water quicker than the other two who have already washed away. He is small but with the ropey muscles you see on chronic heroin users and he can swim, too, and he aims himself to the red rock and cuts a wet swath. Thaddeus tells the boy to scoot back and hold the dog and Bobby does as he is told. The small man gets to the other side of the rock without much trouble and he hoists himself up and his shorts have been pulled off by the current and there he stands naked like some wild being from older times emerging from a wet hell. Thaddeus stands stock still and lets the small man approach.

Bobby holds the dog when it tries to wriggle free.

The men are standing just a few feet away from each other now.

He want the boy there, the small man says.

He indicates Bobby with a tilt of his chin and continues.

And then you and him got some business, he says.

Tell him come on then, Uncle Thaddeus says.

Oh his leg hurt, the man says. Otherwise he would.

The boy stays here with me.

The small man considers this. He looks at the boy. He looks across the river at Blackie who is still yelling but they cannot hear him over the din. Then he looks back at Thaddeus. He appears to be calculating, looking for a weakness, an opening of some sort.

That's no good, the small man says.

He must be tired from the swim but he moves like he isn't and suddenly he has a prison-made shank in his fist that they hadn't seen before. It must have been hidden in his ass crack, Bobby figures. Thaddeus adjusts like a two-hundred-pound cat and takes the man's wrist and he snaps the bones in it like so many dry twigs. Bobby can hear them breaking one by one. Then the smaller man takes a knee and massages his wrist.

Fuck me, he says.

It all goes down so fast.

The dog is going berserk, wants to attack the man, but Bobby holds her.

She has formed a bond with Bobby and Thaddeus and wants to protect them.

Thaddeus has the shank now and he tosses it to the boy. The handle is layers of blue electrical tape and the blade is a filed-down toothbrush. Thaddeus moves so he is standing between his nephew and the strange intruder. His knees are slightly bent.

Go on now before you get hurt, Uncle Thaddeus says.

The small man laughs and looks across the river at Blackie again.

I'ma get hurt regardless, he says.

Pick your poison then.

I'll always take the here and now.

The small man gets up again and issues a step toward Thaddeus. The dog gets loose and locks its jaws into the man's thigh and lets go just as Bobby sticks the knife in the man's calf and withdraws it, leaving an incision. Then he watches his uncle hoist the distracted ruffian by the cock, and with the other hand around the man's neck he holds him high over his head for a beat or two so Blackie can get the full effect. The smaller man toad-pisses himself and it runs down Uncle Thaddeus's arm. Thaddeus regards it with a look of disdain and disgust and he puts that man back in the river whence he came. With only one wing now plus an injured leg the small man cannot muster a strong enough stroke to get back across. Resigned to his fate he puts his head back and circles the drain. Bobby watches him bob and sputter and then eventually disappear.

He pissed me, Uncle Thaddeus says. That little shit.

Thaddeus washes his arm in the river and sits on his haunches. He looks at his brother who is looking at him. They look at each other for a long time. Bobby studies the well-crafted shank and then puts it in his pocket. He looks at his uncle standing there.

Then he looks across the river at his father.

Is he gone to try too now, Bobby says.

Nah, Thaddues says. He gone wait us out.

The dog sits at Bobby's feet and licks its lips.

Blackie is laughing now and looking at the sky turning dusk. He's gesturing as if to claim that the passing of the day is his doing and their undoing. He picks up the clothes and items that Uncle Thaddeus and Bobby had left behind and he chucks them in the river one at a time. A boot, a t-shirt, a billfold that has long been empty. Bobby closes his eyes. He can smell the river and it is a good and clean smell.

He opens his eyes when Uncle Thaddeus clears his throat.

What we gone to do, Thaddeus says. Is head down the river come dark.

Bobby nods his head.

The reservoir will be plugged by then, Thaddeus says. And he's in no condition.

To give us chase.

That's right.

Bobby watches his father across the way, dragging his bad leg around.

But I hope that little fucker can swim, Thaddeus says, indicating the dog.

CHAPTER FORTY

Liz puts an ad in the paper. She says Earl needs somebody to help him around the house for when she's at work. She smiles and tells him that the girl is Jamaican, like that's supposed to be a good thing. That is just a fancy word for nigger as far as he can see. They come up by the busload now to pick field tobacco and cucumbers, worse than the spics. Earl doesn't know where they get them, but he guesses it's cheap labor. Billy Nourse told him that he got a whole family out there hitting the strawberries for five dollars an hour. Then Earl's breath fogs the window behind the couch where he kneels with his chest against the backrest. He can see the river through the trees. He wipes a spot with the heel of his hand. His neighbor is out there cutting down trees for fence posts.

There he is, he thinks. That rat bastard.

Somebody is always stealing something from me now.

If he keeps it up I will have nothing left and that just will not do.

Sharp little pieces of light spill out around the neighbor and it hurts Earl to watch.

He puts his head in his hands.

Please please please, he thinks. I am not one to beg.

Come on mister, a female voice says.

Earl turns around.

She's somebody new.

Earl does not want another dark bitch to touch him. She is not from around here, that's for sure. Maybe Holyoke or Springfield or even Hartford. He tells her that he's going to start counting forks and spoons. She shakes her head and calls him mister again.

Come on mister.

She buttons his church shirt that is white and starched. Then he hangs the stars and stripes out front and there is a wind that whips it around. Then somebody pours him a glass of beer. He has not been in a place like this in years. There are voices and there is music on a little stage. It is too much for him. Tony Overalls used to work for Paciorek Electric and he puts a glass in Earl's hand. Earl focuses on him because he is familiar.

Tony Overalls is talking to the bartender.

Yeah I know this one hey, he says.

What the fuck.

He's lost his wits is all.

Old-timer's disease, the bartender says.

Yeah they found him out back wandering around by the trash.

She would not approve, his wife, but Earl drinks the beer and it goes down good. Then Tony Overalls helps him into his pickup. He talks about what he calls the olden days. The radio plays polka. They drive over Stillwater Bridge where Earl used to jump into the Swift River as a kid. They pass the drive-in theater and the drag strip and the town dump where CB died. Sometimes bats fly as one and form a dark cloud that cannot be explained unless they shit on you. There was one who got himself into the house when they were young and first moved in. Betty called Earl and asked him to get rid of it so he used a ball-peen hammer. It was small but fierce and it did have a certain amount of wingspan and sharp teeth that you might not expect. Earl had smashed it up against the sheetrock and shoved it back behind the wall and she worried about the smell.

If it wasn't one thing then it was always another.

CHAPTER FORTY-ONE

WESTY TELLS THE FAT COP that Thaddeus and Bobby have been seen around town, but more likely they have taken to the backwoods and so they need his particular brand of expertise. He's flattered, of course. They are sitting in the chief's office drinking coffee.

So you need me to track them, the fat cop says.

That's the short of it hey, Westy says. And Blackie too.

And get them all three into custody.

Before they shoot each other in the fucking head.

Probably cheaper to just let them.

No good talking like that.

All right then.

The fat cop takes a long sip of his coffee. Westy leans back in the chief's chair.

And the chief knows, the fat cop says.

Of course.

And has approved it.

Yeah hey.

I only ask cause there was talk of eliminating the budget for a mounted patrol.

Westy leans forward abruptly.

Shit boy, he says. This aint the time to get petty.

The fat cop turns red. He knows Westy is right but feels justified in bringing it up. All right, he says. When you want me out there.

CHAPTER FORTY-TWO

BOBBY HITS HER AND IT feels good. It bothers him that it feels so good. He never thought that he'd ever hit a girl or a woman. But when he sees her he can't help it. Doreen cries for a while and then she stops. Bobby has slipped into town for supplies and is supposed to be robbing Boron's Market. Fat Johnny doesn't say anything and he just sits there.

Bobby finishes the bottle and then he smashes it empty on the cement wall. Doreen walks away and smokes a cigarillo. She doesn't want to look at Bobby anymore. He can go to hell and she tells him so and she cries some more. She once told Bobby if he ever hit her she'd quit him forever and that would be best now, he figures. Fat Johnny clears his throat and Bobby looks at him and he has his hat in his hands, turning it over.

You hit her like you would a dude, Fat Johnny says.

No I didn't either, Bobby says. I backed it off some.

Not her fault really.

What's not.

That she got in that way.

Bobby looks at him hard.

That's not what this is, Bobby says.

Or that there's a posse coming for you now.

What you know about it.

Not much, Fat Johnny says. Just what I hear.

And what.

Well shit boy I think you broke her nose.

Bobby looks over at her and she can't hear them talking and she's still smoking and looking off toward the mountain range that is different shades of green. The sky is gray. There's a heavy mist. Doreen crosses her arms and taps her right foot in the dirt.

Shit, Bobby says.

He walks over to her and she looks at him and she's bleeding.

Her nose is not broken.

You all right, Bobby says.

Motherfucker, she says. You broke my nose.

Ah shit, he says. It aint broke.

She's crying and it takes her a while to catch her breath so that she can speak.

No, she says.

Bobby rubs his thumb at the blood over her lip. She removes the cigarillo from her mouth so he can do it. She takes a final drag and snaps the butt away. He pinches her nostrils between his thumb and finger to stop the bleeding.

Put your head back now, he tells her.

She tilts her head a little.

All the way back, he says.

She puts her head back and tells him she's sorry. Fat Johnny is quiet. Bobby gets the bleeding to stop and takes his hand away and she sniffs. He wipes the blood on his pantleg.

I said I'm sorry, she says.

All right.

I shouldn't of told no one, she says.

Damn girl I told you that.

But I was scared, she says.

All right but I told you what would happen.

I know, she says.

Bobby doesn't know what to say.

She puts her arms on his shoulders and he holds her to him like that. Fat Johnny gets up and comes over and stands just behind her so the boys are looking at each other.

Fat Johnny speaks.

Come on now, he says.

Doreen tenses up and puts her face in Bobby's chest.

All right, Bobby says. I got to go.

Fat Johnny turns and walks to the car. He opens the door and gets in and closes the door and after a few seconds he starts the engine and Bobby can hear the radio. Fat Johnny reaches across the seat and opens the passenger door. Bobby lets go of Doreen and she lets go of him, too, and she looks at his face with her cupped hands over his ears.

Well, he says.

She starts to cry again.

I can't believe you're still going, she says.

Like I got a choice in the matter, he says.

There's always a choice.

Not in this life.

Whatever.

They'll put me away for what I done.

Put that on your uncle or at least his influence.

I won't hang my part on him.

That's not you out there, she says. I don't care what they say.

She touches her nose and winces.

This, she says. Is not you.

But what if it is.

He kisses her on the mouth and there is a bunch of snot running out of her nose now, too. He can taste the salt of it as well as her tears. She closes her eyes and he kisses her for a while. Fat Johnny guns the engine and Bobby stops kissing Doreen and she takes a step back. He doesn't say anything and she doesn't say anything and he turns around and walks to the car. He gets in and closes the door and Fat Johnny already has it in drive and he pulls away and Bobby doesn't look up. The package from Liz is on the seat next to his leg, as well as the items he lifted from the market. He can feel Doreen looking. He can feel her watching. Tires crush stones and dirt and twigs and dry leaves.

THERE IS A FULL MOON and you can smell the hills and Fat Johnny wants to know if Bobby's uncle is truly crazy. They are sitting up top of the water tower. Uncle Thaddeus and Billy Tucker are going to meet them here. Billy Tucker is going to give Thaddeus some other supplies that should last a few weeks maybe. They said to wait until it got dark.

No he's not crazy, Bobby says.

And he means it, too.

He doesn't think it's crazy that drives his uncle or father.

Not any more crazy than any of the rest of us at least, he says.

Well I hear he is.

Not the kind you mean anyhow.

I hear he went to a crazy hospital.

It's not just crazy people there.

Why call it that then.

It's known for that, Bobby says.

Uh huh.

And I guess they got to call it something, he says.

Fat Johnny's car is parked in some dry scrub. There is a train coming. The tower shakes when it goes by and they hold on tight. Fat Johnny is working at something in his teeth with a stick. From where they are sitting they can see the river.

Joe Curry fell off here and broke his neck, Fat Johnny says, changing subjects.

He shows Bobby how Joe Curry fell.

Fuck Joe Curry, Bobby says. That boy always rubbed me wrong anyhow.

I guess he was drunk and not holding on right, Fat Johnny says.

Well like I said.

He's down to Cooley Dick now.

No shit.

It doesn't look too good for him.

Couldn't of happened to a nicer guy.

Bobby can't see the moon anymore, eclipsed by a flat black cloud. Fat Johnny keeps talking but Bobby stops listening. Then there are headlights cutting through the trees, winding their way toward the clearing. Bobby slides on his ass to the ladder and starts to climb down and Fat Johnny follows. The rungs are wet and slick and they move slowly hand over hand and foot over foot. By the time they touch the ground Uncle Thaddeus and Billy Tucker have parked the F250. They're standing in front of it drinking cans of beer and the headlights are still on. It's pretty dark now and Fat Johnny holds his hand out in front of his face. They stop within a few feet of the grown men and Billy Tucker is saying something and Thaddeus is laughing and he looks at Bobby.

Be careful up there boy, he says.

Yeah we know hey, Bobby says.

Thaddeus raises his eyebrows at his nephew and elbows Billy Tucker.

Worse ways to go I guess, he says. Then falling from a height.

What goes up must come down.

Billy Tucker is drunk, that much is clear, but Bobby can never tell with Uncle Thaddeus. Thaddeus looks at Fat Johnny. Fat Johnny looks at the ground. Billy Tucker offers Bobby a can of beer and Bobby takes it from him and opens it. It's cold and good. He gives some to Fat Johnny. Uncle Thaddeus is still looking at Fat Johnny. Not a hard look especially, but not friendly either. It's as though he is troubled, Bobby notices.

Boy you can look me in the eye, Thaddeus says to Fat Johnny.

Fat Johnny won't look yet, but he stops drinking.

Thaddeus knows he's scared.

Come on now, Uncle Thaddeus says.

Fat Johnny looks at Thaddeus and Billy Tucker laughs.

Bobby has not seen his friend scared before. Not just of Billy Tucker and his uncle he expects, but also of this big thing that exists between Bobby and his uncle.

I won't bite now, Uncle Thaddeus says. Come here.

Fat Johnny doesn't move.

No matter what you done heard, Uncle Thaddeus says.

Fat Johnny takes a step and Thaddeus takes one big step and he puts his hand out and so does Fat Johnny and they shake. Uncle Thaddeus is looking at him the whole time. Billy Tucker is laughing and Bobby laughs, too. Uncle Thaddeus waits until it's quiet.

You been knowing about me your whole life, he says. Hearing things I guess.

Right.

Aint no reason to fear me, Thaddeus says. I aint no boogey man.

All right.

Don't believe all what you hear.

Well I aint scared.

Billy Tucker laughs like a stuck pig would snort.

Oh no, Thaddeus says. I guess you're not.

And then just like that he pulls Fat Johnny closer and kisses him on the mouth. Fat Johnny squirms out of his grip and spits and Billy Tucker howls at the moon. Bobby doesn't know what to do and so he just takes another pull from the can of beer in his hand.

What the fuck, Fat Johnny says.

All the shit said about me, Thaddeus says. Never mention of my kissing ability.

Everybody laughs.

Billy Tucker goes to the back of the truck and gets more beers for everybody. Then he sits on the bumper and Uncle Thaddeus sits next to him. Bobby sits in the dirt and Fat Johnny does, too. A moth is drawn to the headlights that are dim now and Billy Tucker notices and gets up and reaches through the open driver's side window and cuts them. He kicks up some of the dirt when he walks. There is a certain smell that Bobby notices on these men. He expects he'll smell that way too, when he is old enough.

CHAPTER FORTY-THREE

SHE CALLS HIM A SONOFABITCH. He lets her call him a few other things. He fingers the ice cube in his glass of Jack Daniels. There are only a couple other slobs at the bar at this hour; Ginnie Lewandoski and her sister and Hawk and Dutch Syska Junior. Sue is really pissed and she lets Westy have it again. He leans back in his chair and closes his eyes.

He waits for the storm to pass.

Don't you shut me out W, she says.

He opens his eyes to register that comment and then he closes them again.

You rotten bastard, she says.

He feels her get up and then he hears her chair slide across the hardwood floor.

Westy eats stale popcorn until she comes back. He knows the routine.

Oh shit I didn't mean it, she says, pulling her chair close to his.

I know you didn't hey.

She leans into him and holds his hand.

I just worry, she says. That you're gone to get caught up in something.

She picks at the pieces of popcorn stuck in his ten-day old beard.

I know you worry, he says.

That and I don't like the idea of you paying Nikki another visit.

It's not a social call.

Well whatever it is I don't like it hey.

I told you, he says. I just got some questions.

I hope that's all you got when you leave, she says. If you know what I mean.

Shit woman.

Shit nothing, Sue says. I know all about Darling Nikki.

Oh yeah and what's that.

She's got loose morals.

Westy laughs at the phrase.

Just then Ginnie Lewandoski spits in her sister's face and they end up on the floor wrestling near the jukebox, and Westy and Sue have to break it up.

A TAN-BACKED COYOTE CHASES A rabbit across the dry shrubs and cuntgrass. Inside, Darling Nikki pours herself a stiff one. Jack and a splash. She drinks half of it and then she looks back at Westy and he is sitting on her couch with his uniform hat in his lap.

Still down at the Greek's are you, he says.

Most nights, she says. You should stop by.

He clears his throat.

Not really my cup of tea, he says.

What's not, she says. You don't like pussy.

Westy laughs because he knew she was going to fuck with him a little bit.

I don't like paying for it, he says after a couple beats. That's for sure.

Who said anything about paying for it.

Westy looks away and clears his throat again.

So you aint seen him since when, he says. Thaddeus that is.

I done told you last time.

I know but I thought maybe you might have new information.

Why have I did something wrong.

You tell me.

She makes an innocent face like she is on stage somewhere. He grins at her act.

I don't recall doing nothing wrong, she says.

Like harboring a fugitive even for just a minute.

Now she smiles and opens her arms as if to ask where she could hide somebody.

Where I'm gone to harbor anything in this shithole, she says.

Westy looks around and nods his head. Her place is small but tidy.

But you can frisk me if you want, she says.

He shakes his head. She's tireless, he thinks.

You sure I can't give you something, she says. A drink I mean.

Well all right then.

Maybe that will get her to talk, he figures. If I play along just a little bit.

She pours him a drink. Brings it over to the couch. She hands it to him and then she sits down next to him, crossing her long legs so her foot is barely touching his shin.

I just want to get that boy out of this, he says. His nephew.

Oh you mean Bobby, she says. What you want with him anyhow.

Shit I don't know, he says. I guess I think he has a chance.

A fucking chance, she laughs.

Yeah hey, he says. A chance.

A chance at what exactly, she says.

Westy takes a sip of his drink and he makes a face when he does it. Darling Nikki sure pours a strong one. She finishes hers and puts the glass on the wood floor at her feet.

I don't know, he says.

Right.

Maybe a chance at not following after his father or uncle, he says.

She nods her head. She figures that is something. She wished somebody had given her a chance. She wished Westy would give her a chance right now, but she hears he's been running around with that skinny little bitch down at the Hot L. Sue something.

She can't stand those goody-two-shoes bitches like that.

What's she got that I don't, she thinks.

Then on a dime she decides to be a little bit cruel to her guest.

But you know it might be too late for him, she says. Too little, too late and all.

He agrees with her to some degree and that throws her off.

She flirts some more until he finishes his drink. When he stands to leave she gets up, too. Leans in and brushes up against him like that. He can smell body lotion. He sees what she's up to, knows her game.

I'm too old for silly games anymore, he thinks.

Darling Nikki walks him to the door and he puts on his hat and says goodbye.

So that's it then, she says.

Unless there's something else.

There's always something else.

I mean about the boy and his whereabouts.

Oh if he's cut from the same cloth, she says. I'm sure he's just fine out there.

Out where.

See, she says. Already I said too much.

You don't have to be scared, he says.

Oh no.

I won't let him hurt you, he says. None of them.

Darling Nikki laughs.

Cops usually bore her but she likes Westy for some reason.

With a straight face even now, she says.

Westy lets out a long breath that smells like Jack.

Them boys do what they want, she says. Always have and you know it.

We got these special places called jail for people like that.

Throwing out these lines like he's in a fucking movie, she thinks.

The brave sheriff war hero come to save the day or whatever the fuck.

Westy fingers the brim of his hat and turns around and walks down the three cement steps to the dirt yard. Darling Nikki watches him cross to the driveway and the town police car. She strikes a pose on the threshold that would bring most men back, but he just smiles as he gets into the cruiser. He drives away slow and she shrugs her shoulders and closes the door with her foot.

PART IV:

*"That weren't nothing but a rabid dog in there
and yeah I killt him dead."*
—Earl Ran DuBois

CHAPTER FORTY-FOUR

THE PIGS ARE QUICK. BOBBY stands off to the side. There are about a dozen of them and they are covered in shit and mud and their own saliva. They are fat, too, and look like good eating. Snorting and squealing and farting, they run to and fro in the twelve-foot-by-twelve-foot square pen. Uncle Thaddeus watches them and waits. There is a runt in the bunch that he has his eye on. The boy is sitting on the wood rail now swinging his legs. There is a bucket of grain in the tack room and he's eating a handful of grain and dry corn that he got from it. He has filled a small green sack. They are always hungry and the bulk of their day is spent looking for food. Uncle Thaddeus reaches down with one hand and picks up the runt he likes. It wriggles and twists and arches, but it cannot escape his grip. He sticks it up under his armpit and it rolls its eyes back in their sockets so you can only see the whites of them. It squeals and squeals. Uncle Thaddeus looks at his nephew and shows his teeth and squeezes the pig.

We'll cook her up and eat good, he says.

Uh huh.

For once in our fucking lives.

All right, Bobby says.

You fill the sack with that other like I said.

The boy holds up the green sack so his uncle can see that it's full.

And there were some old apples back there too, Uncle Thaddeus says.

Bobby jumps down and walks back to the tack room. There's a bushel basket of apples that are mostly brown and soft and rotten from sitting so long. You can smell them and there are flies buzzing around and worms. The boy kneels on the hard ground and rolls his shirtsleeve up past his elbow and sticks his hand in there and feels around. He finds a couple three that are in decent enough shape, red and green. He cleans them on his pantleg as best he can and drops them in the green sack with the grain and corn pellets. The sack has a string so he can close up the mouth of it and he pulls it tight. Then he wipes the mushy film off his arm with a saddle rag and pushes his sleeve back down where it belongs. Uncle Thaddeus stands in the doorway with the pig wrapped up in the thermal that had been under his flannel. The smallish pig is not moving too much anymore, probably from lack of air. Just small twitches and his snout pushing at fabric.

Any luck, Uncle Thaddeus says.

We got a couple three.

A real fucking feast then.

The boy looks at his uncle and almost smiles. He has always been skinny and now he is emaciated. Dark and thick half circles under each eye. They leave the barn together. They are careful to not be seen. It's on Phillippe Devine's property out by the Conway border. The Devines are a wild bunch and will not take kindly to this type of thievery. Uncle Thaddues had hidden his newly stolen bike off in the treeline at the base of the foothills. He'd stolen it from Greg Garnier's shop over to the Chitwood Quarry. A 1967 chopper in need of work, a water faucet handle in place of a light switch. They get to the bike and Bobby takes the pig in one arm and the sack in the other and he positions himself on the back of the seat. They wear welders' goggles to protect their eyes and have given up using the helmets. Uncle Thaddeus mounts and starts the engine and they lurch along the old logging road. Stones and heavy treelimbs and deep potholes. The boy uses his legs to keep from falling off, squeezing them tight against the machine.

Then the chopper coughs and sputters and Thaddeus jerks it off to the side because it's out of fuel. Bobby dismounts and sets his packages down in the dirt and dried dead leaves and he stretches his back and reaches for the sky. Then Thaddeus gets off and curses himself for neglecting to get gasoline. He curses their overall circumstance as well. He fumbles under the seat where there's room enough to store some items, including a long cut of clear tubing and a collapsible gallon-sized plastic container with a red twist cap. He closes the seat and latches it and looks at the boy who's smoking a cigarillo and leaning on a skinny sapling that's knotted and gnarled and oddly misshapen.

You want to wait here, he says.

Fuck no.

Uncle Thaddeus smothers the pig.

Then they work together to hang their bounty so that stray dogs or wild coyote or big cats or black bear will not make off with it. A blue length of nylon rope thrown over a branch and secured around the pineapple-sharp bark of the thing. They use fallen branches to cover the bike a bit so as not to arouse the curiosity of an unexpected passerby. It is turning dusk now, too, and that will work in their favor.

A ways back, the boy says. I saw a couple Asplundh rigs.

Yeah.

The treecutters.

I saw them too hey.

They follow the rutted road back the way they had come. After a while they come to a sand pit where the clearcutting operation has been shut down for months. Whatever week or month it is now. Whatever day. Thaddeus has long since lost track. There are two pickups and a wood splitter and a couple bigger machines that appear to have been abandoned in a hurry, the paint bubbling off of them like skin cancer. Not a soul around. Bobby checks the closest pickup, removes the gas cap and gives sniff. His uncle hands him the clear tubing that has been coiled. The boy uncoils it and holds an end in each hand and pulls it into a straight line. He inserts one end into the mouth of the gas tank of the pickup and he feeds it along until he stops. There is six inches or so left hanging. Thaddeus prepares the plastic container by removing the red top and blowing air into it and massaging it into its proper shape.

He places it on the ground at his nephew's feet.

Have at it, he says.

Bobby bends at the waist and lowers his face and uses his front teeth to pinch the end of the rubber hose that is there. He sucks slowly and within seconds the gold color fuel is evident through the transparent skin of the tube. Then he carefully removes the other end from the gas tank, navigates it to the plastic container and blows from his own end, pushing the liquid out, helping the force of gravity. He repeats this procedure several times until the jug is full. Uncle Thaddeus caps it and claps his nephew on the shoulder.

Swallow much this time, he says.

Not much.

I'll make a right outlaw of you yet.

CHAPTER FORTY-FIVE

THE DOG BARKS AT BOBBY and shows teeth. She's not wearing her red collar now. He puts his hand out and she comes close enough to put her nose against his fingertips. She looks like an Australian dingo. Her ribs are showing and he knows she hasn't eaten in days.

None of them have.

The scent of the pig roasting is unfamiliar by now.

What's your fucking name girl, he says.

She barks at him and he laughs until it hurts.

He saw a show on television about dingoes once.

We got to give you a name.

Hunger is getting to his brain.

He's getting weak and silly.

His head is light.

All right then, he says.

She barks at him some more until even she runs out of bark.

I'll just call you Dingo then.

CHAPTER FORTY-SIX

THE NEIGHBOR'S WIFE COMES OVER and invites Earl to dinner. He shakes his cock at her and she runs back across the street. He stands there holding it and they all look over at him. He wants them to see. It does not even work anymore. That is not what this is about. Then Hank Zukowski is out there. He is an old family friend. He is sitting in his thresher. There is a bit of autumn sun reflecting off of the glass that encases him and Earl does not see if he waves back at him. The sounds of farm work soothe him. He used to work the land like his father before him. He closes his eyes. He's not supposed to get excited.

That fat fucking Jamaican is frying up some kielbasa from Pekarski's off of 116 in Conway. That and some red bell peppers that Earl picked himself. She's singing in there in some godforsaken language. Liz wants her to sleep over, too, sometimes, so that Earl will always have somebody there at night, but he needs that like a hole in the head. He sees the way she looks at him. There is lust in there. They are like animals and she will wait until he's in bed and dreaming and she will slip in there with him like a haunt.

Then there is a loud crash and everything disappears.

Did you see what happened, Liz says.

Mister fall, the Jamaican says.

I know he fell, Liz says.

Mister fall.

I see that.

Yes.

Did you see how it happened, Liz says.

No.

Did he faint, she says.

No I cook inside, the Jamaican says.

You didn't see it.

I hear crash. Mister fall.

All right.

Look at mister, she says. He open eyes now.

All right, Liz says. Help me get him up.

It's too cold, Earl thinks.

These people. Why can't they just leave me alone. There is something that tastes like a ten-penny nail. They put him out in the sun, which is a start. He tells them to get him some towels with warm water if he has any left. If that sonofabitch across the way hasn't used it all up again. Earl doesn't know how many showers one man can take.

There is a warm and wet cloth on his forehead now. It feels good to him. He will not get excited. He tells her not to burn his supper. If she does then he will fire her, he doesn't care what Liz says. She can't run his life. He doesn't know who she thinks she is. Then the Red Sox, those lousy bums, are losing in the eighth inning. His chair is rocking and the radio is coming in good for once and there's a breeze and the smell of gladiolas. A skunk is nosing around the yard. Earl remains still and watches him. What he would give for a pellet gun. He knows he should keep one around and loaded at all times.

He closes his eyes.

His bone-handle pistola is in the basement. He got it off a dead gook in Vietnam. He used to break birds with it, believe it or not. He can picture where it's hidden.

I am going to find that gun, he says to nobody in particular.

He doesn't realize that Blackie has taken it.

Or that his eldest son has plans more sinister than shooting rodents or birds.

What happen mister now, the Jamaican says.

She gets Earl's pants off and puts him in the tub, where he's at her mercy. She uses a big soft sponge and liquid soap. He rests against her bosom because he's too tired to fight anymore. But he thinks somebody should pay for what is happening to him.

CHAPTER FORTY-SEVEN

THE FAT COP SITS ON his horse and nurses a nip of Old Crow. The horse is still but for her tail that is whipping dry at flies. A shiny coat of sweat glossing her black hide. The fat cop strokes the horse's muscle-roped neck with a fat hand and talks softly into her ear.

Take a breather there girl, he says.

The horse nods her head and snorts as though she understands.

We're getting warmer now, he says.

The horse sneezes.

Yeah, he says. I can smell them too.

He is regarded as an expert tracker and he claims it's due to what some consider his dubious heritage. He is descended from the Pocumtuck tribe known for the Battle of Bloody Brook and the killing and scalping of Captain Thomas Lathrop and sometimes credited with kidnapping the women and children of white settlers, and raping them, and hauling them up across the Canadian border. From his steady perch the fat cop studies the ground and listens. He can see where some buck, probably at least a ten-pointer, had bedded down in the tall reeds. He detects the fresh scratch marks of a black bear cub on a tree, the bark shredded and sawdusty. The tap-tap of a woodpecker, the soft hiss of a creek fed from mountain snow runoff, the water of which polishes stones large and small.

CHAPTER FORTY-EIGHT

THE UNOFFICIAL SEARCH PARTY COMES across the old fire pit, long cold. Doreen's father is clearly in charge of the four others. He spits into the pit. Hard piles of dog shit litter the site. Cigarillo butts around the base of a tree. Nobody says a word. There is a hard and constant gust pushing weather down from the north and they are coming up from the south, hoping to squeeze Thaddeus and Bobby out into the open. Mother Nature has partnered with manmade catastrophe to become their unwitting accomplice. Then Blackie emerges from the shadows as though delivered by the wind or some other force of nature. Doreen's father and the others look at him like he's a ghost. He smiles but not nice. They weren't expecting this confrontation. He has caught them on their heels and so they hesitate, which is the worst mistake you can make with a man like Blackie.

CHAPTER FORTY-NINE

BOBBY NEVER DREAMS ANY DREAMS anymore. He's squatting on the ridge of a scarlet rockwall with Dingo at his side. There is a black bear sitting in a wet meadow sucking white ants from a felled beech sapling. He smells the boy and the dog now, too.

CHAPTER FIFTY

THADDEUS SITS ON A ROCK and jiggles fishing wire. The boy watches him and puts a worm on a hook. The dog always at his side now. He calls her Dingo. He and his uncle got the bait from a vending machine tagged Live Bait at the service station in the center of town. They busted open the machine with a tire iron because they didn't have fifty cents. Festus will be pissed when he comes across the results of their most recent act of vandalism. A dozen pink and gray night crawlers packed with dirt into a milk container. The trout is running pretty good. Uncle Thaddeus will be happy to eat some fish. There's a dirty white plastic bucket on the ground next to him and there's some tackle in it. Different size hooks and lengths of wire and a small knife for dressing the catch. The boy casts his line out and it takes a couple tries to get it in the right spot. The dog barks twice.

There you go now, Uncle Thaddeus says.

Think that'll do her.

Unless she scares them off with that barking.

Uncle Thaddeus wants to eat the dog.

He insists it will taste like chicken.

Basically just chink food, he has said many times.

But Bobby has grown quite fond of Dingo and she's all ribs now anyhow.

And the fact that it was a gift from Doreen is important to him.

He has come to think of the dog as a piece of her.

A piece of them.

Bobby shuts up the dog and settles down next to his Uncle Thaddeus. He wraps the line around his wrist a couple times and gives it a tug. He leans forward and then the line goes slack and he sits back. There are trees along the stream and a mill with a water wheel. Bobby watches the wheel turn and there is a beaver-cut log caught in a standstill and he watches that, too. He is shirtless and his uncle is shirtless and their shirts are wet and hanging to dry on a straight leafless branch with socks, as well. They had bathed in the stream, too. They washed their hair and bodies, naked and pale and skeleton bone-hard now with the lingering hunger.

It's just water so there is little they can do for the stench, but they don't smell themselves anymore and aren't around other people for it to really matter. Thaddeus closes his eyes and leaves them closed and rests the back of his head against the tree trunk. He doesn't want to sleep but there's no fighting it. It doesn't feel like sleep anymore. Then his line jerks and tightens and he opens his eyes and looks at the boy who is sleeping now, too. The line doesn't let go and he has a live one. He pulls back in a quick snap and can feel the hook catch on the lip of the trout. It feels small, but big enough for them to eat. The dog gets up and barks, whips its stubby tail back and forth.

Sonofabitch, Thaddeus says.

The boy opens his eyes and blinks and looks at his uncle.

You got one, he says.

He checks his line, too, but there is nothing there and he turns back to his uncle. Uncle Thaddeus stands up to get some better leverage and he pulls the line in hand over hand. Bobby unwraps his line from his wrist and snags it on a piece of bark so he can help. Then the fish breaks the surface and it is silver in the sun and flicking its tail first and then the rest of it. The boy manages to get hold of it and the hook has gone through its eyeball and there is some rust-colored blood. He works the hook out backward and lays the three-pounder on some leaves they've set up and he puts a foot on it and reaches in the bucket for the knife. He uses it to clean the fish, slicing it and folding it open. The innards of the thing still working for a second or two once exposed. Uncle Thaddeus is already starting the fire. He had dug a hole for a pit and surrounded it with stones. Dry leaves and twigs as a base and a teepee of bigger sticks and some other kindling. Logs and heavier branches on standby. There are still some matches left, but they have to be careful. Thaddeus cups his hands and blows at the embers and a thin wisp of smoke. When it catches he straightens up and looks at the boy who is just finishing up.

How's she looking over there son, he says.

He has taken to calling the boy son and Bobby does not seem to notice or mind.

About ready now, Bobby says.

There is a flat piece of tin and the boy puts the meat and skin and bones there. All right hand it here, the man says.

The boy hands it to his uncle. Thaddeus puts the tin on some rocks to hold it over the flames that are licking upward now like the cursed tongues of a hundred hungry demons buried somewhere deep. He stands up and steps back and spits. Bobby walks down to the water and rinses his hands and wipes them sticky in some weeds and then shoves them back in the water and then again until they are not sticky anymore.

Wish we had some bread, he says.

That was the last of it the other night.

Can she bring some more.

He means his grandfather's girlfriend, who had dropped more supplies with them a week or so previous. But that was not a good idea with all the folks on their asses. Meeting up with known people in town. The perfect way to get themselves caught.

I think we got to lay low now, Uncle Thaddeus says.

Uh huh.

That's just the ticket for now.

All right.

Until things blow over a little bit.

Bobby nods his head in agreement. He knows it's true, but he wants some bread and some chocolate and ice-cold beer. He wants these things and more. What he used to have even though it was never much.

He wants to drive around carefree with Fat Johnny and maybe tussle with some other fucking rednecks in a relatively harmless fashion that doesn't lead to a fucking funeral. Doreen. He wants to see Doreen and to put his hand in her hair. To get inside her. He pictures in his mind for the millionth time what them boys done to her and it hardens his heart. And now Bobby's baby forming in that belly.

After them poking and prodding around in there.

It was a trespass that Bobby could not ever forgive.

Maybe when it's dark, Bobby says.

He means maybe they can take the bike into town and do another raid on Rogers & Brooks or Hebert's or Boron's Market. Uncle Thaddeus is nervous about going into town now and he does not answer the boy. He flips the fish with a stick and you can smell it. Seconds later he removes the tin from the flames and puts it down on the ground and puts his burned fingertips into his mouth. They are too hungry to let it cool and Uncle Thaddeus takes the knife from the boy and cuts the thing in half and he gives his nephew the bigger half with the tail and he eats the one with the head, eyeballs intact. They use their hands that have gotten shiny with oil. The bones are small and sharp and they spit them out or lick them onto the backs of their hands like feral cats.

Good fucking fish, the boy says.

His uncle laughs and chews and laughs. Then they stand there. Uncle Thaddeus goes down to the stream and takes a knee and puts his hands in the water. The boy does, too, though the fish stink will not go away entirely. Then the sun has dried their shirts and socks. They get dressed and Uncle Thaddeus pisses on the fire to put it out.

Let's pack up then, he says.

The key to their survival is to stay in constant motion.

The boy gets the bait and tackle together. He rinses the tin they used for cooking. He puts it all in the box and then he puts the box under the seat of the chopper that is leaning against a tree. His uncle kicks some dirt and leaves into the fire pit. He looks up at the sky through the canopy of trees. Dark clouds are forming, shifting ominous shapes.

Looks like rain, Uncle Thaddeus says.

Uh huh.

Might could help us.

Keep them others at bay you mean.

But meanwhile we got to find some cover.

They have a blue tarp and rope that is fine and functional for some mist or light rain or heavy fog, but it will not do in a real storm. Not that half-assed lean-to they contrapt. They need real shelter soon. There is some rolling thunder in the distance.

Coming down from Canada, Uncle Thaddeus says.

Yeah.

Sounds like a real fucking beaut.

All right then.

The boy looks at his uncle.

Let's go hey, Uncle Thaddeus says.

The boy laughs a little bit and puts his hand on his mouth and Uncle Thaddeus throws his leg over the bike and backs off the kickstand and the boy straddles behind. It is a strange thing that links them now: the way they need each other like never before.

CHAPTER FIFTY-ONE

THE BIG ASH-COLORED ROCKS IN the river have been honed smooth over the years. Blackie stands on one that can hold his weight and puts his bad foot out to test another. He balances himself with the dead branch of an oak. About halfway across he stops and with his free hand retrieves a bottle of rotgut from his back pocket and that he had acquired from Doreen's father just before he dispatched him from this bad world. It's not a clear liquid. It burns even his scar-tracked throat and he caps it off and scowls. Slips it back into his pocket. Looks for his next foothold. He shakes his head as it becomes clear that he's going to have to step in the water. Then he takes a knee and unlaces the boot on his injured leg. He removes the boot and the sweat-damp wool sock. He switches knees and takes off the remaining boot and sock, and he stands and puts the socks in his pants and ties the laces of the boots together and hangs them over his shoulder. Rolls up the cuffs of his pantlegs. His feet are white and mapped with green veins and the nails of the toes are yellow and thick and curled at the ends. He fingers his ear and enters the water slowly, holding the stick with both hands now, leaning on his strong leg.

CHAPTER FIFTY-TWO

HIS NAME IS BILL BUT everybody in town calls him Killer. He's standing with his cousin, Frank Devine. They had found the motorcycle where Uncle Thaddeus had stashed it in the foliage. Killer has just finished uncovering it. Frank Devine is saying something, but Bobby can't understand what. Thaddeus holds his hand up and Bobby stays quiet and still. It's the back edge of the men's property and they will not take kindly to any type of poaching. There is a tan burlap sack of birds they had bagged in Bobby's left hand and he switches it to the other while his uncle holds the shotgun in his right hand so that he can hoist it up and fire a quick round. He steps out from the trees and Bobby stays hidden because he knows his uncle wants him to. The Devines look up and see Uncle Thaddeus.

Hello boys, he says.

His sudden appearance and friendly nature catch them off guard.

Killer straightens up and considers the black barrel of Bobby's uncle's shotgun.

What's doing, Killer says.

Just traipsing about.

With that thing, Frank Devine says, indicating the gun.

This is private property, Killer says.

I guess I got a little spun around hey.

What you shooting anyhow.

Dinner I hope.

Well it's off season.

Shit, Thaddeus says. Isn't it always.

Killer and Frank Devine move away from each other as they speak. Making it so Uncle Thaddeus has two targets if it comes to that and it will. They do not appear to be armed but that would be a first. Killer kicks at some dirt with the toe of his boot and spits.

Shit we got fences and signs up everyfuckinwhere, he says.

Oh all right.

Private property and whatnot.

I only seen them just now, Thaddeus lies.

There is knot-barbed wire strung across posts in some spots and walls of stones piled waist high in others. Yellow signs warning of dogs and death and damnation and worse nailed eye level to trees. It is abundantly clear that strangers are not welcome.

Will not be tolerated.

Must be fucking blind then, Frank Devine says to Killer.

Frank whistles a bit of the tune to "Three Blind Mice."

Killer laughs a little and Frank Devine laughs, too, but it isn't jovial. Uncle Thaddeus stands still. The cousins finish with their laughing and they look at each other, speaking some silent language. Then Killer looks directly at Uncle Thaddeus and Frank Devine turns and studies the wooded area behind him. Checking to see if this stranger is alone in his trespass. Bobby becomes his surroundings. He is invisible.

To them both.

To the world.

Even to himself.

Who else with you, Killer says.

Nobody.

Bullshit I hear somebody out there, he says.

Come on out now, Frank Devine says in a louder voice. Come out little mouse.

He whistles again.

Nobody with me, Thaddeus says. What you hear is them birds I aim to shoot.

Bobby stands still and barely breathes. Frank Devine looks right at him once it seems, but he's well camouflaged. They are bluffing and Uncle Thaddeus waits them out. Finally, Frank Devine settles down about it and Killer jerks his thumb toward the bike.

You ride in on that piece of shit, he says.

Then he spits toward the bike.

Yeah.

Well go on and ride out on it then.

And that's that hey, Thaddeus says. Plain and simple.

Yeah just don't come back fucking around here boy.

Thaddeus doesn't believe they are going to let him depart so easy.

This is my pappy's land, Frank Devine says.

Oh I know your pappy, Thaddeus says.

You got no right to be here, Killer says. So go on now.

Well all right then.

Uncle Thaddeus goes to the bike and Bobby takes the flare pistol out of his belt because he doesn't believe either that they are going to let him go just like that. And his uncle wouldn't leave him behind. With a little bit of luck he can hit Frank Devine from where he stands. Bobby holds the flare pistol in one hand and the sack of birds in the other. Uncle Thaddeus keeps his shotgun ready as he rights the chopper and swings his leg over the seat. He turns the key in the ignition and kickstarts the engine that sputters with some water in the fuel line. Killer looks at Frank Devine and Frank Devine reaches down and gets a throwing knife from his cowboy boot. Everybody knows that has become his specialty over time, which is the problem with acquiring a specialty, Bobby figures. Bobby aims at the middle of Frank Devine's back and pulls the trigger and the flare whistles and hits him square and knocks him forward and that dude is sure as shit on fire. He drops the knife and yells and curses, and rolls around on the ground.

Fuck me, Frank Devine says. I'm burning.

Goddamn, Killer says.

He kicks some dirt onto his burning cousin and helps him put out the fire. Bobby can smell Frank Devine's burning clothes and skin and hair. He comes out from behind the tree and his uncle has the shotgun now trained on the pair and he waves his nephew over. Bobby stops and picks up Frank Devine's throwing knife, secures it.

Good fucking shot there boy, Uncle Thaddeus says.

Bobby doesn't say a word.

It's the first time he has ever shot anybody with anything.

He tosses his uncle the bag of birds and Thaddeus fastens it to the seat with bungee chords. Frank Devine looks up and sees Bobby for the first time and his mouth opens but no words come out. He's a true fucking mess. He knows the boy from town. He knows his father. It's a notorious lineage and Bobby's deed here makes perfect sense to him.

Bobby looks away from Frank Devine. He doesn't necessarily want to watch him suffer. A brown-striped chipmunk balances on a nearby tree branch.

Uncle Thaddeus tells Bobby to look at what he done, that it's important to see.

Bobby looks back at Frank Devine.

I know you, Frank says through pink bubbles of saliva and blood.

Bobby looks straight at him and almost smiles.

Then Bobby whistles the tune from earlier, clearly mocking the man.

You little bastard, Killer spits.

Frank Devine is yelling now but running out of voice quick, maybe losing consciousness, going into shock. Bobby has heard about that. It's supposed to help with the pain. From the sound of things he could use some help. Frank Devine regards Bobby again but there is no longer any recognition in his eyes. There isn't much there at all anymore, truth be told. Then Killer holds his cousin's head in his hands. There's gray smoke coming off of him that could be his spirit escaping his fire-broken body, drifting upward toward heaven. Bobby doubts a knifethrower is destined for such glory.

More than likely he is ultimately headed in the other direction.

Uncle Thaddeus slams the butt of his rifle hard against the side of Killer's head, denting his temple, knocking him out cold. He falls in a heap adjacent to his cousin.

Come on, Uncle Thaddeus says.

Bobby gets on the back of the chopper and Uncle Thaddeus turns the engine over and they leave the smell and them others with it behind as the back tire kicks up dark dirt.

CHAPTER FIFTY-THREE

Two days later Fat Johnny wants to know what it was like to kill a man. Bobby doesn't tell him everything because he doesn't know how to say it all, how to put it into words.

Fat Johnny says that Westy has been coming around again. They are sitting in the back room of the Polish Club. Fat Johnny is supposed to be cleaning up and he has sneaked Bobby in and fed him some poor boy sandwiches and flat warm beer and stale potato chips and cold turkey kielbasa leftover from a stag party. Whitey Baggs is getting married apparently. The trees outside the window are dead and bare of leaves.

Fucking cold to be living outside now boy, Fat Johnny says.

It aint so bad.

Winter sure come early though.

Right.

Seen your girl down to Cheapside Bridge, Fat Johnny says.

Not my girl no more I suppose.

Oh she is too.

Bobby looks at his one true friend in this hard life.

She's really showing now, Fat Johnny says.

Bobby tries to picture her like that, but he can't.

That shit binds you together now, Fat Johnny says. Forever.

Bobby looks away.

That's a big word, he says. Forever.

I thought you meant shit.

Bobby laughs.

Bare sugar maple branches are mad and dancing skeletons beckoning him. He can see his and Fat Johnny's breath even indoors, even with the fireplace with a fresh log just tossed in and crackling. Paper-thin black flakes float like broken promises when a pretty girl pokes it with a black iron stick. She looks at Bobby and smiles and he nods.

CHAPTER FIFTY-FOUR

THE FAT COP SMELLS THE campfire again. The horse smells it, too, and shivers. He sits her still and quiet. Dismounts and wraps the leather straps around the elbow of a tree branch. Puts a finger to his lips and looks her in the eye and quiets her. He takes a sugar cube from the pocket of his coat and her lips pull back exposing large yellow square teeth and pink gums. The tongue extends and he puts the treat on it and watches as they both disappear into that maw again. The horse snorts, blowing globs of snot onto the fat cop's arm. He wants to get a closer look at the vagabonds, but prefers to engage them on his mount. That's where he feels strongest and most capable. As though he and the horse are at least equal parts of something more effective. Standing on his own two feet he cannot impose his will on others in the same way. And without him the horse is just a stupid, aimless beast. He feels bad for thinking that and strokes her neck.

Voices now.

He can hear the boy and the man talking.

Watch it now, the man says.

They are cooking something.

Smells like fowl.

Crackling over open flames.

Don't burn it now, the man says.

He stands so he can see them. Thaddeus DuBois is sitting on a rock with his shoes in his hands. He is turning them over one at a time, inspecting each. He appears to be mending them. Bobby DuBois is standing over the crude fire pit they have concocted of stones. There is a small white dog at the boy's feet; the fat cop had detected his scat on the trail and wondered about that, about the sense of taking a pet on the lam. It is a bird they are cooking now. Probably a pheasant. Out of season, of course. He can fine them for that, too, if he wants. Such a minor infraction in comparison. Laughable really. It's cooking on a spit. There is a pile of white and gray feathers nearby. The dog has a mess of feathers stuck on its moist nose.

The dog hasn't sensed them because the fat cop was careful to situate downwind.

He knows a thing or two about tracking.

Should I turn it again, the boy says.

Sure, the man says. Give her a turn.

The boy bends at the waist and turns the spit. The flames lick higher when the juice of the thing drips and there is a sizzle. The dog is paying very close attention to the meat. The man is definitely darning the fabric of his shoes now. He has a needle and thread and a cut of cloth. It looks like a sewing kit. There is a red plastic container cracked open at his tube-socked feet. He holds the needle between his teeth as he talks to the boy and it makes his words harder to discern.

What, the boy says.

The man removes the needle from his mouth so that he can be understood.

Turn her all the fucking way I said.

The boy looks up for a second and then he turns back to the task at hand and does as he is told. Again the flames rise up and again blood drips and sparks. An uncertain dusk is falling all around them. The horse won't stay quiet much longer. She will get restless and snort and shift and snap twigs. This is a fact that the fat cop knows. The man has his shotgun within reach and the boy has a knife and some form of handgun in his belt. Probably the flare he used on Frank Devine. He can see it all. It will be difficult to get the drop on them and the time of day is not in his favor. He should camp off a ways and catch them unawares in the morning. He decides that is the thing. He closes his eyes and pictures it. Sitting high on his saddle with the sun behind him, blinding his captives as they rub sleep seeds from their eyes and scramble for their weapons—but it will be too late for that. He will of course have his sidearm ready. Resting the butt of it on his forearm. Steady. He has bracelets enough and he will link them together and walk them down the mountain to Sawmill Plain Road and then to River Road and then he will radio for a car to pick them up. Then Westy can take them. But not until he does his part.

Let's eat, the boy says.

The fat cop opens his eyes, his vision interrupted but anyhow complete. Dusk is turning to dark. The boy has put the bird on a flat tin plate and he is carving it with the throwing knife from his belt. The man puts his shoes down and gets up and goes to the fire. The fat cop watches the man and he watches the boy and that dog, too. They are getting comfortable in their life out here, he thinks. Really taking to this rough existence. He hears a twig or two snap beneath his horse's hoof. Shit. He holds his breath.

The man looks at the boy, who has stopped eating to listen hard.

What was that, Thaddeus says.

The man turns when he says it and holds his hand up to the boy. The boy stops cutting the bird and he straightens and he turns, also. They are facing the fat cop now, but unable to see him due to his cover. He counts five Mississippis. There's nothing. The man looks at the boy and the boy looks at the man. The boy starts cutting the bird again.

You hear that, the man says.

The dog growls and perks up now.

Bobby scratches her behind the ears.

I heard something hey, the boy says.

Your supposed watchdog aint worth a shit.

Bobby scratches the dog behind the ears again.

Probably a raccoon or a coy dog, he says.

The dog's ears perk up again.

Somebody out there, Thaddeus says.

I figure we'll run into one of them somebodies soon enough.

The man laughs at that. The boy hands him a leg with skin crisp-blackened and hanging off it like a banner for mortality. The man shoves it in his mouth. The boy works on a wing. It is a messy business. They use their sleeves. The dog licks its chops and Bobby gives her a little meat. They settle down as they eat their meal so the fat cop slips away. He backtracks to where the horse is getting ready to fidget some more. He rubs her neck and whispers. She is a good old girl and he tells her so. He walks beside her until he feels they are out of earshot and then he puts his foot in the metal stirrup and then he throws himself on. He will find a good spot now. A little meadow where he can bed down. But he won't start a fire. He won't need one. A few blankets and his bedroll is all he needs. Some jerky and tack to gnaw on. A handful of oats for the horse. He has provisions enough for three more nights out here. He likes to be prepared. Then at dawn he will capture that which he has hunted for so long. When they get to the road maybe there will be a photographer. His picture in the *Hampshire Gazette*. The chief will have to rethink cutting the budget for a mounted patrol then. The horse jerks her head forward so the reins tighten in his grasp and he smiles at her and clicks his tongue.

IN THE MORNING WHEN HE opens his eyes the sun has been in the sky for at least an hour. The fat cop rises and scrambles to collect his gear, and disheveled he returns to the site where he had seen Thaddeus and Bobby the night before, but they are gone. He dismounts and warms himself a cup of water over the smoldering fire pit they had left behind. Sipping coffee with steam rising into his face, he curses a body's need to recuperate and his own proclivity for heavy slumber. Then he starts because the horse stamps her rear hooves and snorts as though she too would like to weigh in on the matter.

CHAPTER FIFTY-FIVE

THERE'S A SMALL WHITE TOYOTA pickup loaded down with fresh-cut fence posts and a large spool of electrical wire. Uncle Thaddeus recognizes the man wearing the blue coveralls. They speak for a minute or two while Bobby watches from the barn. Then his uncle calls his name and he joins the two men. The man in the blue coveralls regards him.

We can stay in his barn for a couple nights, Uncle Thaddeus says.

It will be good to get out of the rain, Bobby thinks.

The man in the blue coveralls spits over his shoulder.

Plus he'll give us provisions, Thaddeus says.

All right.

But first we got to put up this fence for him.

Bobby looks at the posts.

He wants to get it up before the ground gets too hard.

Fair enough.

The man with the blue coveralls drives the pickup slow and tells them in as few words as possible where to put the posts, as well as the six-foot-long galvanized grounding rod. The basic enclosure will ultimately include a pond, a small creek, and two patches of tall grass for the cows to nibble on. Then the man with the blue coveralls leaves them with the pickup and he gets a four-wheeler with a brush hog attachment from the barn and goes to work on the surrounding area.

Uncle Thaddeus and Bobby revert to where they started and take turns pounding the sharpened five-foot fence posts into the hard ground every sixty feet or so. They use a twenty-pound sledgehammer. They tap two small white cylinder insulators into place on each post using mismatched rusty spikes from a cardboard container, about eighteen inches apart, and proceed to hand-wrap the wire one time around for them both and then stretch the spool for the next setup.

Not so tight there hey, Thaddeus says.

All right.

It should be like a rubber band.

Bobby backs up on the wire so his uncle can check it.

That's better hey, Uncle Thaddeus says.

It's not too loose.

It's got to give or else if a cow runs into it she could pull them posts up.

But I figured they could slip out like this.

Not with five thousand volts running through her she won't.

Oh all right then.

Just a little jolt from that will learn them good.

The juice will come from a box with a voltage meter on a wall in the barn, where the man in the blue coveralls can throw a switch when he wants. When they break for lunch the man with the blue coveralls gives them venison jerky and water from a metal jug.

CHAPTER FIFTY-SIX

EARL RESTS FOR A LONG time. Then Westy extracts him from the bog. The gumball lights are spinning. He speaks into his walkie-talkie and pulls Earl by the shoulders and it sounds like a cow pulling her foot out of the mud. He asks Earl about Blackie and them others.

Earl what in fuck you doing out here, he says. All by your lonesome.

Aint breaking no laws.

Anyhow I'm looking for your boys.

Uh huh.

They in it deep now, he says. All three.

All right.

I don't suppose you seen them.

Who's that now.

Westy shakes his head.

Earl Ran doesn't even know who he's talking about.

Westy uses a towel from his trunk to wipe himself clean and then he hands it to Earl. But Earl just looks at it and then Westy does what he can for the older man. There is a ride in the backseat and the world rushes by and Earl Ran presses his face against the glass like a small child. Then Westy is getting the Southern Comfort from the top shelf over the refrigerator along with a couple shotglasses that have thumbprints all over them. He goes over them once and then twice with the bottom of his t-shirt that has come untucked and hangs just below his uniform. He is talking because Earl sees his mouth moving. Then he shakes his head. He pours and sets one in front of Earl and they each take a tug and then he refills. Earl Ran tries to focus, but he is running low on fuel now. The house is empty besides them because Liz is working.

And that nigger bitch quit again.

You might think about assisted living, Westy says.

Fuck you say.

You done lost your damn mind.

Shit boy.

But you're not near as mean as you used to be.

Earl laughs and stands up.

I guess there is that, Westy says.

Then Earl's ears come back and the gravel churns under the thick tires of the squad car. The screen door bangs behind him. Crickets and frogs and the river and the familiar buzzing and sometimes it's all too much. He has to sit down again. Then Liz is in his face. The Jamaican quit again because Earl made her cry. He tells Liz he doesn't need some other nigger bitch around here, too. She takes it in stride like everything else.

I hope you don't talk about me like that.

Like what now.

Nigger bitch this and nigger bitch that.

He dismisses her concerns with a wave of his hand.

That's not how he thinks of her anyhow.

Just get me a chair with wheels, he tells her.

A chair.

My legs need rest and that is all, he says.

He doesn't mention the visit from the police because he doesn't remember it.

THE NEXT DAY SHE GOES to Wilson's in Bucktown and comes back with a box and somebody carries it into the house and Earl watches him closely because he doesn't trust anybody anymore. The stranger unpacks it and takes the cardboard and stuffing away and that's the last Earl sees of him. Liz clears a path among and around the downstairs rooms so Earl can get to everything all right. The chair is the office kind like you might see behind a desk and it sits well. His fingers are the gnarled and knotty branches of an old sycamore tree and he can't get them to work the doorknob. He hits his head against it.

Something pops.

Then he's in Cooley Dick again.

A nurse says something about a concussion. Earl smells pipe smoke and he smells the bleach they use to clean the floors and the small packs of grape jelly they spread on his white toast. The room is white. They tell him that his house is okay. The neighbor saved it with his garden hose. It just burned up some shingles is all. A damn fire had jumped the river. His feet are purple and they stick out and he does not recognize them at first. His own goddamn feet. The curtain moves and then it doesn't. The hands are not gentle and Earl is poked and prodded and something is inserted into his asshole.

Earl Ran, the nurse says.

Right.

Have you been taking your medicine, she says.

Fuck you say.

Are you watching your diet, she says.

Shit.

There are so many voices that he can't possibly remember them all. Things are swollen now and that seems to create a sense of urgency around him, but he is not supposed to get excited. He closes his eyes and counts to ten, twenty, thirty. He can feel his breathing regulate somewhat. Then somebody comes up big in the bottom of the ninth. There is a newspaper in his hands and open in front of him. There is cigarillo smoke rising up from his mouth. The fans at Fenway are making a lot of noise. There is static too which serves him right for living in a house between two mountains. There has always been static. It is part of the game to him. Part of his life and what it has become.

A new set of problems has posed itself. All these pills and he never knows which. Liz helps him by matching the colors to the days, but he doesn't ever remember what fucking day it is. There is a calendar somewhere. He goes from room to room in his chair from Wilson's. There's dirt on the floor and he sweeps and mops the hardwood and linoleum and he vacuums where there is a carpet. He uses stain remover in some areas and scrubs with an old toothbrush. The stains from the fire. Then he needs to rest so he closes his eyes. Then Liz quits her day job at the used car lot so she can monitor him. She tells him she's his girlfriend. She tells him she slings beers at a couple joints for quick cash, but most nights she's off so she can keep an eye on him. She gives him a choice of either her or Kozy Korners and he keeps his mouth shut so he gets her on default. There are certain rules that he establishes from the outset. There are certain rules he lives by.

And she had better abide.

CHAPTER FIFTY-SEVEN

BLACKIE IS SITTING ON THE steps out in front of Schuster's Funeral Home.
A pile of smoked cigarillos at his feet. He is smoking another one and
taking long slow drags from it. It is night. Schuster's is closed. He listens
to a pair of skunks fucking in the bushes. There is a mechanical hum
in the distance. The third-shift generators at the pickle shop he figures.
Then a slow loping figure appears to his right and he registers this
development coolly.

Fuck you, Blackie says through a face full of smoke.

The man coughs and spits. His name is Ed. He is wearing a knit cap
pulled low.

Tribal tattoos on his neck.

Blackie doesn't know what the markings signify—doesn't really care.

Back at ya, Ed says.

Folks call him Ed the Animal, but never to his face.

Blackie moves over and Ed sits next to him and they stare at the
house across the street. There is movement behind the curtained
windows. A family of normal people bedding down for the evening.
Blackie gives Ed a cigarillo and lets him light it from the tip of his own.
They smoke some without conversing. A car passes.

So this thing, Ed says.

Blackie hisses behind clenched teeth.

I don't usually fuck with kids, Ed says.

Don't fuck with him, Blackie says. Just deliver him to me.

All right but you know what I mean.

Blackie looks at him.

This kind of business, Ed says.

Yeah.

Anybody involved gets fucked with a little bit.

Blackie looks back at the house and flicks his butt away from him.

So long as that's clear, Ed says.

You fucking kidding me, Blackie says.

Ed inhales deeply.

You know me, Blackie says.

Ed looks at him and exhales.

Think I give a fuck, Blackie says.

Ed shrugs his shoulders and reaches up and tugs the cap lower.

Just get that little fucker away from my brother.

Ed looks away from Blackie. He looks at his feet.

Nice to see a father who loves his son, Ed says.

Blackie doesn't get sarcasm and Ed remembers that from their time together sharing a cell in Cedar Junction. He's always considered Blackie a fascinating study.

Shit it aint even about that, Blackie says.

All right, Ed says. Tell me again where you seen them last.

Red Rock, Blackie says.

Ed nods his head.

But that was a while ago.

Uh huh.

And then I tracked them again and then I lost them again.

All right.

My brother knows these woods.

I suppose he does, Ed says. But who all else maybe has seen them.

You mean since they been on the run.

Right like maybe they come down for supplies and whatnot.

I guess maybe that Billy Tucker'd be a safe bet.

All right and who all else is looking for them.

Johnny Law of course and some others it seems, Blackie says.

He fingers his ear.

Ed looks at Blackie again and he smiles. It is a smile vacant of teeth. It is empty in most other ways, too. It is not derived from joy. It is surely conjured from a darker place.

That could complicate things, he says.

Right.

Okay then.

You specialize in complicated matters I recall, Blackie says.

Ed regards Blackie and nods his head up and down.

The key is to see the simplicity in even the most convoluted situations, he thinks.

He smokes.

He stands up and spits his cigarillo out and wipes his hands on the front of his pants. Blackie stands up, too. They remain a few feet apart like strangers in line. Ed laughs and nods his head and turns away. He departs in the same direction from which he originally came. Blackie does not watch him go. Then Ed is gone so thoroughly and swiftly it's as though he had never been there or anywhere at all. Blackie pulls the tattered tips of his Navy pea jacket collar up to the bottom of his ears. There is a cold snap in the air and this pleases him as he thinks it will help his cause. For now he will break a window to the cellar of the funeral home and sleep with the corpses tonight.

CHAPTER FIFTY-EIGHT

LESS THAN TWENTY-FOUR HOURS LATER Billy Tucker stumbles solo from the Hollywood. Johnny Cash tunes spill out of the place and then the door closes behind him and the sound is muffled. He doesn't see Ed waiting by his pickup. Ed is counting on that and the fact that the younger man will be out of his mind drunk on a Saturday night. Billy Tucker is afraid he is going to piss himself and he is fooling with his zipper. Oblivious and unconcerned with his surroundings. Just another night out on the town. He leans his shoulder against his pickup and puts his hand in his pants and exposes his cock.

Boy, Ed says. You shouldn't drive like that.

Billy Tucker looks up and sees Ed. Then he looks back down and continues with his urination. He doesn't say anything at first. Doesn't know what to say, really. He immediately recognizes Ed and understands why he is here, that he's looking for Thaddeus and the boy. Blackie went and enlisted him for the hunt. Holy fucking shit. This thing is going to a whole new level now, he thinks. He closes his eyes and makes mud that splashes at his feet. Ed gets splashed on, too, but he doesn't move a bit. He waits almost patiently. Billy Tucker finishes and puts himself away and zips up his pants and really looks at Ed.

What the fuck you want with me, he says.

Not with you.

Well get out my way then.

He tries to muscle past Ed against his better judgment. He figures, what the Christ, he might as well give it a shot. Then the old backwoods assassin takes hold of Billy Tucker's Adam's apple and squeezes just a little bit and lays him down in his own piss in what could be considered a gentle manner. It happens fast and there is efficiency about it. No wasted movement or sound. No anger or emotion in Ed's actions.

All business.

Now let's try this again, Ed says.

Billy Tucker wants to cry and he is not a soft man by any account.

But he's suddenly aware of what his immediate future holds.

Where he at with that boy, Ed says.

Kill me if you want to.

I don't want to kill you, Ed says. But this isn't a matter of wants.

Billy Tucker tries to swallow.

But I will if I have to, Ed says. Do like you said.

Billy Tucker closes his eyes.

After I first do some things that will seem even worse, Ed says.

Then he shoves pissy mud into Billy Tucker's mouth. Billy gags on it and pukes and Ed pinches his ear, turns him over and puts a hard knee between his shoulder blades. Applies enough pressure and then backs off a little. Billy Tucker pukes some more and tries to breathe and when he can finally breathe he does cry a little bit. Ed lets go then. He allows Billy Tucker to roll over and to remember what it feels like to be unfucked with.

Now let's talk to each other like grown-ass men, Ed says.

Uh huh.

All I want is some information, he says. And then you can get on.

Billy Tucker manages himself into a sitting position. He wipes his face with his hand and leaves a streak of mud that looks like war paint. He breathes deep several times. Off toward the creek he can see a rope with a noose dangling from a tree. He figures that Thaddeus and the boy are far enough away by now. He justifies it in his mind that way. Telling himself they had a plenty good head start. Almost believing it, too.

And not fully convinced that it even matters anymore.

CHAPTER FIFTY-NINE

FAT JOHNNY SITS WITH DOREEN. She is showing good now. She asks him for a cigarillo. She tells him how her parents put her out because she refused to let them scoop that thing out of her at the clinic and so she is staying with her great aunt with the horse farm in Indian Falls. The crazy old broad has got her shoveling shit and lugging salt licks to earn her board. He doesn't really know what to say to her so he just listens for a while.

You'd tell me if you'd seen him, she says.

Fat Johnny looks at her and nods his head, but he isn't so sure.

I just want to know he's all right, she says.

I hear you.

That his uncle aint did nothing to him, she says.

Right.

Or that he aint did nothing crazy hisself, she says.

Shit girl.

I mean I won't tell nobody, she says.

I know.

Bobby made him promise since she gave them up the last time.

So you seen him, she says.

No I aint, he says. But I imagine he's all right out there.

How you figure.

We'd of heard something.

She smokes and looks away.

I mean if the law had caught up with them, he says.

But what about them others, she says.

He knows what she means and that she is right. If that other faction gets to them first it might be weeks or months or years before there is ever any solid evidence of it. She looks at him.

What I'm gone to do, she says.

He looks at her blue eyes for a long time and there are tears leaking out of them and onto her cheeks. Fat Johnny doesn't have any experience with female matters such as this. But he thinks she'll do fine. Her aunt has a real nice place out there in the hills.

Oh I think you'll do just fine, he says.

She wipes at her eyes.

At least you got people, he says.

Doreen tries to collect herself.

They can help you with it, he says.

He's talking about the baby, of course.

Doreen knows he is trying to be helpful but that is the last straw. She puts her face in the crook of her elbow and really cries now. Bringing a baby into the world is burden enough but to do it alone and to have it be of such dubious lineage makes the challenge tenfold. But she is a strong believer in fate and she has always figured her destiny is to fix Bobby in some small way and maybe this is somehow her contribution. To bear what she is already sure will be a son. To make him different and better but with all the good parts of his father that will never likely be remembered because of the enormity of this latest string of incidents which is certain to become the stuff of local legend. Bobby is going to make his mark in history as Blackie's boy. The nephew of Thaddeus. Vagabond and vigilante and thief and now killer of men. That is your father, she will say someday.

She has to find him. Fat Johnny knows his whereabouts, that is sure. She calms herself, looks him in the eye, puts her hand on his knee and moves it higher, smiles. Doreen is now quite aware of the power that a pretty girl holds over men and boys.

And that it can work against her, but also in her favor.

Come on, she says.

Fat Johnny looks at her.

What can I do to convince you, she says sweetly now.

Fat Johnny looks at her hand resting on his knee.

He regards it there for a long spell.

HALF A MILE AWAY TONY Overalls uses a red rubber band to squeeze his nappy beard together into a ponytail. He is sitting at the lunch counter at the pharmacy. Pat Crudo is standing in front of him with her hands on her hips. There are ketchup and coffee stains on her white apron. There are crumbs in Tony's beard and on the newspaper that is open next to his plate. The headline is about a wildfire threatening Colrain. Tony is eating a grilled cheese like it's his last fucking meal. The chips are already gone. He looks at Pat.

So you heard about Billy Tucker, he says between bites.

She shakes her head, bored, half listening. Her eyes are watering and irritated.

It appears he hanged hisself, Tony says. Out back behind the Hollywood.

Pat wakes up and lets the news sink in before she says anything.

Oh shit, she says. You mean hanged hisself dead.

From a tree, he says.

Oh shit.

By the creek, he says. Behind the wood.

Goddamn.

His head all swoll up like a fucking Halloween pumpkin, he laughs.

Poor Arlene, she says.

Pat went to school with his mother and remembers her as the nervous type.

Yeah she found him out there, Tony says. After her shift over at Plastics.

Arlene found him like that.

She stopped in for a drink, he says. Or ten.

I wonder what brought that on, Pat says.

I guess she was thirsty.

Pat gives him a look and he laughs.

You always got to be a smartass.

Shit, he says. Who knows what makes a man do something like that.

Pat wonders what's happening to her once quiet and predictable corner of the world. The DuBois boys going all kinds of crazy and now this latest development about Billy who she would never have pegged as the suicidal type. She shakes her head again and takes Tony's plate to the sink. There's a pile building up and she runs water. Tony dumps the crumbs from the newspaper onto the floor when he's sure she's not looking.

CHAPTER SIXTY

ED SMELLS THE FAT COP's horse before he sees the fat cop. Ed is walking carefully. The fat cop is sitting on his bedroll and reading a comic book. The horse shifts and snorts and the fat cop looks up and sees Ed. Ed smiles. The fat cop knows that smile too well, shudders.

Sonofabitch, the fat cop says.

But he is not surprised.

Nice to see you too, Ed says.

The fat cop puts his magazine on the ground and stands up with some effort. He knows better than to make a move for his sidearm. He is very cautious. He faces Ed.

What you doing out here Edward, the fat cop says.

Ed laughs and coughs and spits over his shoulder.

All right then, the fat cop says. That was a stupid question.

He knows full well what Ed is doing out here. Everybody knows what Ed is about, that he is the truest form of hunter. It was a stupid question, but he had to ask.

So anyhow I'll take it from here, Ed says.

Just like that.

That's how I'd prefer it.

You know I can't just let you, the fat cop says.

Ed figured he would say something like that. Chris takes his job very seriously and Ed respects him for that. He reaches into his pants pocket for a pouch of tobacco and some EZ Wider rolling papers and he runs his tongue across an edge of the paper and deftly manufactures a filterless cigarillo while the fat cop stands and watches and considers his situation. Ed hands it to the fat cop and then he rolls one for himself equal in size. He scratches a wood match on his leather belt and lights them both and the two men smoke together. It is an oddly intimate and very peaceful moment that they share.

Will you take care of her, the fat cop says indicating the horse.

Sure, he says. You know I will hey.

Things might be different if I was atop her when you showed.

Don't do that to yourself, Ed says. Cause I mightn't of showed till you got down.

The fat cop finishes his cigarillo and bends over and picks up his magazine and rolls it up and puts it in his back pocket. He picks up his bedroll and fastens it to the horse with the rest of his gear. He strokes her neck and whispers something akin to goodbye.

Rations enough in there, the fat cop says.

All right.

Will maybe last you a couple three days.

Thanks.

Ed nods his head. The fat cop makes a decision in his mind.

Beans and water and coffee and some jerky, he says.

All right then.

Then the fat cop reaches for his sidearm and he sees Ed's boot rise up from the turf and he detects the unmistakable glint of sharp steel and he hears the fabric of his jacket and then his shirt tearing and something else, too. The pop of his gun aimed at nothing. He knows that it won't hurt right away and he is thankful. It is at first a warm feeling and he sits down. Ed helps him rest against a tree. His sidearm is on the ground and out of reach and he can smell the hot powder of it. The horse is standing on three legs. Ed is standing there, too, on one leg and reaffixing the knife into the tread of his other boot. Ed puts his hand in the fat cop's hair like one might do to comfort a small child. He stands there calmly like that until the fat cop leans over and spills a dark substance that becomes oily strings hanging from his open mouth.

Goodbye, Ed says.

The fat cop closes his eyes.

A SUN-STRIPPLED DIMNESS AND SOME wind and the sounds of early morning. Westy takes a knee and inspects the fresh dug dirt nearby the culvert. His partner stands behind him scratching his balls with one hand and leaning on a black rubber-handled shovel with the other. Westy points at the dirt. Cap Warger yawns and sniffs snot and coughs and spits.

Westy looks up at him and frowns.

What you make of it, Cap Warger says.

It's a grave.

Fuck you say.

There's a body in there.

What kinda body.

A dead one.

You mean a human body.

What in fuck you think I mean hey.

Who for fuck sake.

Westy indicates the shovel.

Let's find out, he says.

But who put it in there I mean.

Well that's another thing we got to think on next.

Westy stands up and reaches over and takes the shovel from his partner. He digs carefully out of respect and to preserve the scene of whatever crime was perpetrated as much as possible. It's against protocol but he doesn't have time for protocol right now. Cap Warger breaks a sweat just watching him. He holds a thin red kerchief with a knot at the end to his cheeks and forehead and neck. He'd much rather be sitting in the car. The dirt is not too hard and Westy digs about two feet down around the periphery.

Lookit here, Westy says.

Shit.

Human indeed.

Part of an arm is protruding now from the hole. Westy hands the shovel to Cap Warger and then he squats and uses his hands to clear the rest. He stops and leans back on his haunches when the face is apparent. He looks up at Cap Warger who is unwrapping a narrow blue stick of chewing gum that smells like peppermint.

Oh shit, Westy says as he uncovers the body of the fat cop.

Oh fucking shit is right.

Cap Warger sticks the gum in his mouth, but he does not chew. He steps closer so he can better see the dead man that used to be his colleague and friend. Chris had been missing for some days and even his horse, too. Cap Warger looks down and doesn't realize that his mouth is open; the gum falls out, and he doesn't even notice.

He looks at Westy.

Who would do that then, he says.

He drops the foil gum wrapper at his feet.

I got some ideas, Westy says. But let's get him out of there first.

Cap Warger needs to get sick so he achieves a bit of distance and does so. He listens to the sounds of the shovel. Then they stop and Westy curses under his breath and Cap gets sick some more, doing his best not to stain his shirt and pants.

Fuck this job, he says.

Westy gets the fat cop out of the hole and sets him on a bed of leaves.

He stands next to his new partner and Cap Warger can smell the laundry detergent on Westy's clothes. Probably a big box of powder.

You all right, Westy says.

Cap Warger closes his eyes and nods his head up and down.

Chris was on the wrong side of the law, Westy says. This time in this place.

Cap Warger tries to spit the taste of vomit from his mouth.

There was no room for that out here, Westy says.

Not in DuBois country you mean.

Blackie is a sick enough fuck.

Cap Warger opens his eyes and looks up at Westy but the sun blocks his eyes and he has to hold his hands like a shield and even then he has to shut them halfway. He shakes his head. This is not what he signed up for. He just wanted a little extra income. Westy helps Cap Warger stand up by holding onto his elbow. They face each other and there is silence between them but for the whispered secrets of the river.

We need to be careful, Westy says.

Cap Warger laughs at the understatement.

Careful, he says. LaPinta and now Chris.

Sure as shit, Westy says. We got a target on our back.

Then he laughs, too, and he shows his partner where the heavy hoofprints lead off into the thickening bush country, the trail overgrown with Virginia creeper.

I guess I know them tracks, he says.

He took the horse, Cap Warger says. Jesus.

He shivers.

Then a bug bites him on the neck and he slaps at it and misses and swings both of his hands at the air all around him. It's not just the bug he's swinging at anymore.

Motherfuck, he says to nobody in particular.

CHAPTER SIXTY-ONE

THEY TAKE EARL'S LEG OFF from the knee down. Something to do with circulation and of course his diabetes. It feels to him like the leg is still there and the stump itches sometimes. They fit him for a plastic one with straps and buckles, but it rubs and he can't master the thing so he puts it in the fucking closet with all the other shit. People with strange faces come around and bring casseroles and Liz smiles and is very grateful and Earl tells them to go fuck themselves because he's not dead yet. Then he's in the yard and there's a lawnmower chewing up a stick. It will dull the blade, for Christ's sake. The kid from down the street looks at him and nods and backs up, picks up the stick and chucks it into the treeline. He's a good kid and Liz will pay him from Earl's account. He built a plywood ramp that gets Earl from the porch to the yard. From his moving chair, Earl charts the kid's progress. Front of the house to back of the house to side of the house.

On the stoop there are glasses of tea that has been brewed. Ice cubes crack and squeak and pop and there's a bug suspended in the center of one. Earl feels utterly useless. He closes his eyes. Then there are nimbus clouds and in between them, far away, planets blink. The flashing beak of an airplane inchworms its way south toward Bradley.

It is bleak.

That is the word she has used to describe his situation.

We got to evacuate now, she says.

She tells him that there's a storm coming.

It's a hurricane, she says. As big around as the state of Texas.

He grunts as he pictures the state of Texas on a United States map.

So we got to get gone, she says.

He tells her to fuck off.

I'd rather die here than live somewheres else, he says.

She laughs and calls him a stubborn old bastard.

EARL'S SPIRIT IS SLOW LEAKING. There is the sound of it, it's like smoke. It is like a snake from the garden. Other than the memory he doesn't know what. He chases a real snake with a can of Raid and a book of matches. The ground is wet. He will fry that fucking serpent. She hated them more than anything. In the corner it hisses at him and then disappears. Earl starts to climb out the open window after it until his girlfriend's voice stops him.

Earl Ran, she says. What in the hell.

He looks at Liz and grunts.

This is not the time to play with matches, she says.

He is good and stuck now, you see. Half in the pantry and half out into his rose bush. He straddles the sill and his left stump dangles, swinging like a pendulum, and his right foot kicks over a can of tomato soup. Flakes of white paint peel off against his nose. He drops the can of Raid and the matches in the yard. There is no sign of the snake now.

What in the hell, Liz says.

Stuck.

Earl Ran, she says. What have you got yourself into now.

She considers his new situation from outside, spilling groceries, low fat milk and tubes of frozen orange juice. Then she goes into the house to see if there is a better way to remove him from his current position, but she shakes her head. It is not a pretty sight.

Earl Ran, she says. You are an old fool.

He can smell something big burning across the river. She puts blankets and pillows outside to cushion what she expects to be his fall and then she leverages herself against the red cupboard and with her thick ankles she pushes. The grunts she makes remind Earl of a hog pen and he laughs and at first he doesn't budge, not even a little bit.

I'm glad you find this funny Earl Ran.

Then she really gets behind it and he just lets go and his hip is like a plastic socket in a child's toy. Thorns cut him on the way down and he eats a mouthful of dirt. She takes hold of his head and puts it into her lap and she is rough about the whole thing. She is not an even-tempered one. Then somebody shuts the lights off. Earl's bedsheets smell like mothballs. He doesn't know who is supposed to be washing them. Even though they are white he cannot see them, not even a hint of them, that is how perfectly dark it is. Everything is absorbed into it, even sound it seems.

He is in a purgatory. This goes on forever until the house shifts, creaks. He calls his dead wife's name and of course she does not respond to his cries. He calls her name again and again and again and again.

Help me, he says.

He can almost hear the river creeping up toward his house.

Somebody please help me remember who I am, he says.

Earl Ran pictures the river rising slow like baking bread.

It's going to sweep him away with everything else.

Earl Ran, a voice says. Don't you blubber.

CHAPTER SIXTY-TWO

A BLUE HEAD TURKEY WITH a nine-inch beard holds a garter snake in its beak. Uncle Thaddeus grins. Bobby looks at him. Thaddeus sees Bobby looking and he smiles, shaving cream on his chin and cheek. He shakes his head. Squatting with his elbows on his knees. Pokes a stick at the turkey until that old Tom drops the snake.

I know, he says.

Bobby looks away.

You thinking about your girl again.

Bobby spits.

The turkey stands on one leg while the snake plays dead.

Bobby doesn't say anything and he stops looking at his uncle.

Uncle Thaddeus spits in the dirt, too, and kicks it with his toe.

For the last fucking time, Thaddeus says.

Bobby meets his eyes.

You got to let go, Thaddeus says.

He gets up and with his bare back to Bobby he dips his straight razor in a red pail that is filled halfway with cool river water. Then he dries himself with an old pink oil rag with small fragments of industrial iron wire caught in it.

Listen, Uncle Thaddeus says. We got to make moves.

All right.

And this aint no girl's life out here, he says.

I know but shit.

But nothing, Thaddeus says. That's all she'll ever be.

Bobby nods his head because he is right about that. She isn't cut out for this here.

That's all she'll ever be, Thaddeus repeats.

All right, Bobby says. I heard you.

Just a rotten little cunt, Uncle Thaddeus says.

Bobby sets his jaw.

Don't ruin what we got here between us over a female.

Bobby kicks the turkey and feathers fly and the snake slithers into the tall reeds.

Shit on a stick, he says. There goes that.

Well don't lose the bird now too, Uncle Thaddeus says. For fuck's sake.

Bobby gives the turkey some space; it has been taunting them for hours.

Then Thaddeus turns and looks at Bobby and Bobby looks at him. Thaddeus empties the bucket on the ground and the dirt goes dark and puddles. Bobby rolls up the blue and green sleeping bags, pushing air out of them and brushing away twigs with the back of his hand. Thaddeus pisses a clear orange stream into the fire pit and you can hear it smoke. Bobby takes the bags to the bike and fastens them onto the back and he looks at the sky. Windblown clouds block the sun in a swarm and then disappear.

Uncle Thaddeus laces his boots.

Bobby sniffs at the air.

Boy you got to get your mind right, Uncle Thaddeus says.

All right.

If we gone to do this outlaw thing right.

I said all right already.

Problem is you still got feelings.

Shit.

But you'll outgrow them soon enough.

Bobby stays looking at the sky, squinting against the glare of the new day that isn't his. Not really. It doesn't belong to him anymore. It seems to him that nothing does.

Boy, Thaddeus says.

Bobby is lost to his uncle for a moment.

I said boy.

Bobby looks at his feet.

Look at me now.

Bobby gets a tobacco flake off his tongue and spits it out.

Goddamn it boy, Thaddeus says. Look at me.

Bobby looks at him and he's standing close now and the boy can smell him. Coffee, shaving cream, cigarillos and sweat. The whites of his eyes mapped with red.

But that's my fucking girl, Bobby says.

Thaddeus waits before he speaks.

No because they spoilt your girl, he finally says. Them boys.

Bullshit.

So now she's something else and you got to quit her, he says.

Bobby looks at his uncle and then he looks at his boots.

Maybe they made it easy for you, Thaddeus says.

Bobby looks at his boots and Thaddeus digs in the front pocket of his pants.

You wouldn't of quit her otherwise, Thaddeus says.

Shit.

And you know it.

He's right.

Even after them other boys did her like that, Thaddeus says.

Bobby doesn't want to hear about those others just now.

Stabbing at her guts with their dirty little cocks, Thaddeus says.

Bobby grinds his teeth together.

Shucking your corn they were, Thaddeus says.

Bobby knows his uncle is testing him.

You don't want her shitting that thing out anyhow, Thaddeus says.

Bobby looks at him and then away.

That's the last thing this world needs, Thaddeus says.

Bobby spits.

Is another fucking DuBois, Thaddeus says.

It's true and Bobby knows it. And he still will not quit her, but he won't tell Thaddeus that yet. He looks at his uncle and he looks away toward the river that you can hear through the trees; it sounds like a living thing in jeopardy almost—the way it hisses and gurgles, murmurs and burbles. A last gasp. It's been rising regularly and at a rapid rate as though in promise of a flood. Must be they let the reservoir drain a bit, which is not unusual before a big rainstorm. Then Uncle Thaddeus takes his hand out of his pocket and puts two cigarillos side by side in his mouth that is so thin and straight it looks like it was cut with that straight razor. Then he goes in his pocket again and produces a lighter and he turns the little wheel with his thumb until it catches and he holds the blue-bottomed flame to the tips. Breathes deep the kerosene. Closes his eyes. Puts the lighter away. Hands Bobby one of the cigarillos. Then he opens his eyes and looks at Bobby and Bobby takes the cigarillo and puts it between his own dry lips that are chapped and bleeding in spots. They stand like that and smoke and don't say anything more for a little while. Thaddeus looking at Bobby and Bobby looking away. The tobacco tastes good and Bobby's lungs sting in that sweet way they're supposed to. Then that old turkey makes another run at his leg and he kicks it again and then he chases it around the clearing and calls it names and Uncle Thaddeus laughs at the sight and spits yellow.

Then he gets serious.

Don't let the rest of our dinner get away, he says.

CHAPTER SIXTY-THREE

SUE GETS A STRANGE CHILL. She's sitting on the cement steps that lead to the back door of the Hot L and she holds herself. Eugene will be pissed if she stays away from the bar too long on a busy Friday night. Westy is sitting on the bumper of somebody's pickup truck. He's looking at her and she is doing her best to not reciprocate. He gets up and removes his down vest and hands it over to her. She refuses at first, but she is awfully cold now. She puts it on and it smells like him and she zips it up and she crosses her arms on her chest. He doesn't seem troubled by the weather at all. He looks like he always does.

You're something else, she says.

What's that mean.

She blows a breath out as though to make a point.

It means I can't figure you, she says.

She doesn't want him going out in the woods again with that storm tearing things up. She doesn't want him tangling with the likes of Blackie and Thaddeus and even Bobby now from what she hears, as well as those others. She'd prefer if he'd let things play themselves out naturally. That's how she explained it to him. Just let it go natural.

There's nothing more natural, he says. Than what I'm fixing to do.

And what exactly is that.

He pauses for a heartbeat or two, thinking, unsure how to articulate it.

Right some wrongs I guess.

And why is it on you W, she says. What's it all got to do with you.

Well because it's my job.

You're just a part-time cop, she says. They hardly pay you shit.

He looks at her.

There's nothing part time about it in my mind, he says.

Oh shit, she says. I know.

Sue knows that she crossed a line with him and she stands up and walks over to where he is standing now, too, and she reaches around his waist and puts her hands in his back pockets and stands right up against him. He's already over it and he smiles at her and then through her. She puts the side of her face against his chest and he rests his chin on her head. His breath on her scalp, his heartbeat in her ear. She likes being his girl.

I just worry is all, she says.

All right.

I mean we just got started, she says.

I hear you.

And I don't want nothing to fuck it up.

Then as if on cue Eugene kicks open the screen door that swings noisy on a hinge.

I'm not fucking paying you for this, he says.

Sue doesn't move away from Westy.

All right then, she says.

How about giving my girl the night off then, Westy says.

Your girl now, Eugene says.

That's right.

Eugene makes a face.

Well I guess she could do worse, he says.

I already have, she says.

Have you now.

Plenty of times, she says.

Westy laughs a little at her spunk. This girl is all right in his book.

Eugene disappears back inside the bar and Sue and Westy stand together for a few more minutes and somewhere in the distance is the sound of a lone six-string guitar being plucked. After this moment Sue will always equate guitar music with safety and warmth.

CHAPTER SIXTY-FOUR

A FOOT OF RAIN HAS fallen and even broken some kind of record for that. There's a four-wheeler parked and running near the culvert so Bobby takes it and rides it into town with the dog in his lap. He doesn't consider this act stealing since the ATV was basically abandoned. Fat Johnny doesn't look any different, but he says Bobby does. It is cold enough and Johnny is wearing a deerhide-colored chamois shirt over the top half of a red union suit. He has brought Bobby some gear, too, and he puts it on: wool cap, gloves, thick gray socks, a poncho. Fat Johnny is sitting on an old oil drum that is flipped on its side and Bobby sits there next to him with Dingo resting at his feet, cleaning herself. They're under a tin awning behind the service station where old cars go to die. There is Mrs. O's Oldsmobile up on blocks. Whitey's Cadillac with its hood open like the jaws of a sun-faded, red-rusted creature—its innards ripped out and spread around in the mud. Others in various states of disrepair as though somebody forgot about them.

So you're all right out there, Fat Johnny says.

We're not drowned yet, Bobby says. If that's what you mean.

That's something in this shit.

He indicates the rain.

Right.

Jesus Christ that rain.

We're all right so far.

Maybe this fucked-up weather will help.

If it doesn't kill us maybe it will.

They even prayed on it down at the church, Fat Johnny says. The weather.

Your father and them.

Right.

No shit.

Calling it the work of the devil, Fat Johnny says. The cold and the rain.

I guess that sounds about right.

Bobby figures he's got first-hand familiarity with the devil's work by now.

Fat Johnny doesn't say anything for a while and neither does Bobby.

Fat Johnny has a bottle of Old Crow and he takes a snort and hands it to Bobby and he pulls on the thing good and hard until he is warmer inside. Then he hands it back to Fat Johnny and he twists the cap back on and puts it between his legs and wipes the back of his hand across his nose. He kicks the heels of his boots against the hollow drum. There is a sack of things he brought for Bobby to take back into the woods. Food and blankets. Some stuff Liz had given him to pass on. Bobby looks through it and looks at Fat Johnny and nods his head and says thanks without using the exact words for it.

That enough for a spell, Fat Johnny says.

Got to be I guess.

They sit as the sun goes down behind the drugstore rooftop. Dusk is a welcome gift now and always. Fat Johnny opens the bottle of whiskey again and he drinks a mouthful and so does Bobby and then he swallows and it sits scorching in his gut. Fat Johnny caps the bottle and hands it to Bobby. He puts it in the bag with the other items.

You might be needing that, he says and laughs.

Uh huh.

A stiff drink now and again couldn't hurt.

No it never does.

Bobby laughs, too. He slides off the barrel and stands up and Fat

Johnny joins him. Bobby cinches the bag and throws it over his shoulder and they both get up on the fender of an old Chevy carcass. They climb over the cyclone fence while Dingo finds a spot where she can slide underneath with her belly in the mud. The boys land on the other side in the lot behind Bill's Package Store. The rain is falling hard like blacktop. There's a crushed Bud can and Fat Johnny kicks it and it skids ten feet in front of them.

Then the wind lifts that can and it disappears.

Dingo howls.

See you next time then, he says above the din.

Yeah all right.

Unless this thing wraps up some way.

There's really only one way.

Shit boy I hope you get out of this okay.

Bobby looks at Fat Johnny. There are too many violent intentions now to not result in a purer form of violence. He knows this to be true. It is not going to end well, this ordeal. They face each other in the shadow of the building and Fat Johnny puts his hand in Bobby's, but just for a moment

Bobby had left the four-runner nearby a feeble sapling. Fat Johnny watches him get on and fire it up and pull out into the puddle street. Bobby does not turn the headlamp on but had hoped to find his way by the rusted light of the quarter moon. He doesn't wear a helmet but covers his eyes with a pair of welder's goggles that are clear and plastic and bugs have died on them. It's difficult to see and dangerous to be driving with the sideways rain pelting him. He follows Sugarloaf Street to Main Street to Route 5 and 10. He turns left at the drive-in theater. The roads are empty but if anybody sees him or slows down he's prepared to ditch the rig and run for it.

His uncle is waiting for him back at camp. Smoking and drinking and eating the stringy meat of a skinny coy dog he killed with a rock. He is probably ruminating on the impending hurricane and its deeper meaning. He'd warned Bobby to be careful once it became clear that the boy was dead set on going into town. He was concerned that he'd get spotted or leave a trail. He also worried that his nephew wasn't going to return on his own accord. That he'd go find Doreen and disappear. But even though Bobby entertained the idea, it isn't really an option. He has to see this thing through.

CHAPTER SIXTY-FIVE

FOUR MILES AWAY AS THE crow flies and beneath a canopy of trees Uncle Thaddeus chews the meat. There is blood on his chin. The heat of the campfire on his face. Shadows playing tricks and the night is near complete. He is nude and resting on his haunches just a few feet from the feeble flames, his tender ball sack swinging inches from the muddy ground with a gang of black flies swarming around his scrotum, buzzing like electricity and seeking warmth. They'll be dead soon enough but even the smallest of God's creatures have been confused and confounded by the unseasonal weatherfront.

His thick fingers are pulling meat from bone. Shoving it and fat into his mouth. His beard is littered with morsels of food. As he chews he hums a tune that has been stuck in his head all day. That Segar song about playing with his band on the road. He can't remember all the words, but he knows the tune well enough. He seems relaxed and perhaps even careless, but he's very attuned to his surroundings. Thaddeus listens.

The sounds of the river and the rain and the wind.

Then there is another sound.

Uncle Thaddeus does not look surprised.

He sighs.

His clothes are hanging on a branch on the bank, no time to retrieve them now.

He listens so hard his ears hurt.

Uncle Thaddeus picks up his shotgun.

It's a horse. He's certain of that.

Then he gets up and nonchalantly tosses the brittle bones of the coy dog into the fire and walks toward the river and his clothes. He knows he's being watched. It's probably the smoke of the fire that has done it but the cold snap justifies the risk in his mind. Freeze damn near to death. He'd rather take his chances with a man or even a group of men. Then he hears another snort. A tree branch cracks. Nothing else and he fingers the Remington's trigger and grip. His eyes are well accustomed to the blackness by now. The wind runs around him like a pack of wolves, slowly getting closer, moving in for the kill.

CHAPTER SIXTY-SIX

LIZ WHEELS EARL RAN TO the window that looks east because that's the view he likes best. Skyscraping pines atop Bull Hill forming a sawtooth horizon. The waters of the Swift River now rising and seeping into his acreage, creating swamplike conditions. A billow of black clouds floating. She holds a can of beer to his mouth and helps him tilt his head back and he shuts his eyes to the familiar taste and then licks his lips. He leans forward and looks out the window. The eggshell paint around it is chipped. And the glare from the fog plays tricks on his pockmarked face and for a few seconds she sees his younger self, his two grown sons evident. It unsettles her and she wonders what will become of the boy now. Some rolling thunder in the distance is difficult to decipher as such at first.

Look at that wind and rain, she says. Jesus.

It'll flood, he says in a rare moment of clarity.

Yes, she says. It will at that.

She clicks her tongue against the roof of her mouth.

Earl Ran turns and looks more like himself now and not like those he spawned.

Shut them windows good, he says.

All right.

And get them chickens in.

She clucks.

Them chickens been in for a while now, she says.

All right.

We ought to leave this house, she says. Before the river picks it up.

Earl Ran laughs.

I'd rather die here than live anywheres else, he says. I told you a million times.

She knows he means it because he says it often enough.

But she'll do her best to relocate him.

Liz takes a sip of his beer and it is warm and she nods her head and reassures him by putting her hand on his shoulder. It will soon be over; she can sense that much for sure. Then he is gone again in his head to the sad place where he goes. A stream of spittle from the side of his mouth, eyelids half-mast. She dabs at it with a tissue, puts the tissue in the roll of her shirtsleeve, finishes his beer, puts the empty can on the windowsill. Liz knows there's a baby boy coming and she has prayed to some unknown god that they take him far away from this place that has already damaged him. She has prayed that the river will smash this house and all it represents to pieces. She hears the call of a small bird searching for cover and then she sees it, darting, a splash of blue on its chest.

CHAPTER SIXTY-SEVEN

THE BURNING RED OF EARLY swamp maples and then a singular stand of white birches and then a picket fence snaking along a hillside. The ATV dies before Bobby gets back to camp. He leaves it in a ditch and shoulders his load and proceeds on foot with Dingo running ahead of him and doubling back every now and again. It's raining sideways. The bag is heavy and Bobby stops to rest under the sagging roof of an old tobacco shed. Mouse-brown boards are termite-chewed and hanging by a thread. He sits on a corn crate and gets the bottle of Old Crow out and he twists the cap until it falls away and the fumes of the thing reach him someplace deep. Rats that he can't see scurry in the dark innards and the dog barks. Dust in Bobby's throat is scratching, making him cough and spit. He sits there and drinks until it's gone. In no shape now to hike. He closes his eyes for a bit.

WHEN HE OPENS HIS EYES a few hours later Fat Johnny is there shaking him by the shoulders. Bobby is still drunk and cannot focus and it takes him a minute to register.

Hey boy, Fat Johnny says. Now what the fuck.

Bobby rubs his eyes with his knuckles and Fat Johnny helps sit him up and Doreen is there, too. Bobby looks at Doreen and she looks at him and she starts to cry.

She looks different with a big belly. He tells her that.

Saw the four-wheeler back there, Fat Johnny says.

I ditched the fucker when it wouldn't run.

Bobby remembers now what has brought him to this place.

What has brought each of them.

There's a break in the rain now, Fat Johnny says.

He sees the empty bottle and he picks it up and looks at it and then he looks at Bobby and he laughs. He puts the bottle on the ground and punts it away. It smashes on a cement foundation corner.

Guess you got thirsty, Fat Johnny says.

Right.

Don't sleep here, Fat Johnny says.

All right.

Rats'll eat your dick off.

Too little and too late, Doreen says.

She rubs her belly.

Fat Johnny laughs but Bobby feels like shit.

Then Fat Johnny and Doreen help stand Bobby up and it is not an easy task and he gets sick and sits back down and gets sick some more until there isn't much to it. He hasn't had a meal in days. He dry heaves. Doreen places the flat of her hand on his back.

Come on, she says. You got a fever now too.

Bobby coughs up some more.

Come on and get it out of you, she says.

Bobby gets sick until he's done and then they help stand him up. He gets his legs under him pretty good and leans on them and they walk to Fat Johnny's brother's car that is still running. Bobby opens the door and gets in with Doreen and she is looking at him and crying still, but not talking to him, and Fat Johnny goes back and gets the rest of Bobby's stuff. He puts it in the trunk. Then he closes the doors and goes around and gets in the driver's side. The radio is off and the engine is skipping like crazy, pistons misfiring.

Leaky head gasket, Fat Johnny says.

They sit there with the heater pushing warm air all around the interior.

So where to, Fat Johnny says.

Fuck if I know.

All right.

Only one place I can go.

Shit.

And you know I got to go alone.

Well maybe there's options.

Shit.

Bobby doesn't know what else to tell him. If he doesn't go back to camp then Uncle Thaddeus will come looking. If Fat Johnny and Doreen take him to camp then they will know where it is, where they are hiding out. Not that they would tell anybody on purpose. But he understands how these things work. How information can get flipped.

And if he shows his face in public he'll be arrested or worse.

I mean there's always options, Fat Johnny says.

I don't know that's true anymore, Bobby says.

Because he doesn't.

Not for me anyhow, he says.

Then he closes his eyes again for a time.

THEN IT'S DAYTIME AND RAINING again like a motherfucker and he's stretched out in the back seat of Fat Johnny's brother's car with his head in Doreen's lap and she's smoking a cigarillo and the smell of it makes him almost feel better. A bit of hail hits him on the face like spit from the partway open window. Dingo licks his hand. The radio is playing old-school polka. He sits up and Fat Johnny hears him, looks around at Bobby and Doreen.

Look what the cat drugged in, he says and laughs.

Doreen runs her fingers through Bobby's hair that hurts.

His head hurts.

My head hurts, Bobby says still fuzzy from the alcohol.

No shit Sherlock, Fat Johnny says. You drank a fucking gallon.

You're real sick too, Doreen says.

Bobby uses his sleeve to wipe the fog from his window so he can see where they are. There's the tobacco shed. They haven't moved from the same spot. That's good, he figures. He's surprised that Uncle Thaddeus has not come across them yet. Maybe something has happened. There's a bad feeling building up inside him like a volcano.

Doreen sees it and speaks.

You gone to be sick again, she says.

That's not it, Bobby says. I'm all right.

He can't stop his body from shivering like a hound shaking off pond water. Fat Johnny turns in his seat so he can face Bobby somewhat. He sucks on a cigarillo, blows the white skinny smoke over his shoulder so it wisps out the window. He taps the dashboard with his free hand, keeping beat with the goofy fucking music he likes so much. Bobby puts his head in his hands and squeezes his eyes tight, trying to lose the cobwebs. Dingo starts barking at shadows and the sound of hail on the roof of the car.

I should get, Bobby says and Doreen puts her hand in his.

She shakes her head.

Not with it like that out there, Fat Johnny says.

Fuck that, Doreen says. Let's take the car and go wherever.

This car.

Johnny says we can.

He looks at Fat Johnny for confirmation.

And go where exactly, Bobby says.

Wherever, she says. Colrain.

Colrain.

I got people up there, she says. You know that.

She's serious and Bobby can hear it in her voice, a tone he hasn't heard before.

You're serious, he says.

As a heart attack.

Fucking Colrain.

Colrain is just a few towns over, but it might as well be a million miles away.

Better then living in the woods, Fat Johnny says.

Clearly they have discussed this together.

You know they can find me there too, Bobby says. In fucking Colrain.

Who can.

My uncle and father and everyfuckingbody, he says. The cops.

They can find us anywhere, Doreen says. It don't make no difference to me.

Oh no.

Except this way we can be together, she says.

He looks at her and then away.

That would be something, he says.

Fat Johnny smokes some more and then he reaches in his jacket pocket and gets Bobby one, too. Lights it and hands it over. It's a bit damp from the weather but nicely rolled. Bobby takes a puff and then another. He looks his girl straight in the eye.

I got to tell my uncle, he says.

All right.

Settle things with him, he says. You know.

Right.

But I got to tell him myself, Bobby says. On my own.

Like that then.

I think I owe him that, he says. He did all this for me.

Bobby indicates toward the deep woodlot when he says it. Doreen stays quiet for a while and she sets her eyes to a faroff point past the windshield and the foothills.

No, Doreen says. He did all this for hisself.

Bobby spits.

Fuck it, Fat Johnny says. I'ma go with you.

Shit.

You're in no condition, Doreen says, to go alone.

Fuck me.

Bobby tries to dissuade his friends, but he's too sick to make a strong argument and they won't budge. He tells Doreen to stay behind at least, but she insists on coming.

You're not leaving my sight, she says. Never again.

Shit.

Not ever again.

It could get bad.

What's bad, she says with a short laugh. I aint scared of bad no more.

Oh no.

They done all the bad they could to me already.

Oh no they aint.

That's the thing he hopes she'll never fully understand.

They finish their smokes and Fat Johnny rolls his window down and they toss them into the mud. Fat Johnny starts the engine and they drive to the fork at Diorio and cut east and the logging road ends at a trailhead barely visible. He parks and shuts her down. It is raining hard now. Fat Johnny has ponchos in the back and they put them on.

And this might come in handy, he says.

He produces his nigger beater from under the spare tire and sticks it in his belt.

Bobby laughs at the feeble weapon and coughs blood into his hand.

CHAPTER SIXTY-EIGHT

AFTER HIKING FOR A STRETCH the rain yields to an eerie calm and they come upon the abandoned campsite. Uncle Thaddeus is not around, but all his gear is accounted for.

Where in fuck did he go, Bobby says.

They decide to take a break before circling back and Fat Johnny goes up the hill with Dingo to scout a bit. Bobby lifts up Doreen's shirt and poncho and puts his hand on her white stomach and she looks at him. He looks at her face and then he looks at her stomach. There's a blue vein intersecting her naval. He runs his finger along it. Her skin is tight. She shows him where the baby's head is likely to be. She refers to it as a boy.

How you know it's a him, Bobby says.

A woman knows such things.

What woman is that then.

Even in this condition she looks more girl than woman.

She knows it's true. She laughs a bit and Bobby does too and it feels good.

Then they stay quiet for a long while.

It's your son, she says, and her voice breaks when she says it.

Right.

Just so you're sure on that, she says. I aint been with nobody.

All right then.

And it wasn't from…that other thing.

She smiles awkwardly and chokes up a bit like she might cry.

Well, Bobby says. I hoped as much.

Doreen collects herself.

What will we call him then, she says.

I don't know any good names.

We could call him after you.

Let's not even give him a name.

Doreen laughs.

A name is like a noose around your neck.

Doreen looks at Bobby and he looks at her.

Her tits got big too and Bobby tells her so and she smiles. Then he puts his ear against her belly and he closes his eyes. She puts her hands in his hair. He thinks he hears his son forming in there. Maybe floating in her warm fluids. Anyhow he hopes this new DuBois is made a little bit different. That he can shake the legacy that has chased Bobby to this particular precipice. Then the baby boy senses Bobby and jerks about in there.

You feel that, she says.

I feel something, Bobby says.

That's him kicking.

He's scared of me already, he says. The little fucker.

Bobby was taught early and often that a son should fear his father.

No, she says.

No what.

That's not it, she says. He's not fucking scared of you.

But then she cries because she thinks maybe he's right.

Then she rocks back and forth and she hums a lullaby that Bobby doesn't recognize. She cradles his heavy head in her hands. And his unborn son rests. And Bobby finally closes his eyes again and he is so fucking tired. He breathes deep: burning pin cherry and Tamarack and Mountain Ash. Then he listens to the bloated river snaking alongside Route 2 toward Charlemont from Perry's Pass to Whitcomb's Summit.

IT'S AN OTHERWORLDLY SCENE THAT they stumble upon under Stillwater Bridge. There's a big dead black horse with its belly torn open and its gut-pink insides spilling out and steaming. Straddling the horse is a man wielding a knife with a steel blade as long as half his arm. Bobby doesn't know or recognize this man. He's inked up like crazy, dark tattoos creeping out of the neck of his shirt like wild ivy. The river is running high and fast. Wind-whispered trees all around are about all they can hear. Fat Johnny is still and with his mouth open, Doreen is shivering and the dog is furiously licking at herself. Across from the stranger and about twenty paces off is Bobby's old man. They are talking to each other, but Bobby cannot hear them because of the water and the wind. But it appears to be conspiratorial in nature. Blackie has Earl Ran's bone-handle pistola in his grip, at his side, resting against his hip. A healthy wad of chaw visible in his cheek.

They have not seen the boys and Doreen and so the youngsters don't move.

Then Bobby sees Uncle Thaddeus.

Bobby is not religious, but there is something Christ-like in his uncle's current appearance, an image from the Bible. Burrs and debris forming a crude crown of thorns on his head. He's seated naked and bloody in a metal chair that had likely been long abandoned at the edge of the river. He's bound to it crudely with the horse's reins. Slumped forward with his head hanging, long hair covering his face, and he has been badly cut. Chest and stomach and arms. Blood and mud-caked. Bobby can see that he's alive, but maybe barely because his broad shoulders rise weak with each breath he takes. One of his legs appears to be broken the way it's wrong-twisted. Fat Johnny starts to say something, but Bobby shuts him up. The smell of the horse and something else, too.

Bobby, Doreen whispers. What's that smell.

That's death, he says. That's what death smells like.

Doreen is shivering again. They're not far from his grandfather's property line now. He tells her to go on ahead to the house up there and see if Liz can let her rest for a while. He tells her to go ahead and take the dog, too. Dingo will keep her safe. She doesn't want to at first but he

convinces her. He puts his mouth on hers. She smiles. Then she's gone
and the dog is gone too and Bobby and Fat Johnny climb a tall tree to
watch.

CHAPTER SIXTY-NINE

THERE IS A SLOW BEND in the long road up ahead. A duck hawk is making curious circles and casting a silhouette of itself. Ed watches the big bird of prey and guesses its wingspan at forty inches. Could probably swallow a fucking housecat, he thinks. The hawk pumps its wings and they thrum and the air vibrates and he laughs, marveling at the awesome display and imagining field mice pissing themselves in fear. Then Blackie clears his throat and spits, thereby removing Ed from his moment of reverie. Blackie fingers his ear.

You can feel it in the air, he says. More storm coming.

Ed regards the sky.

That was some messy business, Blackie says.

Like I warned you.

And still no boy then.

He can't be far.

Our time is short now.

Ed is certain of that as well.

Hard to imagine that was your brother hey, he says.

Right.

After you done him like that.

Well, Blackie says. I haven't ever really imagined him as such.

He draws his cap down when he says it, puts a square-edged thumb in his ear.

You aint bothered by it, Blackie says. Are you now.

It's just a thing I noticed.

Ed isn't bothered by much. That is what makes him good at his chosen line. But he is a keen observer of human nature, which is also a proven attribute. And the emotions that Blackie is demonstrating are threatening to derail them from their original purpose. He's too angry. Anything but dispassion is going to get them caught, Ed is certain. He looks at Blackie and then he looks up at that hawk still hovering among the airborn ash and then he studies the surrounding woodlot. Bending trees and he can smell the river.

The air is still and then the wind howls and surrounds them.

Well, he says.

Blackie grunts.

I'm not sure how much you truly need me now, Ed says.

Blackie sees this coming and he already has the bone-handle pistola ready when Ed's boot jumps up toward his jugular. And simultaneously it seems the hawk angles groundward and swoops and flaps madly and grasps a fat gray squirrel in its talons.

CHAPTER SEVENTY

THERE IS A SINGLE SHOT fired somewhere nearby on this side of the river and Earl thinks it sounds like his bone-handle pistola. Something bad is happening. Earl Ran is not supposed to get excited. He's not supposed to blubber. And he's not supposed to shoot at the neighbor's dog when he shits under his porch. Earl can smell it from a mile away. That there is a mongrel and good-for-nothing. His bone-handle pistola is not where he left it. Not where he pictured it. Goddamn it to hell. It is not a good day. He finds the pellet gun instead. The dog yelps and sidesteps awkwardly into some shrubs and Virginia creeper. Earl sends a couple more slugs in his general direction to make his point loud and clear. There was nothing else over there. It was just that damn dog. That green poncho was maybe blown in from the wind. It maybe was on somebody's clothesline and it landed here innocently enough. Earl doesn't care what they say. Earl Ran DuBois would never shoot one of his own. Especially not a girl in that condition.

WHEN LIZ DISCOVERS HIM HE'S just barely breathing. Sprawled on the ground where he fell from the porch, from his chair. The Benjamin 397 a few feet away. She goes inside and calls 911 and then she kneels beside him and tells him everything is going to be all right.

It's gone to be all right, she says.

Fuck me.

Help is on the way.

How many times has she used that exact same phrase on him, she wonders.

How many times will she use it again.

And how much more of this can she really take.

The roar of the wind like the sound of God ripping the tin roof from a shed.

Earl Ran is disoriented.

He mumbles scattered words about that damn dog next door getting into his garden patch. She holds his head in her lap, strokes his hair, wipes drool from his bottom lip. He cranes his neck, blue veins popping, and looks toward the treeline with a sudden sense of urgency and then she gets a sick feeling in the pit of her stomach. Something about the abrupt shift in his demeanor triggers her maternal instincts.

Oh no, she says.

The ground around them feels like a wet fucking sponge.

No, he says. It was just a damn dog.

Please, she says. Jesus no.

Earl Ran looks at her.

What have you gone and did now, she says.

The dog, he says. Just a dog I tell you.

She doesn't even really have any inkling about what could be troubling her. She doesn't give a shit if he were to shoot a stupid dog. But she senses something much worse. And she has learned to trust her instincts over the years. She drops his head un-gently and he curses at her and she fast-walks and pushes branches aside and slips on her ass a bit down the muddy bank. A swatch of blonde through the low foliage. It's a girl tucked into the fetal position. Liz gets up close and recognizes Doreen as well as the small white dog with its brains spilled all over the carpet of leaves—Bobby's canine sidekick. Liz rushes to the girl and checks her vital signs and it's not too late. Earl Ran got her straight through the shoulder. Maybe we can save the baby too, Liz thinks.

She puts her hands on Doreen's belly.

Doreen opens her eyes and looks at Liz.

You, Liz says. Are gone to be all right.

But my son.

We got to get him out of there, she says.

Liz tells Doreen to wait and she passes Earl Ran on her way to the barn.

You shot the poor girl that's carried your great-grandson, she says.

Hell you say.

She ignores him.

He closes his eyes.

The next sounds Earl Ran hears are the muted cries of a newborn baby. The next visage before him is Liz pushing a mud-covered girl across the driveway in a red wheelbarrow. A bloody bundle in the pale girl's arms as she bounces along. Liz using her thick legs to push them up the hill to safety. It strikes Earl Ran as funny. He turns his head to watch and laugh and then they disappear from his sight. Then he feels himself being lifted off the ground, as though he's levitating, as if he's being procured by the angry hand of the Almighty, which he almost finds reassuring. But in nearly the same exact moment it occurs to him that he wouldn't do heaven's work well. So he tries to secure himself with his right elbow hooked around a tree in his yard that eventually gets uprooted and he begins to drift along with it. The fucking river finally got me, he thinks. Living beside the threat of it his whole life. He watches more trees on his property and along the disappearing riverbank lean and slowly fall. Then he closes his eyes. The trees are dead, he thinks. God and the trees are dead. Laughter fills the ravine with echoes.

CHAPTER SEVENTY-ONE

THE JUDGE LETS BOBBY STAY with Westy and Sue for a while, until his fate is decided in court. He has to wear a black electronic band around his ankle. Westy drives him over to Pat Crudo's so he can try to make things right with her at least. She's sitting in one of the chairs on her porch. She smiles which is more than he could have hoped for already.

Bobby, she says.

He stands in front of her with his hands in his pockets.

Westy and Sue stay in the pickup.

I heard you had quite the time, she says. And you got sick.

Yes ma'am, he says. I forget what they call it.

You look all right now.

I guess I'll live.

Won't we all.

Pat laughs a little nervously when she says it.

Well, she says. We talked about you working it off.

All right.

The stuff you stole and whatnot.

Right.

Me and Westy did, she says.

That's fair enough, he says.

These steps sure need fixing, she says. You might notice.

Bobby regards the short set of stairs leading up to the porch.

Maybe you can start with that, she says.

Westy and Sue honk the horn and drive off and wave at them. Pat stays on the porch and Bobby goes into the barn to get some tools and random scraps of lumber. There's a piece of two-by-ten good enough for the stringers and he finds several lengths of old decking that will be sufficient for the tread. Using a sheet of plywood and two sawhorses he sets up a workbench in the yard. He takes measurements with tape and records them with a flat carpenter's pencil on the backside of a dated piece of newspaper advertising Gromacki Insurance. Then he plugs an orange extension cord into the outlet by the cellar door and connects the other end to a skill saw with a dull-rusted blade so that he can first notch the stringers. Sue smokes a cigarillo and alternates between watching him work and napping. She opens her eyes when she hears him pulling nails and ripping out the old set of stairs with a crowbar and the claw end of a hammer. She gets up and goes inside and comes outside with a cold can of beer for Bobby.

Take a break there, she says.

All right.

He drops the hammer in the yard and joins her on the porch.

She opens the beer and hands it to him and he takes a long tug.

She hands him a lit cigarillo and they both smoke in silence for while.

I heard you got a kid now, Pat says.

Yes ma'am.

Well, she says. That's good news.

Is it now.

Pat laughs.

You tell me, she says.

Bobby thinks for a minute.

He looks like his momma at least, he says.

Pat laughs and Bobby does too.

The sun is shining brighter than it has in a while and Pat goes inside to get a hat. Because of her condition she's extra sensitive to daylight and when she returns her eyes have teared up. She drags her chair deeper under the overhang and into the shade.

Bobby gets up.

Look, he says. I'm sorry about what I done.

I know.

But I wanted to say the words out loud.

Thank you.

I didn't mean nothing by it.

I know you didn't Bobby.

You always treated me good, he says. Which is more than I can say for most.

CHAPTER SEVENTY-TWO

FIRST BOBBY PUTS AN OLD chair in the back of the pickup and fastens it there with some rope. Gets it centered and straight so it won't move. Then Fat Johnny helps with the body. It's heavy and awkward but they get it on board. Strap it in so it will look at first as though Earl Ran DuBois is just sitting there. But for his head flopping around like that. And the smell that will carry for a long ways, the black flies that live in his nose holes.

It was a wish Earl Ran had expressed many times over the years.

When I die, he had said. Drive me through Stillwater.

Right down the middle of Main Street.

A final fuck you.

Bobby's not doing it for his grandfather, though. Not really. It's more selfish than that. He can't explain it. But now that he is so completely alone it seems appropriate. Earl Ran and Blackie and Uncle Thaddeus are all dead, gone to a place that suits them better. Bobby has been left to forge his way solitarily perhaps or maybe with a girl and a child; the decision which path he takes will be made by others, it seems. And so he feels obligated to make this dramatic gesture as if to say: I'm still right fucking here.

Fat Johnny messes around under the hood replacing a worn-thin alternator belt. He skins a knuckle on the manifold and curses under his breath. Bobby hands him a spray can of de-ruster so he can loosen the rogue bolt. Fat Johnny taps it with a rubber mallet. Bobby watches him and smokes a cigarillo. There is sweat on his lip and the dark stories of the Swift River that he can barely hear now. The good bones of Earl Ran's house survived the storm and flood but barely and Liz is letting Doreen and the baby live there. The yard is littered with ruined furniture and wall hangings and carpets and such. Liz doesn't approve of the grand finale, but she watches Bobby and Johnny fix the pickup, standing in the crooked water-warped doorway with Doreen and the fat crying baby.

TOWNFOLK STARE AND POINT FINGERS at them like they're a float in some ghastly Day of the Dead parade. Bobby drives far below the speed limit through the center of Stillwater. Sue is standing in front of the Hot L with a handful of regular customers. She waves but he does not wave back. He laps the common three times to give everybody an eyeful.

Festus from the service station steps into the street and hollers for Bobby to stop.

Fuck you doing that for boy, he says.

Bobby brakes and stops the pickup until Festus gets back onto the sidewalk.

That's some sick-ass shit, Festus calls after him.

Bobby ignores him and keeps driving.

He follows the road until it runs parallel to the muddy river that has finally settled down. Bobby drives for miles through Stillwater and Bucktown and Indian Falls and everything has been ravaged. It makes him think of the pictures he has seen of the bombed-remains of war-torn places. It conjures images of the apocalypse. Everything looks different, the low-hanging fog that clings desperately, the grey landscape where once the lush colors of autumn flourished. It's alarming and sad but also wields promises of a fresh start. Bobby takes a deep breath and holds it in his lungs. Each stretch of South River Road, each slow bend, each adjacent and abandoned cornfield, each empty meadow brings the possibility of something new. Then among the tree skeletons there is a Northern Red Oak with barely a leaf missing—somehow untouched by the recent calamity. Bobby stops the pickup and leaves the engine running and gets out and walks until he is standing on the wet ground beneath the full branches. Rich ruby and orange and a warm fudge brown. It's perfect. Bobby knows that tomorrow will be different and its leaves will lie in thick mats around the trunk, but today it's holding on.

ACKNOWLEDGMENTS

The author would like to thank David Poindexter and Sonny Brewer
for their skill, patience and constant encouragement.